Anna Weston

Published by Hedera Books
Alderbrook
Springvale Road
Headbourne Worthy
Hampshire SO23 7LF
England

A CIP catalogue record for this book is available from the British Library.

ISBN 0 9537554 0 1

Anna Weston

Brenda Finn

A sequel to *Emma* by Jane Austen

Hedera Books

Chapter 1

'Mama! Did you know that the Coles are leaving Highbury?' cried Selina Elton, slamming the parlour door in her haste to pass on the news.

'My love, I wish that you would close the door more quietly,' said Mrs Elton fretfully, looking up from her household accounts, 'and do not throw your bonnet down in that vulgar way. Now, what nonsense is this about the Coles?'

'Augusta and I have just heard it from Miss Bates. We went to Ford's to buy some ribbon and met Miss Bates at the door. It must be true for Miss Bates had it from Mrs Cole herself.'

'And where, pray, is Augusta now?' asked Mrs Elton. 'You girls seem to spend your whole mornings dawdling about the town.'

'Oh, she's still with Miss Bates. She could not get away, you know, Mama. But I made an excuse then ran away home so that I could be the first to tell you.'

Mrs Elton felt aggrieved that Mrs Cole had not made her the first recipient of such a momentous piece of news. She piqued herself on being first with all the gossip, though now Highbury had grown from a village to a prosperous small town she found she had time only for the doings of the first families. The inferior families had to shift for themselves, and be married or buried or run mad without the aid of Mrs Elton.

'I expect Miss Bates has got hold of the wrong end of the stick,' Mrs Elton said, musing. 'Though I always thought they were over-stretching themselves by having that great house built. Too ridiculous!'

When the Coles had first come to Highbury some thirty years earlier, they had lived quietly with no pretensions. Mr Cole was in trade, and as his fortune increased so their ideas became loftier, and they began to keep dinner company and bought a grand pianoforte. Fortune continued to smile on them; their family increased, causing them to build on to their house and add to their number of servants. Some years went by; Mr Cole by now had set up his carriage, and began to consider whether to give up his present house, in the centre of Highbury, and commission a new house to be built on a fine site in Donwell Lane, only a few hundred yards from the Abbey gates. This plan was finally put into execution some five years before our story begins. Whether it was this last expense, for the house had been very costly, that had over-stretched his purse, or whether it was that trade in general had been undergoing a recession, the fact was that he had been feeling the pinch for some time. He also suspected that he was being cheated by his man of business, necessitating a removal to Whitechapel, to the house where he had been born.

Mrs Elton had come to Surrey upon her marriage meaning to be first in everything, but the years had left her a disappointed woman. Her once handsome *caro sposo* had grown fat, and his good humour had turned to petulance when his dinner was late or his daughters extravagant. He was still the admired and respected Vicar of Highbury, but Mrs Elton had lost all hope of being the first lady of Highbury society. Shortly after her own wedding, Mr Knightley of Donwell Abbey had married Miss Woodhouse of Hartfield, uniting wealth and good breeding, much to Mrs Elton's chagrin. For a while she could sneer at them privately for staying at Hartfield with old Mr Woodhouse, who could not be left alone in his infirmity, but after four years Mr Woodhouse died, and the Knightleys removed to Donwell Abbey. Other families of quality settled in Highbury, then another misfortune befell Mrs Elton when Mr John Knightley, Mr Knightley's younger brother, gave up the practice of law in London and brought his wife and six children to Hartfield. Isabella, his wife, was delighted to return to her childhood home, to be near her sister at Donwell, and to take the place Mrs Elton had hoped that *she* might one day occupy. And now this final blow, the Coles, her closest friends, were leaving. It was too provoking!

Mrs Elton had never been more than handsome, even in her youth, and now she was only a well-looking woman of a certain age. The elegance of her dress could not make up for the crow's foot about the eyes, or the disagreeable pursing of the lips which was her habitual expression. Nothing was ever quite right for Mrs Elton. In her mind she went over old grievances. Her husband lacked ambition, and Highbury was so quiet there were scarcely any eligible young men about to be teased and tormented by her daughters with arch looks and sharp set-downs, such as had given pleasure to her own youth. With an effort she turned back to her accounts.

Just then, Mr Elton came in with his elder daughter Augusta. 'So it has been decided at last,' he said, beaming with satisfaction at being party to the secret for some weeks. 'Mr Cole is to give up Donwell Court for his London house, where he will be nearer to his warehouses, for he has had some losses, you know, my love.'

Mrs Elton looked down at her accounts with a frown. Mr Cole was not the only one. 'I dare say that is not the only reason,' she said, in an ill-natured tone. 'Those Cole girls will never find husbands if they stay in Highbury, for though they are good-humoured enough, they are decidedly plain.'

'Oh Mama!' cried Augusta, 'How can you say that? Harriet Cole is a sweet girl, and my particular friend.'

'She may have been your friend last year,' said Selina, 'but I rather fancy she is *my* particular friend now.'

'Girls, please! Whether she is your friend or not does not alter the facts. You and Selina have, I flatter myself, inherited something of your mother's handsomeness, so you do not realise what a disadvantage it is to be small and ill-favoured.'

'Well, I shall miss her,' said Augusta, as she went to take off her bonnet.

'Perhaps she may invite me to stay with her in London,' said Selina. 'I should like that of all things.'

'Perhaps, child, but do not bother me now with your chatter. I must finish these accounts.'

Mr Elton's income had not increased with the years. Mrs Elton, said to be heiress to ten thousand pounds, had brought considerably less than that sum to the marriage. They had lived in some style in Highbury Vicarage for the first few years, but the costs of a growing family, and Mrs Elton's own extravagance, made her feel it a blessing that there were only two children, now aged nineteen and seventeen. Mrs Elton was more correct in talking of her daughters' appearance than fond mothers usually are, for they were indeed handsome girls. Augusta was tall with quiet good looks, and Selina was strikingly pretty, short and plump with blonde curls and blue eyes.

Mr Knightley of Donwell Abbey returned from a meeting with Mr Cole and told the news to his wife.

'So Donwell Court is to be let,' she said thoughtfully. 'Did Mr Cole say what kind of people they are? I am a little anxious, as they are to be our nearest neighbours.'

'Yes, Emma. He said this morning that they leave on Monday sennight. You and the girls will call on Mrs Cole, I trust? It would be felt as such an attention.'

'I think, Mr Knightley, you may rely on me to do what is right. I will go tomorrow. But who are the new tenants?'

'They are a family called Walters. Colonel Walters has retired from the Army and wants a settled home.'

'And what of Mrs Walters? Are there any children?'

'Now, Emma,' said Mr Knightley, laughing, 'I know nothing of the rest of the family. Mrs Cole, I dare say, will be happy to supply you with all the details.'

Emma Knightley at forty-one was still a remarkably handsome woman, healthy and vigorous. Her husband, though now seven or eight and fifty, still retained his firm, upright figure, and ruddy complexion. His beloved Emma had made a few changes to Donwell Abbey to create a more comfortable home when they were finally able to take up residence there on the death of her father. The four years they had spent at Hartfield were not without difficulty for Mr Knightley. Irritated by roaring fires and quiet querulousness, he had gone to consult with his bailiff, William Larkins, more often than was strictly necessary, but his real regard for Mr Woodhouse, and his love for Emma enabled him to bear his troubles with good humour. The dear kind old man had fallen asleep in his chair one day after dinner and had not woken up; his end as peaceful as his life had been.

Although deeply saddened at his death, Emma found consolation in her two little girls, then aged almost three and ten months respectively. Little Emma with her chestnut hair and bright hazel eyes was the image of her mother, while Georgiana was darker with her father's grey eyes. They had both grown up to be fine girls; Emma at eighteen was beautiful and intelligent, though a little inclined to be serious. She was her father's particular favourite. Georgiana had not such regular features, but the play of expression on her face and her candid grey eyes made her often seem the more attractive of the two.

On the morrow, Mrs Knightley, accompanied by her daughters, called on Mrs Cole. As they entered the drawing room they found themselves forestalled by Mrs Elton, her daughters, and Miss Bates. Mrs Cole, almost overcome by a visit from Mrs Knightley, bustled about to find them the best seats, and to offer food from the beaufet.

'So many kind friends,' she murmured, 'and here are Mrs Elton and Miss Bates . . .'

'Oh, Mrs Knightley, how do you do? And Miss Knightley and dear Miss Georgiana,' said Miss Bates starting up from her seat in her eagerness to welcome them. Miss Bates was quite an old lady, daughter of a former Vicar of Highbury, who had known Mrs Knightley in her infancy. She was now a little bent, and occasionally hard-of-hearing, but she had lost nothing of her quick interest in her neighbours, or the kindly nature which saw good in everyone. Unfortunately, she was still a talker without very much to say.

Mrs Elton greeted Mrs Knightley with an artificial smile, and continued to speak loudly to Mrs Cole.

'So, you sly thing, you would not say anything until it was all settled. Of course, Mr E. had it from Mr Cole this month and more, but he is so discreet. He never breathed a word of it to me! I dare say you were surprised, Mrs Knightley?'

'I was indeed, and may I say, Mrs Cole, how very sorry we shall be to lose you.' Mrs Cole blushed with pleasure.

'But do tell me,' interrupted Mrs Elton, 'who we are to have as our neighbours. I do not require great riches or resources you know, but let them at least be gentlefolk.'

'Oh, I assure you, ma'am, that Colonel Walters is quite the gentleman, and his lady is a very free-spoken, genteel person; from Ireland, I think she said.'

'Then I shall not be ashamed to call on her,' said Mrs Elton.

Mrs Knightley tightened her lips, but kept her disgust to herself. She had always disliked Mrs Elton, thinking her pert and ill-bred, and nothing had occurred in the twenty years of their acquaintance to improve that opinion.

'Have they a family, Mrs Cole?' she asked.

'Two sons, ma'am, and a daughter who is an invalid, I believe.'

'Are they little children, ma'am?' asked Selina Elton eagerly.

'No, the young men are grown, and the young lady is fifteen or sixteen, I believe.'

'Oh then, Mama, we shall have some beaux in Highbury, for there are few enough, if you do not count the Knightleys.' She gave a sly glance in Mrs Knightley's direction.

'Really, Selina,' said her sister angrily, 'your head is always full of beaux.'

'And so is yours, for you told me yourself that you liked a certain person whose name begins with H.'

'That will do, Selina!' said Mrs Elton sharply. Turning to Mrs Knightley and trying to smile she said, 'My girls are so high-spirited that sometimes they forget their manners, but you must admit that your eldest nephew is a fine gentleman.'

Mrs Knightley had heard enough.

'Come girls, we must not keep the carriage waiting. Miss Bates, may I be of service to you?'

'Oh, how very kind, but dear Mrs Elton brought me in her carriage.'

So with many expressions of thanks from Miss Bates and Mrs Cole ringing in their ears, the Knightley family departed.

In the carriage Mrs Knightley gave vent to her feelings. 'That odious woman! To be so rude to poor Mrs Cole with her 'let them at least be gentlefolk'. Everyone knows that Mr Cole made his fortune in trade, but he is more genteel than Mrs Elton.'

'I do not think that she meant to insult Mrs Cole, Mama,' said Emma.

'No, but to insult by accident is even worse.'

'Oh, nobody minds Mrs Elton,' said Georgiana, 'but that silly Selina . . . she gives herself such airs with those curls and finery, and her everlasting talk of beaux, I have not patience with her.'

'Certainly, Augusta seems to have more sense, but they are both vulgar, silly girls, and I beg you will have as little to do with them as possible. 'Beaux' indeed! How I detest that word!' said Mrs Knightley.

In the confined society of Highbury it was not easy for Mrs Knightley to avoid Mrs Elton, try as she might. She was able to maintain an air of distant civility, but her patience was often tried. It was a cause of further irritation to her that their daughters were much of an age, and she often heard them being compared by the gossips in Highbury.

'It seems that Augusta has set her cap at our cousin Henry,' said Emma with a mischievous smile. 'I wondered why she had been so particularly charming to me of late, and Bella says the same.'

Bella was their Knightley cousin, the only girl in a family of five brothers since her sister Emma had died in infancy. Her eldest brother, Henry, was the young man in question. He was six-and-twenty, tall and handsome with an easy, indolent nature, and a passion for hunting, who divided his time between Highbury and London, where he occupied his father's house in Brunswick Square.

His brother John was a year younger, quiet and studious and, though not plain, was not as handsome as his brother. Bella came next, then George. The two younger boys were away at school.

'Oh, pray do not say so!' cried Georgiana, with a merry laugh. 'The prospect of uniting our family with the Eltons would give Mama a fit of the vapours!'

Mrs Knightley smiled wryly. It was but true that she would hate it of all things, but 'swooning' and 'vapours' were happily not in her nature.

Chapter 2

Within a month of the Cole's departure the Walters family was settled in Donwell Court, and receiving visits from all their neighbours. Mr Knightley was among the earliest of them. He returned home very pleased with the acquaintance. 'Colonel Walters is a sensible man,' he told his wife. From Mr Knightley this was high praise. He was a sensible man himself, plain-spoken to the point of bluntness, but unfailingly kind and courteous.

'I hope that does not mean he is dull,' said his wife, with an arch look.

'No, Emma, do not try to provoke me,' said Mr Knightley, smiling. 'He is a man of information who has travelled widely, chiefly in India. His wife, too, is a most amiable woman, and I am sure you will be delighted with them.'

The Colonel and his lady returned the call on the following day. Emma and Georgiana, who had not quite finished dressing, were drawn to the window by the sound of a carriage. Looking down they saw a slight, almost girlish figure being handed down from the carriage by a tall young man with black, curly hair. He happened to glance up and smile, and the girls drew back in some confusion.

'Be quick and tie my sash!' cried Georgiana, 'We must go down at once.'

They hastened into the drawing room and were presented to Colonel and Mrs Walters and their son, Tom, who had a merry smile and a charming air. Colonel Walters was a man of medium height, between forty and fifty, with an air of calm authority. Mrs Walters was a pretty woman, a little faded but still looking younger than her forty-two years. She was fashionably dressed, had a low, pleasant Irish voice, and was quick to praise everything in Highbury.

'And how do you like Donwell Court?' asked Mrs Knightley.

'Oh, we like it very well. As I am sure you know, ma'am, it's a fine modern house with every comfort. I could wish that the pleasure grounds were more extensive, though. My daughter, Anne, is not very strong, and likes to exercise when she is well enough by walking about the garden.'

'Yes, Mr Cole often talked about buying the pasture land behind the house to make into a garden, but it came to nothing.'

Mrs Walters spoke pleasantly to the two girls, though Emma was the only one who replied. Georgiana sat blushing and trying not to catch the eye of Tom Walters.

'My poor Anne is sometimes low-spirited because of her illness, and does not often accompany me on my morning calls. Otherwise I would have brought her with me and left this great fellow at home.' Here she cast a loving glance at her son, who was looking a little shy. 'He has just come home from Oxford, and I am glad of it, for I like to have all the family together.'

As they were leaving, she asked the girls with great kindness to visit her daughter, and they promised to do so as soon as they could.

The following morning brought a note addressed to Miss Knightley. It was from Mrs Walters inviting the girls to visit her daughter the following day, if their Mama could spare them, saying as an extra inducement how eager Anne was to meet them.

'May we go, Mama?' asked Georgiana anxiously.

'Of course, my love. I intend to visit your Aunt Isabella, so I can take you in the carriage, unless you prefer to walk.'

'Oh, yes, it is only a short walk, and it has not rained for days so the lane will be dry.'

'As Miss Walters is an invalid, you had better take some fruit from the hot-house. The peaches are ripening fast,' said Mr Knightley.

The two young ladies set out the following morning early, with a basket of the best fruit their hot-houses had to offer. It was a fine June day, with hardly a breeze to stir the white dust. Halfway along the lane they were met by Mr Tom Walters and another gentleman.

'Here you are at last!' he cried, sweeping off his hat with a low bow. 'My mother said you were coming to visit Anne.' Then with mock solemnity he went on: 'Miss Knightley, Miss Georgiana, may I present my elder brother, Mr James Walters?' Mr Walters smiled and bowed.

'You must forgive my brother for sounding like the Master of Ceremonies at an Assembly,' he said. 'It is only an excess of high spirits.' Tom Walters winked at Georgiana, who could hardly keep her countenance.

'It is most kind of you to visit my poor sister,' he went on. 'Miss Knightley, may I carry that heavy basket for you?'

'Oh, look, James,' cried Tom, 'what wonderful fruit! How very thoughtful of you, Miss Knightley. There is nothing Anne likes so much as a ripe peach.'

'Indeed, it was my Papa who thought it would please your sister,' said Emma, 'but I wish the first thought of it had been mine now I know it will give pleasure to Miss Walters.'

Mr Walters was a little taller than his brother, but not so dark nor so strikingly handsome. He had a pleasant manner, and Emma liked him immediately. They were met at the front door by Mrs Walters, and ushered into a small parlour which opened on to the garden. Here a pale, thin girl of about sixteen was lying on the sofa. Seeing her visitors she rose quickly to her feet to greet them.

'Oh, please, do not disturb yourself!' cried Emma, stepping forward eagerly to take the thin hand held out to her.

'Anne likes to sit in here on sunny mornings so that she can look at the garden,' said Mrs Walters. After ringing the bell for some refreshment she said: 'Come James, come Tom; leave the young ladies to become acquainted.'

After a little awkwardness at first, the young ladies soon found themselves laughing and chatting as naturally as they did at home. When Mrs Walters came back an hour later she found Anne sitting up, her cheeks flushed quite pink with pleasure.

'Now, Anne dear, you must rest,' she said firmly.

'Oh, ma'am, I hope we have not stayed too long,' cried Emma in dismay.

'Not at all, not at all! I can see you have done my darling good, but she must not be allowed to over-tire herself.'

'Please come again soon,' said Anne shyly, 'and please convey my thanks to your Papa for the lovely fruit.'

As they were leaving, the two brothers came out of the drawing room and offered to escort them home. Emma, unsure if this were quite proper on such short acquaintance glanced enquiringly at Mrs Walters, who smiled and motioned with her hand as if to say 'Go along with you!' Georgiana was already half way down the sweep, chatting animatedly to Tom, and it seemed natural to Emma to walk a little way behind with James.

'Have you travelled much, Mr Walters?' she asked.

'My brother and I were born in India,' he said, 'but we were sent home to school at an early age, and spent our holidays with an uncle in Hampshire.'

'And was Miss Walters born in India too?' asked Emma, fascinated by the novelty of meeting someone who had lived in such an exotic place.

'Yes, but the climate did not agree with her, so as soon as he could, my father applied for a posting nearer home, and they have been in Ireland for the past six years. Tom and I were entered at Oxford, so we have spent little time in Ireland.'

As they parted Mr Walters said: 'I hope we shall have the pleasure of seeing you again soon, Miss Knightley.' Emma blushed and smiled and said all that was proper. She had never met a young man among all her acquaintance who was as amiable as Mr Walters, and it was evident her sister thought the same of Mr Tom Walters.

'Let's go upstairs for a comfortable coze,' said Georgiana, leading the way to the bed-chamber they had chosen to share when the time had come for them to quit the old night-nursery. Their father had been surprised at the time, and had asked them it they would not rather have a room each. 'Lord knows, the house is big enough,' he had said, but the girls were adamant. In the privacy of their bedroom, which was large and comfortably furnished, Georgiana sat on the bed and watched while Emma took off her bonnet.

'I am sure we shall become great friends with Anne, for she is the sweetest little thing!'

'And with her brother, Mr Tom, too, if I am any judge,' said Emma archly. 'But really, Georgiana, it is rather soon to be calling Miss Walters by her Christian name.'

'Oh, Emma, you sound just like Mama! I'm sure she will not mind us calling her Anne. She is so young for her age, and shy. I think she needs bringing out.'

'Certainly she does not seem to have mixed in society as much as most girls of sixteen because of her infirmity, but she is not at all stiff or unfriendly. Perhaps you are right, and Anne it shall be.'

After dinner Mr Knightley joined the ladies in the drawing room. He was not a man to sit long over his port once the cloth was removed, and even when there were visitors he ensured that the gentlemen did not keep the ladies waiting too long. The girls had been entertaining their mother with an account of their visit, and Mr Knightley himself came in for a description of the furnishing of the pretty little parlour that Anne had for her own use.

'We had such fun, Mama!' said Georgiana, artlessly.

'I had not realised a visit to an invalid could be so entertaining,' said Mrs Knightley, with a sly look at her husband.

'They are such a warm, open-hearted family, Mama, it would be impossible not to like them,' said Emma.

'And Mr Tom Walters is so kind to his sister,' said Georgiana. 'He was telling me he has been learning to turn wood on a lathe, and has made her the sweetest little butter churn, so that she can amuse herself by playing the dairymaid.'

'Is she not too grown up for such childish pastimes?' said Mr Knightley. 'I understood she was some sixteen or seventeen years old.'

'She is just sixteen, Papa, but because she goes out so rarely she is full young for her age. She is glad to catch at anything, I dare say, to relieve the tedium.'

'Then we must get her to Donwell. It is not good for a young lady to be so confined. As she was so pleased with our fruit, perhaps she should come and eat our strawberries. The early varieties are already ripe. What do you say, my love?'

'Oh, Papa, what a charming idea! Isn't it, Mama?' cried Georgiana.

'Yes, it reminds me of when I was young,' said Mrs Knightley, with a fond look at her husband. 'If Miss Walters is conveyed here in her father's carriage, and spends most of her time in the shade, I do not think that the fatigue would be too great.'

'You will not forget to invite Mr Walters and his brother too, Mama?' asked Georgiana, a little anxiously.

'Certainly, if you wish it. Perhaps your cousins would like to come, and we must include the Eltons, and Miss Bates.'

'Oh, Mama, not the Eltons!' cried Emma, in dismay.

'I am sorry, my love, but it must be so. Are you afraid that they will disgrace you before our new friends?'

'No, I think not . . . at least Selina will giggle and flirt, but since they must already be acquainted with the Eltons I'm sure they will know what to expect. Mrs Elton and her *caro sposo* will by now be on intimate terms with all the family, and probably call even Colonel Walters by his Christian name!'

'Oh, Emma, for shame! You must not speak of your elders so.' Mrs Knightley could remember only too well a time when she herself had been saucy about the Eltons, and had been chided by her friend and governess, Miss Taylor, or rather Mrs Weston, as she had become. It was hard sometimes to play the disapproving Mama, when her daughters' opinions so closely echoed her own.

Mrs Knightley duly wrote her invitations, which were accepted by everyone. The party was to be the following Tuesday. The invitation was received with complacency by Mrs Elton, and with little short of rapture by her daughters. Augusta immediately began to plan a new trimming for her best straw hat, and Selina thought that Henry Knightley would find her irresistible in her new sarcenet.

'I remember we used to have such sweet parties when first I came to Highbury,' said Mrs Elton, 'but latterly we seem to have left off, I hardly know how. When I came here as a bride Knightley gave a strawberry party in my honour. He would not listen to my ideas for a rustic theme, I remember, though the weather was so fine we could have dined *alfresco*. I was to have gone on a donkey, but unfortunately one could not be found. Ah, me; such happy times.'

Mr Elton had been in London on business for some days, and returned that evening looking serious, his broad, red face much paler than usual. Mrs Elton and her daughters were in the drawing room, where Selina was trimming a bonnet.

'Augusta, I must speak to you at once,' he said to his wife.

'Of course, my love, but do you not want any dinner? I was not sure when you would be home . . .'

'No, I thank you,' he said impatiently, 'I dined at an inn. Please to come at once.' Turning abruptly he led the way into the breakfast parlour. The two girls continued to chatter on.

'I saw Henry Knightley today, Augusta,' said Selina. 'He wore a grey coat, and was being driven in his father's carriage.'

'Did he speak to you?' asked Augusta eagerly.

'No, he was too far away, but I'm sure he would have done if he had seen me.'

'I wonder where he was going,' said Augusta. 'He usually rides to Kingston, so perhaps . . .'

Suddenly there came a great shriek from the breakfast parlour, causing Selina to drop her scissors. This was followed by raised voices and the sound of sobbing. The girls looked at each other in astonishment.

'That cannot be Mama,' said Augusta, 'it must be one of the servants. Ring the bell, Selina, and ask what is happening.'

Before she could do so, however, Mr Elton strode into the room, his face suffused with anger.

'You had better go to your mother, Augusta. I am going out.' With that he marched out of the house, slamming the door as he did so.

Augusta and Selina hurried into the breakfast parlour, where they found Mrs Elton seated at the table, her face covered by a handkerchief, sobbing uncontrollably.

'Mama, what can have happened? I have never seen you cry,' said Augusta, frightened. Selina began to cry in sympathy.

It was some minutes before Mrs Elton could speak, and when she did it took even longer for her hearers to grasp what she was saying.

'Papa has lost all his money? Surely you cannot mean it. You must be mistaken, Mama,' Augusta said in an incredulous tone.

Selina's wails became even louder.

'I am not mistaken!' said Mrs Elton irritably. 'Do you think me deaf or stupid? Oh do stop that noise, Selina, you are making my head ache!'

Augusta's heart sank. What would become of them? There would be no more silk dresses, no balls; they might even have to give up the carriage. She was not a particularly cold-hearted girl in general, but at this moment she had little sympathy to spare for her parents; her thoughts were all for herself, for who would marry a portionless girl?

In a calmer tone Mrs Elton said: 'I do not perfectly understand all the details, but it seems our affairs have not been in good order for some years. The sugar plantations have suffered heavy losses, and your father was advised to restore our fortunes by investing in trade with the Indies. The ship that was to do so . . . (here her voice faltered) . . . the ship has sunk, and our cargo is lost. We are ruined.'

There was a long silence. Mrs Elton had aged ten years in ten minutes.

'Is there *no* money left, Mama?' asked Selina helplessly.

'A little. The living is worth but £250 per annum. From what is invested in five per cents we should receive perhaps £200 or a little more.'

'Then we are sunk indeed,' said Augusta, and as the awful realisation dawned, they all began to cry afresh.

That Sunday Mr Elton chose to preach on the text: 'Lay not up for yourselves treasures upon earth, where moth and rust doth corrupt, and where thieves break through and steal: But lay up for yourselves treasures in heaven, where neither moth nor rust doth corrupt, and where thieves do not break through and steal: For where your treasure is, there will your heart be also.'

A noise, something between a choking sound and a cough, was heard from the vicarage pew.

Chapter 3

Emma Knightley woke early on the day of the strawberry party, anxious that nothing should occur to spoil their plans for the day. She went over to the window and looked out. The day was fine, with a slight haze, promising heat later on. Her movements roused Georgiana who rose quickly. The finer points of dress were soon settled, and they came down to breakfast looking fresh and pretty, Emma in blue, and Georgiana in white. Breakfast was quickly over, and the dining-room laid with a cold collation. The visitors were to arrive some time after ten o'clock.

First to arrive were Mrs John Knightley, her daughter Bella, and her sons John and George. Mrs Knightley's husband had grown more ill-humoured and taciturn with the years, and could rarely be prevailed upon to join any party of pleasure.

'Where is Henry?' asked Emma, looking about for her eldest cousin.

'Oh, he has gone off to Brighton, if you please,' said Bella, scornfully. 'He seems to spend most of his time idling about in some watering place or other. I really have not patience with him.'

'Then there is one young lady of our acquaintance who will be bitterly disappointed,' said Emma with a smile.

'You mean Selina Elton, I suppose?' said Bella. 'I do not know how she dares to think of Henry. With all her airs and graces she must know that she cannot compare with the fine ladies of Henry's acquaintance.'

'Oh, I warrant Selina thinks herself a match for any man, even someone as fashionable and charming as Henry, but I rather thought it was Augusta who cherished a particular fondness for him.'

Emma was right in this; Selina Elton was ready to flirt with any man between eighteen and fifty, but it was her sister who occasionally dared to hope that Henry Knightley would speak to her with kindness. She did not condition for more.

The Walters family was next to arrive, both sons solicitous for their sister's welfare. Finally the Eltons arrived, bringing Miss Bates.

'Oh, Mrs Knightley,' she said, as she stepped down from the carriage, 'what a perfect day! So kind of you to invite me. Miss Knightley, how do you do? Very well, I thank you, a slight cold, nothing to signify . . . at my time of life you know . . . and there is Miss Georgiana. How handsome young Mr Walters looks. Mustn't let him hear me . . . oh see, he bows. Oh, Mr Elton . . .' The rest of her words were lost as the company entered the drawing room.

After a very short time the young people were tempted out into the open air, and accompanied by Mr Knightley, made their way to the strawberry beds. Anne Walters walked between her two brothers, leaning heavily on Tom's arm. After finding her a comfortable seat in the shade, Tom said: 'I will fill your basket for you, Anne,' and walked off with Emma and Georgiana. Bella, having introduced her brother John to Mr Walters and left them chatting a little way off, found herself accosted by Selina Elton.

'Oh, Miss Knightley, I felt sure your brother, Henry, would have been here today,' she said fretfully. 'It is too provoking, for I wore my pink sarcenet on purpose, though Augusta said the strawberries would be sure to stain it.'

Bella tried to say something civil.

'I saw him go, you know, though at the time I thought he was only driving to Kingston. Has he gone far?'

Annoyed by her presumption, Bella was not inclined to tell her anything, but she was forced to say: 'He is gone to Brighton and we do not know when he intends to return. Now, Selina, shall we join the others?'

A little later, Georgiana, not wanting Anne to feel left out, came to sit with her under the tree, bringing with her a few of the choicest berries.

'Oh, you are so kind!' cried Anne. 'I have had such enjoyment sitting here and watching you all. The pretty colours of their dresses make the ladies look like butterflies, flitting about.'

They were soon joined by Tom, who flung himself down on the grass, saying he was exhausted. Georgiana, looking into his basket where there were very few strawberries, said: 'I think you have eaten more than you have picked. I should not care to employ you as a day-labourer!'

Tom laughed and rolled over on to his back. Idly chewing a piece of grass, he said: 'You are quite right, of course, Miss Georgiana; I am an idle fellow. Picking strawberries is too easy. What I need is an arduous quest, which would tax all my resources; rescuing a fair maiden or slaying a dragon perhaps.'

'Unfortunately for you, there are no dragons in the vicinity,' said Georgiana tartly.

'Are you quite sure?' said Tom, looking meaningfully at Mrs Elton, who was walking by just then and scolding Selina for some imagined fault.

There was a reproachful 'Oh Tom!' from Anne, but Tom was quite unrepentant, and Georgiana could not help laughing.

The rest of the party now appeared, and walked about in a more leisurely fashion. Mrs Elton seemed to wish to secure Colonel Walters' attention to herself, while Mr Elton trailed behind, looking glum. Mrs John Knightley had remained indoors, saying the heat was too much for her. On hearing this from his wife, Mr Knightley returned to the house to keep her company. As they walked about, comparing the flavours of the various strawberries, Mrs Knightley felt a touch on her arm. It was Miss Bates, looking sad and thoughtful.

'Ah, Mrs Knightley, I cannot help thinking of those who are no longer with us; dear Mr and Mrs Weston, and dear Jane.' Here she wiped away a tear. Mrs Knightley was touched.

'Do not distress yourself, dear Miss Bates,' she said gently, and leading her to a shady arbour, she sat down beside her, and gave her all her attention.

'I still cannot get over it, though it must be seven years ago. To die so young - only three and thirty! And poor little Anna, how is she? Does she write to you often?'

'She wrote more frequently when first she went to Enscombe, but now she leads such a busy life she has little time for correspondence.'

'Ah, Mrs Knightley,' said Miss Bates, fondly, 'My dear Jane was such a regular correspondent. I had all the news from Enscombe while she lived; I could wish that Mr Churchill were just such another, but come, (rousing herself), this is too much like repining! I should be grateful to have so many kind friends about me, in my old age.'

The 'Jane' referred to was Miss Bates's niece, brought up for a time by her aunt and grandmother when her own mother died, and destined to be a governess. Some twenty years earlier she had had the great good fortune to marry Mr Frank Churchill, a dashing young man, and heir to great estates in Yorkshire. His natural father, Mr Weston, had been a native of Highbury, but being widowed early he had sent his young son to be brought up by his mother's family in Yorkshire; he was adopted, and took his uncle's name. About a year before his son's marriage to Jane Fairfax, Mr Weston himself had married Miss Taylor, Mrs Knightley's former governess and close friend, and they had had one daughter, Anna.

All went well with both families for a few years, then Mrs Weston died suddenly in giving birth to a son, who out-lived his mother by only a few days. Mr Weston felt it deeply; never was there such a wife, such a paragon of all the virtues; but a man with such a cheerful, sanguine disposition was not long in repining, and soon found great comfort in his little daughter, Anna, then some three or four years old. Mr Weston out-lived his wife by a few years, then died suddenly when Anna was ten. By this time old Mr Churchill had also died, and Frank had succeeded to the estate, which was considerable. Mr and Mrs Frank Churchill, who had no children of their own, were glad to have the charge of the little girl, but scarcely had Anna grown to love Enscombe and her new Mama when Mrs Churchill's health declined, and she was carried off by the consumption which had killed her own mother.

Mr Churchill's grief was great, and he tried to assuage it by travelling abroad, leaving Anna to the care of a governess and the servants. The governess ensured that she learned her lessons, but took no other interest in her. Though she never met with any positive unkindness, Anna was first with no-one, which made her deeply unhappy. So many losses in her young life made her feel nothing was safe or secure. For ten years she had been the fondling of her elderly father, indulged in every whim, but now she was left for long periods to her own devices. She became wild and wilful, riding about the countryside with only a groom for company. The governess, alarmed, wrote to Mr Churchill, who returned as soon as he could, but the damage was done. Anna Weston at fifteen was determined to be in charge of her own destiny. By coaxing and cajoling she persuaded her guardian to take her abroad, and spent long periods in France and Italy. By the age of seventeen she was fully mistress of Enscombe, and could persuade Mr Churchill, whose easy indolent nature was always wont to do what seemed easiest, to do anything she wished. This then was the history of Anna Weston.

Mrs Elton was loth to seek the society of others in her unfortunate circumstances, but having accepted Mrs Knightley's invitation she felt it to be impossible to offer her excuses and remain at home. Her daughters, in any case, were very eager to go, and she was not in the habit of denying them anything; so it was in a very subdued frame of mind that she found herself walking about the grounds of Donwell Abbey. Since her husband's confession the previous week, she could scarcely speak to him with civility. She constantly relived those terrible moments; his shame at first, her disbelief, and then the torrent of angry words which had flowed from her. Not that she was sorry for that; she could not forgive him, and wished to see him suffer, but she also wished no hint of the true state of affairs to escape to be talked over by all the second and third rate of Highbury.

How they were to manage, which servants were to be given notice, and moreover, what excuses were to be made, were all her concern. Even her attempts to appear great in the eyes of Colonel Walters - 'my brother, Mr Suckling, . . . extensive grounds of Maple Grove, . . . the great carriage which had replaced the barouche-landau,' were spoken of without her usual animation. She had warned her girls to say nothing, but was not easy in her mind about Selina, whose tongue was all too apt to run away with her. As she looked down the gravel walk, scarcely attending to the civilities of Colonel Walters, she saw Selina talking to Bella Knightley. 'Oh, those Knightleys!' thought Mrs Elton. 'How they would gloat if they knew.'

Just then they were all invited into the house to eat cold ham and chicken. To her amazement Mrs Elton found herself being addressed by Mr Knightley, who offered her his arm, saying: 'You do not look well, Mrs Elton. I fancy the heat does not agree with you.'

'Oh, Knightley,' she said, with an attempt at a smile, 'You are quite the beau!' but did not have spirits enough to continue. After escorting Mrs Elton indoors, Mr Knightley was obliged to attend to his other guests.

Miss Bates was talking to Mr Elton, but hurried over when she saw Mrs Elton standing alone.

'My dear Mrs Elton, tell me it is not true!' Mrs Elton looked at her in some suspense. 'I mean about the carriage,' went on Miss Bates. 'Dear Mr Elton has been saying he does not take enough exercise, and intends to walk or ride about the parish in future, instead of using his carriage. Surely this cannot be good for his health? I fancied he was a little hoarse on Sunday. And if you give up the carriage . . . dear Miss Augusta and dear Miss Selina have so many engagements . . .'

'Nothing has been decided yet, Miss Bates,' said Mrs Elton, sharply, 'but it is all too true that Mr Elton needs exercise. Come, Mrs Knightley is waiting for us to be seated.'

After eating and drinking and growing cool, the young people were eager to be out of doors again. Emma and Georgiana were not unwilling to lead the way, and they were closely followed by James and Tom Walters, and their Knightley cousins. As Augusta and Selina rose up from their seats to follow in their wake they were stopped by a call from their mother.

'Augusta, Selina, come here if you please!'

'But Mama,' cried Selina, 'We were just going with the others to Abbey Mill Farm. Georgiana says they have a sweet little Alderney and . . .'

'We must go home at once,' said Mrs Elton, in a tone that brooked no further argument. 'Please tell your Papa that I have a headache, and wish to go home,' and as Selina hesitated, 'at once, do you hear?'

Selina did as she was bidden, complaining bitterly under her breath, and the Elton family took their leave accompanied by Miss Bates. Colonel and Mrs Walters began to be anxious about Anne, and left soon after, asking that a message be sent to their sons to tell them to walk home at their leisure. This allowed Mrs Knightley to settle down to a comfortable chat with her sister.

'My dear Isabella,' she said, sitting beside her on the sofa, 'I am afraid you have had little to amuse you here indoors, while we have been walking about outside.'

'Oh no, my love, I do assure you, I have had much to interest me. Your dear husband has been showing me all the curios we used to love to look at when we were children. I am only sorry that my wretched state of health prevents me from coming to Donwell as often as I could wish. Dear Dr Perry is so attentive, and has such a pleasant manner, quite like his dear father.'

'Yes, how is Dr Perry, and Mrs Perry? My own health is so good I rarely consult him, now the girls are grown. It seems so strange that he should live at Randalls; when I drive by I half expect dear Mr Weston to come striding out to meet me.'

'Ah yes, how I miss them,' said Mrs John Knightley. 'I had a letter from Henry yesterday. He says he has seen Anna in Brighton.'

'Oh, how strange!' cried Mrs Knightley. 'I was speaking of her to Miss Bates only this morning. Did Henry say how she looked? It is an age since I last saw her.'

'Henry does not mention her health,' said her sister doubtfully. 'Emma, I do not at all like this fashion for spending so much time in watering places. The damp and chill can be very bad for the constitution, Dr Perry says.'

'I did not mean to enquire about her health exactly,' said Mrs Knightley. 'I am sure she is well. I hear she has become quite the fine lady, though, and am anxious to know more.'

'Oh as to that,' said Mrs John Knightley,' I could not say. Henry met her at the races, and again at Lady Maria Dalton's, but young men are not communicative, Emma.'

Between the two sisters there was a wider gulf than the six or seven years that separated them in age. Mrs John Knightley, like her father before her, had lapsed into gentle fretfulness, and anxiety about her own and her children's health. Since her children no longer needed her, this was her sole source of occupation and amusement. Her sister, on the other hand, never knew what it was to be unwell, and took a lively interest in all the doings of Highbury and Donwell. She was kind, clever and charming; her only faults were an inclination to be too nice about the distinctions of rank, and a propensity to condemn as foolish any course of action she would not have pursued herself.

The young people, meanwhile, having visited the pretty little Alderney and her calf at Abbey Mill Farm, were invited into the house by Mrs Martin, the farmer's wife. All the Knightleys were completely at home here, for their mothers had been friends years ago, and the children had spent many happy hours together running about the fields and struggling to ride the old donkey.

Mr and Mrs Martin had a numerous family, the eldest being a young man of nineteen, who in manners and education was far above the rest. This Robert Martin had always been friends with George Knightley, who was a year or two older, and they soon went off to inspect Robert's new hunter. Mrs Martin was delighted to be presented to the Walters brothers, and her eager civilities soon put her visitors at their ease.

Having partaken of some refreshment, the young people set off for home, leaving George behind. Tom Walters walked between Emma and Georgiana, giving all his attention to the latter. Mr Walters walked behind with Bella and John. Emma was privately amused at the conversation between her two companions. They were talking of India.

'And did you ever see a snake when you were there?' asked Georgiana.

'Oh, dozens of them,' said Tom carelessly. 'Once when I was about to take a bath, one wriggled out from under the tub!'

'Oh dear! How very shocking,' said Georgiana. 'Whatever did you do?'

'Why, I whacked it over the head with Papa's walking stick, which happened to be near at hand.'

'Oh, Mr Walters, how brave! For you must have been very young at the time.'

'Indeed, I was not nine years old.'

Seeing that the two young people were so engrossed in each other as not to want a third, Emma dropped back a little, and was soon joined by her cousin, John.

'You look fagged, Emma. Here, take my arm,' he said.

Emma, who was not in the least tired, felt she could not decline, and took his arm with as much grace as she could muster.

'Look at those two in front of us, with their heads together. I hate all this 'love' business, don't you?' John was not in a happy mood, perhaps resenting, not unreasonably, the arrival of two fine young men, who might capture the attention of all the unmarried ladies for miles around. 'Take Tom Walters, for example; he seems a decent enough fellow - capital horseman - but when young ladies are present he is all bows and smiles. I cannot understand it.'

'Perhaps he wishes to make himself agreeable,' said Emma.

'Aye, agreeable!' said John, as if such an idea would never occur to *him*. 'Do ladies find that sort of thing agreeable? And his brother is just the same.'

Emma glanced behind her. Indeed, Bella seemed to be finding Mr Walters very agreeable, and Emma felt a pang of quite unreasonable jealousy.

The following day Mr Knightley returned from riding out early to find that his daughters had gone out, and that his wife was alone in the morning room. It was another bright day, and the room was filled with sunshine.

'Emma, I am glad to find you alone, because there is something I wish to talk over with you.'

'By your expression I fear it is something disagreeable,' said his wife, laying aside her embroidery, and looking up at him expectantly.

'Certainly it is a serious matter. I had a long talk with Isabella yesterday about Henry, and I am not pleased with what she told me.'

'Oh dear,' said his wife, playfully. 'What scrape has he got himself into this time?'

'Emma, the young man is six and twenty. How you and Isabella indulge him! It is not a 'scrape' as you call it which has displeased me, but rather his whole way of life. He travels from one watering place to another in search of frivolity and amusement, and even when he is here or in London he does nothing good or useful. He is idle and expensive, and does not improve with age.'

'But my love,' said his wife soothingly, 'if his father and mother do not mind it, I do not think there is anything *we* can do.'

'Oh, but John *does* mind it. I spoke with him this morning, and he says Henry is making his mother ill with worry. He is so concerned that he has written to Henry to ask him, or tell him rather, to come home to Hartfield as soon as maybe.'

Henry Knightley was not a wealthy young man, though his behaviour might lead one to suppose otherwise. His father made him a handsome allowance, and paid the expenses of the London house, but Henry had expectations of future wealth, and behaved accordingly. It was a great sadness to his uncle, Mr Knightley, that he had no son, and that in the absence of a male heir in the direct line, the whole of the Donwell estate (except for the thirty thousand pounds that Mrs Knightley had brought with her on her marriage) would devolve upon Henry at his uncle's death.

Mrs Knightley was naturally concerned that anything should occur to make her husband angry, but she had always been particularly fond of her eldest nephew, and could not believe him to be really bad, She comforted herself with the thought that he would settle down when he was married, and resumed her needlework.

Emma and Georgiana, meanwhile, had been visiting Anne Walters, where they had encountered Dr Perry. Mrs Walters had been alarmed at some little disorder of Anne's the previous evening, and had sent for the doctor. He was able to reassure her that Anne was merely fatigued from her exertions the previous day, and would be better in the morning, which proved to be the case. Dr Perry was just leaving Donwell Court as the girls arrived, and he paused to exchange civilities with them. He was a charming and courteous man; a great favourite in Highbury, where he lived in some style, and had recently set up his carriage.

'I suppose this fine weather means you have fewer patients than usual, Dr Perry,' said Emma, with a smile, after enquiring after Mrs Perry and all the little Perrys.

'Yes indeed, Miss Emma, this dry, warm weather is most beneficial, especially to my elderly patients. Miss Bates was telling me only yesterday that she was feeling quite well; no fatigue at all after her visit to Donwell. Though I was called out twice last evening; once to Miss Anne, and then, just as I was sitting down to a late dinner, I received a message that I was wanted at the Eltons, where I encountered Miss Bates.'

'Mrs Elton is not ill, I hope,' said Emma, curious to know the reason for his visit.

'No, no, not ill exactly; some little crisis of the nerves. Elton thought it best to call me in, but really, it was not necessary. Good day to you, ladies,' and with a touch of his hat he was off.

'A crisis of nerves!' cried Emma to Georgiana. 'That does not sound like Mrs Elton. I did not know she had any nerves.'

They found Anne in very good spirits, longing to talk over her visit to Donwell with them, and they all spent a very happy morning. The young gentlemen were out, so Emma and Georgiana walked home alone. In Donwell Lane they fell in with Selina Elton, who turned to walk back with them.

'We do not often see you out alone, Selina,' said Emma.

'Oh, I could not stay indoors a moment longer - all that wailing and shouting. Augusta was occupied with Mama, so I came alone.'

'And how is Mrs Elton now?' said Georgiana, with a glance at Emma. 'We heard from Dr Perry that she was unwell.'

'I wish Papa had not thought it necessary to consult Dr Perry,' said Selina, with some spirit. 'Mama had a fit of hysterics last night, and again this morning, but that was only because . . .' here she paused, realising she had said too much. 'Dr Perry's draught has been of some use, and now Augusta is sitting with her.'

'I am very sorry to hear it,' said Emma, and was surprised to find that she meant it. Something very dreadful must have happened to disturb Mrs Elton's customary air of self-satisfaction.

At the corner of Donwell Lane they parted, and the girls hurried home to share the interesting news. Their parents were still in the morning room, as they came in to impart what they had heard.

'What can have happened to discompose Mrs Elton in this way?' wondered Mrs Knightley. 'She did not seem in spirits yesterday, but I thought it was only the heat.'

'I was speaking to Elton yesterday,' said Mr Knightley, 'and I understand they have suffered some financial losses. Mrs Elton has taken it very badly, and blames poor Elton. I have never seen him look so miserable. It is not something they will be able to keep secret for long, but I would ask you, Emma, and you, Georgiana, not to be spreading any rumours about Highbury. It is a severe blow to their pride and I pity them.'

Both the girls agreed eagerly that they would say nothing, but in vain. Before nightfall it was all over the parish that Mrs Elton, accompanied by her elder daughter, had departed on a long visit to her sister, Mrs Suckling, of Bristol, leaving her husband and her younger daughter to the mercy of the gossips.

Chapter 4

The fine weather broke at last in heavy rain and thunderstorms, keeping all but the most hardy indoors. Life was beginning to seem tedious to the two Knightley girls, with no walks or visits to friends, when Mrs Knightley received a letter from Mr Churchill. While his father was alive he had often visited in Highbury, but they had seen little of him in recent years, so it was with some surprise and great curiosity that Mrs Knightley opened the letter.

It was a short letter, mostly taken up with compliments, and fond memories of Highbury and Donwell. His principal reason for writing was to ask Mrs Knightley to invite Anna Weston to stay at Donwell for some months. He was to go abroad, and had intended to take Anna with him, but a slight accident to her ankle, leaving her unable to walk, meant that Anna could not accompany him. He said 'it would do her good to recuperate among friends and in quiet surroundings.' Mrs Knightley was all excitement, and began to consider which rooms would be put at her disposal, for visitors to Donwell were infrequent. Mr Knightley did not feel quite the same degree of rapture over the projected visit, and said so.

'Anna will not like our country ways. She has grown so fine she will fill the girls' heads with all manner of nonsense, and all our peace will be gone.'

Mrs Knightley, who sometimes found life a little too peaceful, refused to acknowledge the slightest difficulty in Anna's visit, and sat down to write to her immediately. Emma and Georgiana were overjoyed at the prospect of a fine lady in the house. They had only imperfect recollections of Anna, as being thin and quiet, but they comforted themselves with the thought that she must have changed a great deal, and speculated at length on the fashions, and clothes, and the number of servants she would bring with her to Donwell.

Anna replied with great civility to Mrs Knightley's invitation, and expressed a degree of pleasure in its acceptance, which she was far from feeling. She had been more than a little put out by being prevented from accompanying her guardian to Paris, till assured by her friend, Lord Urswick, that nobody would be there in July and August in any case.

On receiving Anna's reply, Mrs Knightley took the good news first of all to Hartfield. Here she found her sister lying on the sofa in the drawing room, nursing a headache. The two youngest boys were home from school, which might be contributing to her discomfort, for they seemed unable to do anything quietly. Their father was out, so they were lost to all restraint. One of them was making paper boats, which the other was trying to seize, and there was a good deal of rolling about and shouting.

'Boys! Boys!' said their mother, fretfully. 'Here is your aunt come to see you; please do not make so much noise!'

'It has stopped raining,' said Mrs Knightley, looking hopefully out of the window. 'Perhaps you could sail your boats on the stream, Charles.'

'And I can try to sink them!' cried Frank, the younger boy, eagerly.

Some argument ensued, but finally, with only a loud slam of the door by way of leave-taking, they ran outside, and the two ladies were left in peace.

Mrs Knightley told Isabella of Mr Churchill's letter, and Anna's proposed visit, which had the effect of making her sit up and become quite animated.

'I hope you will not find it too fatiguing, Emma,' she said, 'but you can always come here for a little peace and quiet.'

'Do you think that is likely? No, Isabella, I am never tired when I am doing what I like. But what news of Henry? Do you expect him soon?'

'His Papa wrote and told him to come home directly,' said Isabella, relapsing into fretfulness, 'but he says he cannot; he is promised to some friends at Weymouth, and it will be the end of July before he can come.'

'But that is three weeks off!' cried Mrs Knightley. 'Surely he would not dare to disoblige his father in this way?'

'Oh, he says this, and he says that, about 'obligation' and so on, but I am sure he is determined not to come. His father is very angry, and who can blame him?'

Mrs Knightley could not stay to hear any more of the wilful Henry, as she wanted to call on Miss Bates. She had once found Miss Bates's society irksome, when she was young and foolish, but now she had a very real affection for the old lady, and knew that her present good news would be just the sort to delight her.

Before the marriage of her niece, Jane Fairfax, Miss Bates had lived with her aged mother in very straitened circumstances, but Jane's marriage had made everything easy. Mr Frank Churchill had settled a generous annuity upon her, which enabled her, after the death of her mother, to remove to a snug little cottage at the other end of the High Street to Hartfield. Here Mrs Knightley found her, sitting near the window which looked out on to the green court before the house, and which gave a good view of everyone who passed on their way to Kingston. Everything was neat and shining, from the rosy-cheeked maid who opened the door, to the brass fender which winked in the firelight.

'Oh, Mrs Knightley, such an honour!' cried Miss Bates. 'Please be seated, ma'am. Hannah, I am sure Mrs Knightley will take a glass of Madeira.'

Mrs Knightley waited until the servant had brought the wine, then told Miss Bates about the forthcoming visit.

'Oh, how wonderful! I began to think I would never see dear little Anna again, though I should not call her 'little'. She must be a grown woman by now. Dear me! Mr Frank Churchill always writes to me at Christmas time, or thereabouts, but I do not know how it is, gentlemen are not so . . . how shall I put it? . . they do not tell you all the little details . . . not but what he is a very good correspondent, but not like my dear Jane. Little Anna, how thin she was, but such pretty dark hair!'

Mrs Knightley let her chatter on, knowing how much pleasure her visit was bringing.

'I must wait upon her, Mrs Knightley, as soon as she arrives, though now Mr Elton has given up his carriage I am shut up more than I would like. Dear Mr Elton, so very kind, but I am sure I can walk to Donwell if the weather is fine. It is not so very far.'

'Miss Bates, you must not think of doing such a thing! What, walk to Donwell! It must be a mile and a half, at least, and in this weather too. Our carriage is at your disposal, but I am sure Anna will come to you.'

'Oh no, that would be doing me too much honour,' said the good old lady. 'Aunt Hetty' she always called me; such a sweet little thing, and no blood relation at all, but yes, 'Aunt Hetty' it was. Oh, must you be going, ma'am? Well, I am much obliged to you.'

On the following Tuesday, a fine day, as Selina Elton came out of the pastry-cook's shop, she paused in astonishment to watch a strange procession coming down the High Street. In front was a large, open carriage, in which sat a lady, and a gentleman who looked familiar to Selina. The gentleman had a smiling, open countenance, and Selina guessed that he must be Mr Churchill, escorting his ward to Donwell Abbey. The lady was handsome and richly dressed, with a haughty air, but she smiled graciously as Selina made her curtsey.

'She is a pretty little thing, with those blonde curls,' said Anna. 'Do you know her, Frank?'

'I think she is the vicar's daughter,' he replied, 'but it is so long since I was in Highbury last that I cannot be sure.'

'Perhaps I might befriend her while I am here,' said Anna, with a sidelong glance at her half-brother.

'Now, Anna, I beg you will behave yourself while you are staying at Donwell. Mrs Knightley has some very starched notions.'

'I cannot think what you mean! Shall I call her 'Aunt', do you think? I did when I was a child, but perhaps 'Mrs Knightley' would suit her better. You are making me quite alarmed at the prospect of meeting her again.'

Behind the carriage came an open cart, laden with boxes, and this was followed by a smartly dressed groom, riding a bay, and leading a glossy chestnut. Another servant, and Anna's lady's maid, had arrived at Donwell the previous day, to ensure that everything was ready for their mistress. The procession passed, and Selina turned for home, thinking she had never noticed before how quiet it was on a Tuesday afternoon in Highbury.

The following day, the first people to call on Anna were Mrs John Knightley and Bella. In the drawing room they found Mr and Mrs Knightley, their daughters, Mr Churchill, and Anna. After welcoming Anna with many exclamations of pleasure, Mrs John Knightley apologised for the absence of her husband, but 'he never made morning calls', and said how delighted she was to meet Mr Churchill again.

'Unfortunately, ma'am,' he replied, 'I am just about to leave. I only came to escort Anna, and of course to pay my respects to our dear friends here,' with a bow to Mrs Knightley.

'Oh, Mr Churchill, must you go so soon? It is so long since we have had the pleasure of seeing you.'

'Of course, I could not leave without the pleasure of meeting you, my dear Mrs Knightley, but I fear that if I stay to meet all our old friends I will never get away. I am just about to call on Miss Bates, on my way back to London, so I dare not stay a moment longer,' and with a hearty handshake, and bows to the ladies, he was gone.

While her mother was engaging all Anna's attention to herself, Bella went over to the table where her cousins were sitting.

'What excitement, girls!' she said gaily. 'Did you ever see such a gown? - and her hair - my dears, how very plain we will look in her company!'

They all glanced across at Anna who was reclining on the sofa, placed near the fire which had been lit for her benefit, the day being overcast.

'She has a *French* maid, Bella,' whispered Georgiana, her eyes wide, 'and Anna can speak French like a native . . . at least, it must be so for it does not sound like the French we learned from Miss Sharp; I cannot understand a word of it.'

'We went up to her room yesterday evening,' said Emma, 'to see if she wanted anything, but it was all done. She says she does not know where to put half her dresses, and as for Marie, her *bonne*, she could be mistaken for a fine lady herself.'

Just then, Bella was summoned to join the party near the fire.

'Bella, *Bellissima!*' cried Anna, offering her hand. 'Forgive me, I cannot get up,' gesturing to her ankle, which was bandaged neatly, but did not look at all swollen. 'You are grown so tall, I would not have recognised you.'

Bella hardly knew what to say, and coloured a little. After all, it was not for Anna to play Lady Patroness, being two or three years younger than Bella. Mr Knightley, who was growing tired of Anna's affected airs, looked impenetrably grave.

Another party of friends arrived, among them Mr Elton and Selina; refreshments were offered, and soon there was a happy, informal atmosphere, Mrs Knightley liking nothing so well as to entertain. Mr Knightley was called away on business, no doubt to his relief, and Selina Elton ventured to approach the sofa.

'Come here, child, and sit beside me,' said Anna, patting the seat.

Selina was torn between pride at being noticed, and chagrin at being called 'child'. She sat down timidly, and Anna went on:

'Did not I see you yesterday in the High Street, coming out of the pastry-cook's?'

'Yes, Miss Weston.'

'And has your Mama no servant she can send on such an errand?'

Selina was mortified, and dared not admit that her father now only kept two servants, both of whom had been otherwise engaged.

'Indeed, I do not usually go, but Papa was tired and fancied something sweet, but the fire was out . . .'

'And what is your name, child?' said Anna, as though Selina had not spoken.

'Selina Elton, ma'am, Miss Weston I mean, but really I am not a child, I am seventeen,' and Selina blushed at her own daring.

There was a brief silence, then Anna burst out laughing.

'Well, Selina Elton, you must come and see me again, and if you are really good Marie shall arrange your hair. You might be a beauty one day, if we can get rid of those curls.'

Selina bit her lip in mortification, and feeling she was being dismissed, went over to the window, where no-one would see that her eyes were brimming with tears.

The parishes of Donwell and Highbury were fluttering with the excitement of Anna Weston's arrival, rather as though a peacock or some other exotic bird had come to live in the farm-yard with the ducks and Buff Orpingtons. Mr Elton's church was left almost empty, as the youth of Highbury made excuses to troop off to Morning Prayer at Donwell church for a glimpse of Anna Weston in the Abbey pew. For the first two Sundays they were disappointed, Anna's injury preventing her attendance, but on the third Sunday in July their patience was rewarded and their curiosity satisfied, as Anna swept down the aisle in a rustle of silk and lace; and after that no other topic of conversation was heard, among the servants, the young, and sometimes even their Mamas.

Georgiana was overawed by everything to do with Anna; the lace from Ghent, the silver brushes, the blond tortoiseshell of the dressing cases, all worked with the initials A.W., were sources of amazement to a girl hardly out of the school-room. At first Emma was also amused and interested, but by the end of the second week of Anna's visit she was becoming heartily sick of the whole enterprise, and wished that Anna would go. Her conversation, liberally sprinkled with French and Italian phrases, seemed affected to Emma; and Anna was so patronising about the little shortcomings of the place, that Emma was in danger of saying something sharp. As this would never do, she kept out of the way as much as she could.

There had been a host of visitors to the Abbey; Mrs Walters had called with Anne, then, a few days later, James and Tom Walters came to pay their respects. Anna flirted outrageously with them, which made Tom laugh, and James blush. Emma began to feel that she and Georgiana were no longer the first young ladies of the district; a new and disagreeable experience.

The gentlemen called again, and were prevailed upon by Anna to support her out to the stables, where she wished to discover that her horse was being well looked after.

'He's a fine fellow, sure enough,' said Tom, admiringly, patting his neck.

'I fear he is not getting enough exercise,' said Anna, looking at him critically. 'Do you ride, Mr Walters?'

Mr Walters owned that he did.

'Then perhaps I might prevail upon your kindness, and ask you to exercise Bellerophon for me,' turning on him her sweetest smile. 'It will only be for a few days. Dr Perry says I shall soon be fit to ride again.'

Mr Walters could hardly refuse, though Tom was the sportsman, who spent all his winters in the hunting field, and was feeling aggrieved at being left out.

'That means I shall have to come up here every morning,' said James ruefully, as they left for home. 'What a bore!'

'But you might catch a glimpse of the beautiful Miss Knightley,' said Tom, playfully, 'and that would reward you for all your efforts.'

On their way home they met Selina Elton, looking sweetly pretty in pink, coming to spend the day with Anna, who had made quite a pet of her. Selina for her part was glad of anything that would take her from home, for she missed her sister sorely; and being singled out by Miss Weston was restoring all her self-consequence. She found Anna walking with the aid of a cane in the rose garden.

'I never seem to see the Miss Knightleys any more when I come to Donwell,' said Selina.

'No, they have just gone out with their Mama to pay some calls, which is what I must do now that my ankle is almost better, and you, child, shall come with me.'

They sat down in the shade of a large cedar.

'You have never told me how you came to sprain your ankle, Miss Weston,' said Selina.

'No, and I do not intend to, since it is a very shocking story. Let's just say I had a riding accident. Oh, Selina, don't you find it dull in Highbury? I was having such fun in London, till my brother found out . . . well, we said we would not speak of it,' and she yawned prodigiously.

Selina reflected that she had said no such thing, and would like of all things to hear the very shocking story; not that it could be so very shocking, for Miss Weston was a lady.

'Who shall we call on first?' said Anna. 'I know, tomorrow, if I am permitted the use of the carriage, we shall call on Miss Bates. Would you like that, Selina?'

Selina was disappointed.

'We see Miss Bates nearly every day at the Vicarage, or at her cottage,' she said doubtfully. 'I do not think you will find a visit to Miss Bates very exciting.'

'Ah, 'bread and butter first' as my old nurse used to say. *Then* we may look for some cake!'

Chapter 5

The following morning Anna, accompanied by Selina, called on Miss Bates.

'Aunt Hetty!' she cried, as they were shown into the parlour. Miss Bates hastened forward, all smiles, to welcome her, and received a hearty kiss on the cheek.

'Here, look what I have brought you,' said Anna, gaily, taking a large parcel out of Selina's outstretched arms.

'Oh, no, you are too kind!' said Miss Bates, 'Whatever can it be?' She sat down to unwrap the parcel, which proved to contain a beautiful Indian shawl.

'Oh, my dear! I shall be too fine - only look, Selina, it is from Kashmir. I must confess, I do feel a draught in the evening - oh, thank you, thank you!'

Miss Bates was quite overcome, and sat stroking the shawl with tears in her eyes. 'But, bless me, I am forgetting my manners, pray be seated, Anna. Selina, please sit here,' and ringing the bell for some refreshment she sat smiling from one to the other.

'Selina, dear,' went on Miss Bates, 'Have you heard from your Mama recently? I did not think that dear Mr Elton seemed quite in spirits on Sunday, when I last saw him. He must be missing her.'

'Yes, we heard yesterday. Mama wrote to say she is enjoying her visit - exploring to Clifton, and revisiting old haunts. I believe she intends to visit Bath to try the waters. As you know, ma'am, her health has not been good lately, so really, I do not know when she means to come home. Augusta sends her best respects to you.'

'Ah, dear Augusta! How I miss them both. Your Mama was always a good friend to me, Selina.'

Anna, who could take no part in this exchange, was moving about the room, and examining all Miss Bates's little treasures; the cross-stitch sampler made by old Mrs Bates, when she was only seven years old; the handsome work-box from Miss Bates's niece, Jane; the silver cream jug, and the pretty porcelain, all brought back happy memories of Anna's own childhood.

'Aunt Hetty, there is only one thing you lack,' she said.

'And what is that, my love?' asked Miss Bates.

'Why, a cat of course,' said Anna.

'A cat? Yes, we had a cat once - he was a good mouser - but I did not like his way of chasing little birds. He caught one once - bad Puss! - and brought it indoors, a poor little jenny wren; so when he ran off last year, I did not get another.'

'Oh, you must have one, and I shall seek one out. A dear little tabby kitten, with a bell round its neck, to warn the birds. Come, Selina, I think I know just where to find one'; and leaving Miss Bates open-mouthed, she swept out to the carriage, with Selina in her wake.

'Coachman, to Abbey Mill Farm, if you please,' she said, 'and stop at Ford's on the way.'

Selina felt there could be no greater joy than this; to be sitting outside Ford's, perched up high in the Knightley carriage while all the world walked by; and to be able to pay off old scores by snubbing all but a chosen few; this was recompense indeed for the sufferings of the past month! Miss Weston was not long in making her purchases, and they drove on to Abbey Mill Farm. Selina begged to be allowed to wait in the carriage, as they drew up by the broad gravel walk, saying that there had always been a coolness between the Farm and the Vicarage, she did not know why.

'Very well, child,' said Anna, 'you wait there. I shall not be long.'

While she waited Selina looked about her, but there was nothing to see; only the ducks on the mill pond, a man leading a cart-horse along the lane, and some boys fishing in the mill stream.

'Good morning, Miss Elton.' Selina started, and turned to find herself addressed by Robert Martin. 'Won't you come inside, ma'am, out of the sun?'

Selina declined, feeling uncomfortable. 'I am sure Miss Weston will be out soon,' she said.

'Miss Weston?' said he, surprised. 'I thought it must be Mrs Knightley, calling on my mother.'

Selina had always been told never to speak to the Martins, but really, this young man was so pleasant and respectable, she felt there could be no harm.

'Miss Weston has come for a kitten,' said Selina, 'at least she thought there might be one . . . It is for Miss Bates, you know.'

'Well,' said Mr Martin, doubtfully, 'one of the cats did have kittens six weeks ago, but how could Miss Weston know that?'

'Because, Rob,' said a voice from behind him, 'there were always kittens here when we were children,' and Anna came down the path, carrying a small bundle.

'Miss Weston,' said the young man respectfully, and touched his hat.

'You did not call me 'Miss Weston' when I ran you out at baseball,' said Anna, gaily. 'Here, Selina, take this,' and placed the kitten in her lap. The kitten mewed, and clawed at the fine lawn. 'My gown will be ruined,' thought Selina.

'No, ma'am, but times have changed,' said Mr Martin, gravely. He was interrupted by his mother, who came to press them to come into the house.

'I am sorry, Mrs Martin, but it is not in my power. Mrs Knightley will be needing the carriage, and I still have to take the kitten to Miss Bates, but I will call on you again, if I may,' and with a smile at Mr Martin, which he did not return, the carriage drove away.

'How do you like Rob Martin?' Anna asked Selina. 'He is a fine looking man I think.'

'Oh, he is well enough for a farmer,' said Selina, with a haughty air.

'His *father* is a farmer, certainly,' said Anna, 'but as Mr Knightley's friend he is accepted everywhere; and Robert has been educated, and even as a child he was cleverer than most of the young men hereabout. Besides, he is the heir to all this, which is a very pretty property.'

Selina was not convinced; there might be some who would not object to Robert Martin, but her sights were set on being something much higher than a mere farmer's wife.

Miss Bates *said* she was delighted with the kitten, which came complete with basket, collar and bell; but Hannah, her little maid, was overjoyed at the prospect of a companion in the kitchen, and bore it away with care.

After leaving Selina at the corner of Vicarage Lane, Anna hastened back to Donwell. It was getting late, and Mrs Knightley was tapping her foot impatiently as Anna came in.

'I am sorry, Mrs Knightley,' she said, 'you must have been wanting the carriage this hour or more, but I have had much to do.'

Emma and Georgiana looked at each other expressively, but said nothing. Mrs Knightley smiled graciously, and enquired after Miss Bates.

'Oh, she is quite well, and so pleased with the kitten I fetched for her from Abbey Mill Farm.'

Mr Knightley lowered his newspaper, and looked gravely at Anna.

'Was it necessary to use the carriage for that purpose?' he asked, not unreasonably. 'Are there no servants to be sent on such an errand?'

'Oh, as to that,' Anna said, carelessly, 'I wished to go myself. I have a great fondness for little Mrs Martin, and thought it would be amusing to see them all again.'

'You paid a call on Mrs Martin?' said Mrs Knightley.

'No, I only went round to the stables to see the kittens. I told her I had no time to stay longer, for I knew you were waiting for the carriage. Now, if you will excuse me, I must go and rest. My ankle is very painful,' and she limped slowly to the door.

There was silence for a few moments, then Mr Knightley said, in a tone of calm displeasure: 'You must have a private word with that girl, Emma; she does just as she likes. I met young Walters in the stables this morning, come to exercise her horse, if you please. She orders everyone about as if she were the Queen of Sheba!'

Emma and Georgiana tactfully left their parents alone, and went out into the garden, privately intending to profit from the news that one of the Walters' brothers was coming early each day to ride Bellerophon.

Mrs Knightley felt that her husband was blaming her unreasonably for Anna's improper behaviour, for really what was to be done? Anna would soon be one-and-twenty, and had a generous allowance from her guardian. The whole income from her parents' legacy would become hers absolutely in a short time; moreover her expectations of one day inheriting Enscombe made her a very rich lady indeed. She was accustomed to having her own way, and irritating though it was, Mrs Knightley resolved to let matters stand for the time being.

The following morning Emma woke early, to another fine day. Telling herself that a little exercise before breakfast was good for the constitution, she dressed and stole out without waking Georgiana. Her walk took her in the direction of the stables, where there was no sign of Mr Walters or his brother. Disappointed, she turned away, but encountering Miss Weston's groom she discovered that 'the gentleman had ridden out an hour ago, and would probably be back shortly.' With renewed hope she set off down the avenue, and pausing at a stile, was rewarded by the sight of two gentlemen riding up the slope towards her. It proved to be Mr James Walters, riding Bellerophon, and Robert Martin on a handsome grey.

Mr Walters dismounted and led his horse towards the gate, while Robert Martin, after bidding Emma 'Good day', wheeled round and cantered away.

'Do you mean to walk further, Miss Knightley?' asked Mr Walters, closing the gate behind him.

'No, I was just about to turn back when I saw you across the field. Have you had a good ride?'

'Yes, it has been most instructive. I was fortunate enough to fall in with Mr Martin, and he has been showing me over the farm.'

'Oh, are you interested in farming, Mr Walters?' said Emma in surprise.

'Certainly. Why should that surprise you? Mr Knightley takes a keen interest in everything that happens on the estate, doesn't he?'

'Oh, Papa has always been a country gentleman, interested in country pursuits, but I had thought that you . . .' here she paused, for what had she thought? That he was content to be as idle as her cousin, Henry? Fortunately for Emma Mr Walters broke in on her thoughts.

'My family has estates in Ireland, Miss Knightley, and one day I shall go there, and have charge of them.'

'Then why has your father settled in Highbury?' asked Emma; then blushed in confusion. 'Forgive me, Mr Walters, that was an impertinent question.'

'Not at all, not at all. You see, my father is the younger of two brothers. My uncle died a bachelor last year and the estate passed to my father, but by then he had decided the climate of Ireland was too soft for my sister.'

'Soft?' said Emma, puzzled.

Mr Walters laughed. 'It's what my mother says. 'It's a fine soft day.' You or I would say it was pouring with rain!'

'And when will you go, Mr Walters?' asked Emma in suspense.

'My father is anxious that I should go there perhaps as early as the autumn.'

Emma's heart sank, and she could find nothing to say. They had almost reached the top of the avenue when they saw Anna coming towards them.

'You are an early bird, Emma,' she cried. 'I was just coming to see if Mr Walters had returned with Bel,' and she patted the horse affectionately.

'Yes, here he is, safe and sound. He is a powerful fellow, Miss Weston. You must be a very good horsewoman to be able to control him. I should not have said he was a lady's horse.'

'No; my guardian was most alarmed when I bought him, but he goes like the wind, which is just what I like. Have you ever ridden across the moors in Yorkshire, Mr Walters?'

'Alas no, ma'am, but there is some pretty wild country about Innisdoon, our house in Ireland.'

Emma had hoped that Mr Walters would join them for breakfast, but he and Anna went into the stables together, still deep in conversation, and Emma felt that she was forgotten. Sadly, she turned away, and walked slowly back to the house.

'You were out early this morning, Emma,' said her father, as she took her place at the breakfast table.

'Yes,' said Georgiana, 'why did you leave me to sleep? I should have liked a walk in the cool of the day as much as you do.'

Emma, not being able to think of any reply, busied herself with toast and butter.

'Mama,' said Georgiana, 'could you just give Anna a hint that we are tired of seeing Selina Elton here every day? She keeps popping up everywhere . . . I swear I saw her in the butler's pantry yesterday.'

'My love,' said Mrs Knightley, 'if you and Emma tried to be more welcoming to poor Anna, she might not seek such undesirable company.'

The door opened and Anna came in briskly, bringing a breath of the stables with her. Mrs Knightley hastily began talking of something else.

'I must say, I like your friend Mr Walters,' said Anna to Emma. 'He is a capital judge of horseflesh.'

Mrs Knightley was shocked. Mr Knightley gave Emma a quizzical look, and she blushed.

'He is not my friend, Anna,' she said coldly. 'He is my friend's brother. If I meet him I am obliged to be civil.'

'Aye, you had an air of great *civility*, I thought, when I saw you walking up the avenue with him this morning.'

'Georgiana, you wanted to visit Miss Bates to see her new kitten, I believe,' said Emma hastily, and got up from the table, leaving her breakfast unfinished.

'Did I?' said Georgiana hurrying after her. 'I thought we were going to visit Anne. I haven't seen her for ages.'

'I could hardly say we were going to Donwell Court after what Anna just said,' said Emma, as soon as the door closed behind them. 'Let us be quick and go out . . . anywhere!'

Their walk to Miss Bates's took them past Donwell Court, where, on an impulse they turned in, to ask Anne to accompany them.

'It will be quite a long walk for her, but she has been so much better lately,' said Georgiana.

Anne was in the front garden with her mother, helping her to cut some roses, and readily agreed to go with them, so they set off to walk to Highbury, a distance of about a mile.

'I happened to see your brother this morning,' said Emma. 'How kind of him to offer to exercise Anna's horse.'

'I am not sure that he offered, exactly,' said Anne, with some hesitation. 'Miss Weston put it to him in such a way that he could not refuse.'

Emma was pleased with the hint that he would have liked to refuse.

'In any case,' said Anne, 'he says that Miss Weston means to ride out herself on Saturday, now her ankle has healed, so James need only go out with Bellerophon once more.'

They had just reached Ford's, and were pausing to admire the bonnets in the window, when they saw John Knightley coming out of the farrier's yard. As he had no other business, he offered to walk with them to Miss Bates's. Anne was feeling a little tired, and was glad to take John's arm.

'John, have you heard from Henry lately? I thought he was coming home at the end of July,' said Georgiana.

'Yes, a letter arrived only this morning for my mother. Another sharp word from my father seems to have done the business, and brought him to heel. He comes home on Saturday, and is to bring his friend, Lord Urswick, with him. That has put my mother in quite a state, I can tell you!' and John laughed, rather unfeelingly.

'I do not believe I have had the pleasure of meeting Lord Urswick,' said Emma. 'What sort of man is he?'

'He is about my age, or a little younger; not tall, not very handsome - very dressy though - my brother has known him forever in town,' said John. 'My father does not like the friendship, and thinks Lord Urswick is a bad influence on my brother.'

'And you, Mr Knightley, what do you think of him?' asked Anne.

'Why, Miss Anne, I would say that if he were not a lord I would think him a trifling, worthless fellow.'

They had now reached Miss Bates's cottage, where John turned back, saying he had not time to go in. Miss Bates was always glad to welcome visitors.

'I seem to be quite the fashion nowadays,' she said happily, 'for you have just missed Mr Elton. Poor man, he looks quite ill. I am not sure that dear Selina is quite ready to be mistress of a household. With her Mama away, and most of the servants gone, the dear old Vicarage is not the place it was. Poor dear Mr Elton!'

Anne was glad to rest, and play with the kitten, and the girls stayed longer than they had intended, to give her time to recover her strength. At last, as they prepared to leave, (Miss Bates saying: 'Must you go so soon?' though they had been there nearly an hour) there was a knock at the door. They heard a gentleman's voice, and Mr Walters was shown into the room.

'Forgive me, Miss Bates, for intruding . . .' he began, but his words were cut short by a torrent of civilities from Miss Bates - offers of refreshment, expressions of obligation, and invitations to take a seat. He waited politely for her to finish, and then went on: 'Thank you. ma'am, but I cannot stay. I came to fetch Anne home; my mother was becoming anxious, fearing the walk might have proved too much for her. Miss Knightley, Miss Georgiana,' he bowed. 'If you are ready, might I escort you all?'

All three girls rose; Anne languidly, and the two Miss Knightleys with alacrity. The pavement of the High Street was not wide, and as Anne needed her brother's arm, Emma and Georgiana walked behind them. It was not until they reached the gates of Donwell Court and Georgiana had walked into the garden to admire a particularly fine white rose, that Mr Walters had an opportunity to speak to Emma.

'I missed you this morning,' he began, pleasantly. 'One moment you were there, the next you had gone; I began to think that meeting you in the avenue had all been a dream.'

'I knew that breakfast would be waiting, and in any case, Anna was talking to you . . .' Emma blushed, feeling slightly foolish. Mr Walters always had this effect on her. She longed to be able to speak to him with the easy playfulness she had observed when her sister spoke to Tom Walters.

'Aye,' said Mr Walters, ruefully, 'when Miss Weston speaks, all must obey, but I am sorry we parted so abruptly. Do you ride, Miss Knightley?'

'Not since I was a child. We do not keep a horse that would be suitable for a lady to ride, but it is no hardship for Georgiana and me, for we walk everywhere!'

'Then I shall be denied the pleasure of *riding* out with you and your sister, but perhaps if you go out on one of your walks another day with Anne, I may be allowed to accompany you?'

'I should like that, sir,' she said, with sparkling eyes, and calling to Georgiana, she took her leave with many smiles.

On the way home Georgiana said: 'Anne is sure that her brother likes you very much, Emma.'

'I am surprised she would mention such a thing to you, Georgiana. How did you come to be speaking of it?'

'Oh, I saw how he looked at you, so I asked Anne if she thought her brother admired you, and she said 'Yes',' said Georgiana, artlessly.

'She could hardly do otherwise,' said Emma laughing. 'Really, Georgiana, you should guard your tongue.'

'But I thought you would be pleased. He really is a most agreeable man, Emma, though he is so quiet, not at all like his brother.'

'He is not merry like his brother, certainly, but I do not find him quiet. Tom seems so young to me, and like all young things he is playful. I prefer a more serious man - Mr Walters reminds me a little of Papa - but I should like Tom Walters as a brother,' and she stole an amused glance at her sister, who blushed, but looked gratified.

'Oh, Emma, he has such a merry laugh, he makes me want to laugh with him; and those blue eyes . . . blue eyes have always been my favourite. I wish we could have a ball at Donwell! I am sure he must dance well for he does everything so gracefully.'

Emma could see that Georgiana was falling in love with Tom Walters, and hoped that her feelings were returned. She *thought* that Georgiana was a particular favourite with him, but he was so charming with all the ladies that she could not be certain.

Chapter 6

Saturday came, and Anna rose early, determined to exercise Bellerophon herself. Mrs Knightley was uneasy, but Anna assured her she would not go far. At first she was content to canter around the paddock, her groom waiting patiently by the fence; but the day was so fine that she was tempted to go further, and taking the Richmond road she trotted through the woods, eventually reaching higher ground. From here she could see for miles, and reined in her horse to admire the view. Her groom suggested anxiously that they should turn for home, fearing she would tire herself, but Anna dismissed his suggestion peremptorily.

About half a mile away she saw a carriage just breasting the hill. Even at that distance the equipage was so distinctive that Anna felt certain it belonged to her friend, Lord Urswick. Hardly waiting for her groom to follow, she set off at a good pace down the hill, and cantered to the top of the next eminence, where she espied the carriage, now only the distance of a furlong away. Taking off her hat, with its curling feathers, she waved to the carriage, which soon drew alongside.

'Miss Weston,' said a drawling voice, 'what do you mean by gadding about the countryside in this hoydenish fashion?' It was Lord Urswick, accompanied by Henry Knightley.

'Anna, how d'ye do?' said the latter. 'I'm surprised to see you riding so soon after your . . . accident.'

'Are you? I am surprised to see Lord Urswick dressed in such light colours. I thought you would be dressed in mourning, my lord.'

'Why, pray?' said his lordship, startled.

'Why, for the thirty guineas I won from you when last we met!' and all three of them laughed merrily.

'I hope *that* story has not become current in Highbury,' said Henry, uneasily. 'My father is already angry enough, without discovering what part I played in that little escapade.'

'Have no fear, dear Henry,' said Anna, 'no-one shall hear of it from me. Though I did just drop a hint of it to Selina Elton . . . but she is the soul of discretion.'

'If she has told Selina Elton, it is all up with me, Urswick,' said Henry, gloomily. 'She is such a little shatterbrain, she has probably already told half a dozen people.' Anna only laughed.

'I had not expected you to arrive so soon,' said she, as her horse began to move restlessly. 'You must have left London at dawn.'

'Not so,' said Henry. 'Urswick has an aunt who lives at Richmond, and that is where we spent the night; but we must not detain you - your horse is eager to be off, I see.'

'Coachman, drive on,' said Lord Urswick. 'Good day, Anna, we shall meet again soon.'

To do Selina justice, it must be said that she had told no-one of the circumstances of Anna's accident, not least because she had heard nothing more from Anna beyond the broad hint of its being a 'shocking story'. She was afraid that Anna was tiring of her society, for the last time she had called at Donwell Abbey Anna was not at home, and no message had been left for her. Until then, Selina had not been aware how much she enjoyed being able to visit freely and roam about the grounds, but she knew that without Anna's protection she would no longer be welcome. She had always been more than civil towards Miss Knightley and her sister, but suspected that they did not like her.

It was late Saturday morning, and Mr Elton had gone over to the church for a wedding. Selina was restless, dissatisfied with her circumstances and missing her sister. She found it hard to settle to any employment, with no Mama to scold her for being idle, and sat, lost in a reverie; because of this she did not hear a knock at the door, and was unaware of there being a visitor in the house, when Miss Weston was shown into the room. This was the first time she had ever called at the Vicarage, and Selina was suddenly conscious of the deficiencies of the place. One or two valuable pieces of furniture had been sold, and there were dark patches on the once pretty wall-paper where they had stood. Moreover, there was an air of neglect which Mrs Elton would never have suffered to remain, and Anna's eyes missed none of it. Selina thought she looked particularly fine in her dark green riding habit, and said so. A look of hauteur passed across Anna's face, but she merely said:

'Selina, I can only stay a moment, for I am on my way home, and Bel wants his stable.'

'Oh, Miss Weston, I heard that Henry Knightley is coming home today. Do you know at what time he is expected?'

'I believe he has already arrived. I had the pleasure of seeing him and his friend while I was out riding.'

'Do they mean to stay long?' asked Selina eagerly.

'I cannot answer for Lord Urswick, but Henry's father intends that *he* should stay, at any rate. Now, Selina, I would ask that you do not call at Donwell for the time being. My time is so occupied now that my ankle is better, that I cannot say with any certainty what my plans are.' Turning to go, for she had been standing all the while, she said carelessly: 'I expect Mrs John Knightley will give a dinner for Henry, and no doubt you and your father will be invited. No, do not trouble your servant, I can find my own way out.' With that she was gone, leaving Selina more discontented and aggrieved than before.

In order to make room for Lord Urswick, Mrs John Knightley had sent the two younger boys to stay at Abbey Mill Farm, which delighted Frank and Charles, for there was always much for the boys to do there. Gentle Mrs Martin let them feed the pigs, and collect the eggs, and during their previous visit they had had a splendid rat hunt in the big barn. Mr Martin good-naturedly let them try their hand at hedging and ditching, or harnessing the big plough horses, as long as they were not unruly or foolish. It was to be their last childish holiday; Charles, at fourteen, was going to London to join his father's former chambers, and Frank, through the good offices of a distant cousin, was off to join the Navy, after his twelfth birthday.

Bella Knightley was delighted to have her eldest brother home once more, for she loved him dearly, in spite of his faults. She had had some private hopes of Lord Urswick, which were dashed when she saw him in the flesh. He would not do; she could find no fault with the tying of his cravat, nor with the style of his coat, and his drawling comments were amusing for a while, but he would not do. His manners were too easy, and worse, she suspected him of being a rake. John Knightley, who had met Lord Urswick before, did not care for his way of addressing Bella, and was minded to speak to him about it. In fact he found his proximity irksome, and kept out of his way, going often to the Vicarage, where it was the society of the father rather than the daughter that he sought. John had always admired Mr Elton, and found much in common with the solid, prosing clergyman. Selina's hopes were raised by his first visit, but soon found that he was impervious to the dubious charms of a simpering face, and an ill-informed mind.

A few days after the arrival of her son and his friend, Mrs John Knightley called on her sister to invite the family to dine the following Tuesday. Georgiana was delighted at the prospect of meeting a lord, and said so to Bella.

'You will not like him,' said Bella decidedly. 'He is a foolish fellow, who drinks too much wine.'

'But is he handsome?' asked Georgiana, hopefully.

'No, not at all. He is barely as tall as I am, and if it were not for his fine clothes you would never guess he was a lord.'

'Oh, that is too provoking!' said Georgiana.

'Poor Georgiana has had her expectations raised by Anna,' said Emma, laughing. 'Anna finds him very amusing. She thought it great sport, when they were all in Brighton, that he had a coat made in the style of a hussar's jacket, with *red velvet* lining.'

'Oh, Anna is as bad as he is!' cried Bella. 'Everything that would irritate in general, *they* find amusing; what is praiseworthy they mock. I do not know how you can bear her, Emma. She drives me to distraction, and I am rarely in her company.'

Fortunately Anna was not present to hear this spirited critique, having gone out riding, as usual.

'I am about to call on Mrs Walters, to invite them,' said Mrs John Knightley, 'then I shall call at the Vicarage. One must be very careful not to slight the Eltons in their present unfortunate circumstances.'

'You are right, of course, Isabella,' said Mrs Knightley. 'I feel quite sorry for Selina, though I never thought I should hear myself say so. Anna has been making a pet of her, but now there are other distractions Selina is quite forgotten. Not that I think her a suitable companion for Anna, but in some ways she is still a child, and Anna should not trifle with her.'

Tuesday came, and a large company assembled at Hartfield. Mr Knightley had offered to send his carriage back for the Eltons, but as it was a fine evening, Mr Elton civilly declined, saying they would walk. He felt the loss of his carriage to be a grave blow to his dignity, and was quite short with Selina when she tried to interest him in which gown she should wear.

'Oh, anything, anything, so long as you are decently covered. No-one will be looking at you in any case.'

Mrs Knightley arrived first, with her daughters and Anna, Mr Knightley having been called away on business unexpectedly, but meaning to join them later. They entered the drawing room, which already seemed full; Mrs John Knightley was seated by the hearth which was empty for once, it being August; Mr John Knightley, with an air of disgust, was being addressed by Lord Urswick, whose attention Henry was trying to engage to himself, no doubt fearing what he might disclose. Mr Elton came in with Selina, looking hot and discomposed. After greeting everyone with a show of civility, he drew John Knightley to one side and engaged him in conversation, leaving Selina to shift for herself.

'Come and sit by me, my dear,' said kind Mrs John Knightley. 'What news of your Mama?'

Selina sat down beside her on the sofa, and answered politely enough, but she was longing to be with the other young people, who, with the informality of cousins, had gathered together at the other end of the room.

Colonel and Mrs Walters, with their two sons, were the last to arrive. They had left Anne at home, partly on account of her youth, but mostly because they thought she would find an evening party too fatiguing. The young gentlemen were soon drawn to the lively group by the window, and Selina thought how fine they looked; all the gentlemen tall, save for Lord Urswick, who nevertheless carried himself so well and was so beautifully dressed that he might be called a 'well-looking man'; Bella and her two cousins quietly elegant, and Anna, in a rich gown adorned with lace in the latest fashion. Selina was overjoyed when Mrs John Knightley said: 'Thank you for giving me news of your mother and Augusta, but you must be longing to join the others. See, Anna is beckoning to you.'

Selina was in raptures at being presented to Lord Urswick, and blushed and smiled becomingly. Now that she was back in favour, she was ready to worship Anna as a goddess. Anna was not really beautiful, but she was striking, and so animated that she made all the other young ladies feel like schoolgirls, awkward and plain. All the gentlemen, except John Knightley, stood around her admiringly. John alone seemed unaffected by her, and began talking to his cousins.

'Where is George this evening?' asked Georgiana.

'Oh, he is out somewhere with Robert Martin. They talked of shooting rabbits. He hates formal dinners and dressing up, and gets out of it when he can. I wish I could, but my mother wanted me here, especially since my Uncle Knightley cannot be with us.'

Mr James Walters had left the group around Anna and came to stand beside Emma, who said: 'Look at Anna - how she shines! The gentlemen seem to find her fascinating.'

'Indeed,' he said, 'she is very different from any other young lady I have ever met. She has travelled so widely, and has such lively conversation she is excellent company in a gathering such as this.'

Emma feared he was making comparisons unfavourable to herself, but only said: 'She is certainly very lively,' as a burst of laughter came from the group.

Mr Walters looked down at Emma's beautiful face, with its candid expression, and said: 'I do not think Miss Weston will marry early. She is handsome certainly, and an heiress, but I could not see her providing the solid comforts most gentlemen require in their home life. It would be parties and gaiety every day of the year.'

'I love parties,' said Emma, thoughtfully, 'but you are right. Too much gaiety makes me tired and cross, like a child that has eaten too much sweet stuff. Then I long for a country walk, or to sit quietly at home with my father reading his newspaper and my mother at her embroidery.' Mr Walters looked as though he thoroughly approved her sentiments, delivered in such artless fashion.

Emma was delighted the evening had begun so well, and took her seat next to Colonel Walters with pleasure. His elder son was at the other end of the table, next to Bella, and opposite Anna and Lord Urswick, but Emma felt sure he would come to her again, when they had returned to the drawing room. Colonel Walters was an amusing and eloquent talker, and Mr John Knightley felt he had not been so well entertained for years. He envied Colonel Walters his rajahs and tiger hunts, but decided on reflection that the heat and flies of Surrey were quite enough for him.

The Colonel then turned to Emma, and engaged her in conversation. He seemed anxious to find out more about her, and was warm in his praise of her kindness to his daughter, Anne.

'She has been so much better of late, Miss Knightley,' he said, 'I think that the Highbury air agrees with her. Her appetite is increasing, and she has lost her pallor. Let us hope she suffers no reversal when her brothers are away.'

Emma's mouth went dry, and she had difficulty in swallowing. Fortunately, Henry, who was seated opposite her, asked the question she was unable to put.

'Do they mean to be away for long, sir? It will be a great shame if they do, for I was hoping to improve our acquaintance.'

'My elder son must visit our estates in Ireland, and his brother has decided to accompany him. They are to leave on Friday. I hope it will be a short visit, but there have been some little local difficulties; a hayrick set on fire, and a barn burnt down; so it may be some weeks before they can return home.'

Mrs Knightley, who was seated next to Henry, noticed the look of dismay on her daughter's face, guessed its origin, and kindly changed the subject.

There was a pause while plates and dishes were removed, and there was still a lull in the conversation at their end of the table after the next course was served, and the servants had withdrawn. Not so with the group around Lord Urswick, who had been drinking freely, and whose voice had grown louder in consequence.

'You should have been there, Miss Knightley,' he said to Bella. 'The best horse race I ever saw!'

Anna was doing her utmost to change the subject.

'Mrs Knightley,' she said hastily to her hostess, 'I seem to remember there was a circular dining table at Hartfield when I was a child.'

'Oh yes, now you mention it, there was. What a good memory you have, Anna! My dear father did not really give dinners; just a few friends now and then.'

'Five o'clock in the morning,' said Lord Urswick, determined to finish what he thought was a capital story. 'I never was up so early in my life. Only a few troopers in Hyde Park at that time.'

'When we came to Hartfield we found it would not do,' went on gentle Mrs Knightley. 'There was scarcely room to seat our own family, let alone have room for visitors, so we purchased this handsome table. My dear husband is so hospitable; he is never happier than when he sees it filled.'

Anna gave Lord Urswick a look which defied him to continue, but she might have saved herself the trouble.

'I say, Knightley,' he called down the table to his friend, Henry. 'I was just saying, I never thought she'd beat you. Cost me thirty guineas, but it was worth every penny!'

'I do not perfectly understand you,' said Mrs John Knightley. 'Was *Henry* racing in Hyde Park?'

'Yes ma'am, but that's not the cream of it. Your son let himself be beaten by a lady.'

There was a silence broken by a small exclamation, as Anna knocked over her wine glass. After the subsequent bustle of servants clearing her place, and replenishing her glass, conversation was renewed. Tom Walters was openly amused, and tried to catch Anna's eye. His brother spoke quietly to Anna, as if to shield her from impertinent remarks. Mr John Knightley looked grave, and said quietly to Henry: 'Tomorrow, if you are disengaged, I should like to speak to you in the library.'

When the ladies retired, Anna withdrew to make some adjustment to her dress, which had become splashed with wine. She might also have thought it prudent to be absent at this time, fearing something more than a scolding from Mrs Knightley. Bella was serving the tea and coffee, helped by her two cousins, and Mrs Walters was chatting politely to Selina Elton, which gave Mrs John Knightley an opportunity to say to her sister: 'Do you think Anna was the lady in question? Ah, Emma, if only her dear Mama had lived, Anna would not have turned out so wild.' Mrs Knightley was inclined to agree but, without a mother's partiality, could not help censuring Henry for his part in the escapade.

No more was said by them on the subject, as the gentlemen were coming in, and they were soon joined by Mr Knightley, who had walked up from Donwell. Henry, aware of his uncle's poor opinion of him, was heartily glad he was ignorant of what had taken place, at least for the time being. After half an hour there was music; Bella began, but though she played well she had no voice, and soon gave way to Emma, who played and sang some Irish airs, finishing with *Fly not yet*. Then Anna was prevailed upon and, with some reluctance, led to the pianoforte. Her playing was excellent, and her rich contralto voice filled the room, as she sang an aria from an Italian opera. Selina Elton was heard to remark: 'Oh, Lord Urswick, it is as good as a play to see her face change like that. I wish I knew what she was singing about.' She was hushed by Bella, as Anna struck up the plangent chords of Dido's dying song *When I am laid in earth* . . . by Purcell. The words of the second line 'May my wrongs create no trouble . . .' were particularly apt in the circumstances.

The party began to break up; Anna was collecting her music together by the pianoforte, when she was approached by Mr Walters, presumably to congratulate her on her singing. Emma was quick to notice this, having been in hopes of speaking to him again herself. To her astonishment, she saw Anna press a small package into his hand. He coloured, and hurriedly tried to put it into his pocket, but it was too large for that. Turning away from Anna abruptly, he followed his parents out of the room. Emma was puzzled and distressed; could there be a private understanding between Anna and Mr Walters? She had no time to consider the matter, before being hurried away by her father who was to send the carriage back for Mr Elton and his daughter. Mr Elton had stationed himself by the drawing-room door, where, between bows to the ladies, he was speaking privately to John Knightley. As Emma passed them, she heard Mr Elton say: 'Now that you have made up your mind, you should lose no time in speaking to your father.' Emma was too dispirited to wonder for more than a moment what it was they were discussing, and was glad to be handed into the carriage by her father.

Chapter 7

Henry Knightley was dreading the interview with his father that Wednesday morning, so he arranged to ride out early to clear his head. Unfortunately, Lord Urswick insisted on accompanying him, on a horse which he said, scornfully, was 'little better than a hack.'

'You had better not let my brother hear you say that,' said Henry, as they set off. 'It was good of him to lend you his horse, and by-the-by, Urswick, I have not done berating you. I am not at all pleased with your conduct last evening.'

'Oh, pooh,' said his lordship, 'I told that story at Lady Gleaston's, and they thought it a capital jest.'

'At my expense,' said Henry, dolefully.

'No, my lad, at mine. I was the one who forfeited the thirty guineas, remember!' Henry tried not to smile. 'And I tempered the wind to the shorn lamb, you know, being aware that this ain't London society. I could have told the whole truth about Anna.'

'What? That she wore breeches like a boy, and rode astride? My father would have found that very diverting!'

'So I thought! So I thought!' cried Lord Urswick. 'That is why I did not mention it. I do have *some* discretion Knightley, my boy! And you tried to box her in, which was most ungallant, and injured her ankle in the process. I don't suppose we will happen upon Miss Weston this morning - locked up in her room on bread and water, I'll warrant.'

'Oh, come on,' said Henry, giving up the struggle to be serious, 'I'll race you to the top of the hill.'

Anna Weston rose late, and took no breakfast, to avoid an encounter with Mrs Knightley. She did not regret racing against Henry, knowing that her circle in London found it the best joke of the season. Lord Urswick was not the only gentleman to have lost money on that particular wager. Here in Highbury, though, she had been made uncomfortably aware that country people were different; more upright, and moralistic, they tired her to death. At least, that was what she told herself, but she had a real regard for the Knightleys, and could not help feeling a little ashamed. She did not want those whom she respected to judge her, but was somewhat afraid that they did. Colonel Walters and his lady might not view her as a desirable companion for Anne, lest her innocence be tainted. Anne's brother, James, had not been amused, and cast a warning glance at Tom, when he began to laugh. At the thought of Mr Walters something like a blush spread over her cheeks, which dismayed her, for she had not blushed since she was fourteen. Looking at herself in the glass she thought no man could resist those bright eyes and the glossy abundance of her hair. She smiled, and her teeth were perfect. Mr Walters must be brought to heel. Just then, Marie came in with a message from Mrs Knightley, saying that she hoped Anna was quite well, and would like to see her in the breakfast parlour.

While his brother was out riding, John Knightley went to the library for a word with his father. He found him seated behind the large desk, perhaps thinking that a more comfortable seat might cause him to be less severe on his eldest son.

'I thought you must be Henry - do you know where the fellow has got to?' said his father.

John said something about riding and Lord Urswick, then went on quickly: 'I wanted to speak to you, Father, about my own prospects. I cannot live at home for ever, and was wondering if I might set up my own establishment.'

'Aren't you happy at home, John?' said Mr Knightley. 'I must say that this request has taken me by surprise. Do you intend to support yourself? You have not been trained for any profession, and if your brother were not so extravagant I would say that no profession was needed. You will have Hartfield when we are gone, of course, but with your younger brothers to support, I cannot afford to provide you with a home of your own.'

'I understand your difficulties, Father, but if you will hear me out, I may be able to allay your fears. As you know, I have been spending some time at the Vicarage of late. I admire Mr Elton, and have talked with him at length of the clerical life. He finds it satisfying, and I think it might suit me.'

'What, be a clergyman? But there is no living vacant at present, John. Elton is still a hale and hearty man, and the living at Highbury is a very small one - no tithes you see.'

'But Father,' said John earnestly, 'the living at Donwell is much better. The Rector, Mr Otway, is an old man and cannot live much longer; my Uncle Knightley has no sons, so where else should he bestow it? If you would be so good as to speak to my uncle about it, I shall go back to Oxford and prepare for ordination.'

'Well, bless me!' said Mr Knightley. 'You have certainly put a great deal of thought into this. I must speak to your mother, but it seems a capital idea, John, capital!' and clapping him on the shoulder he indicated that the interview was over.

Henry was waiting outside the door, and whispered to John: 'What sort of mood is he in?' To which John replied: 'He was very affable to *me*.' His father had been standing by the window, mulling over what John had told him, but he took his seat again at the desk when Henry entered. There was a long silence, which Henry thought it politic to break.

'Father, I owe you an apology. Lord Urswick should not have spoken so at dinner last night.'

'I cannot comment on Lord Urswick's actions when he is a guest in my house. No doubt such conversation is amusing in certain circles, among the idle and the vicious.' Henry thought this was a little hard, but wisely made no protest. 'Henry, I must be blunt. You have idled away the past two years, wasting money and doing nothing useful. Indeed, having met your questionable friends - oh yes, everyone knows that Anna is the lady in the case - I would be glad if this were all, but they give me too much reason to fear the worst.' Henry began to say something, but was silenced by a movement of his father's hand. 'No, you cannot excuse yourself, but I am determined to put a stop to your . . . ill conduct. I intend to give up the house in London; henceforth you will live at home, and keep a strict account of your expenditure. I have some plans for your future which I cannot mention until I have spoken to your uncle. Oh Henry, why can't you be more like your brother, John? You may go, but I should be grateful if you would drop a hint to Lord Urswick that his presence in this house is no longer agreeable to me.'

While Henry was closeted with his father, Lord Urswick was still wandering the lanes about Highbury. Henry had hurried home, leaving Lord Urswick enjoying the morning air, but while he still had a mile or two to go his horse went lame, and he was obliged to dismount. Cursing the while he walked on, but the way was secluded and the hedges high, and he soon lost all sense of direction. He was growing hot and tired when he saw some cottager's children playing in the dirt, and ascertained with some difficulty that he was on the right road to Highbury, and that the next turning would bring him into Vicarage Lane.

No sooner had he turned the corner than he espied a trim little figure with golden curls peeping out from under her bonnet, walking a short distance ahead of him. He soon caught up with her and addressed her thus: 'I thought it must be some dryad from the woods, but now I see it is Miss Selina Elton. Your servant, ma'am.'

Selina did not understand the precise meaning of his words, but understood that he meant to be gallant, and was gratified.

'Lord Urswick,' she said with a little flutter, 'I had not thought to see you here in Vicarage Lane. Have you been far?'

Lord Urswick explained what had happened; she was all sympathy and concern, and begged him to take some refreshment at the Vicarage. Charmed by Selina's pretty face he accepted, though he was only a short distance from Hartfield. He might also have been desirous of avoiding his host until the business with Henry was over.

Mr Elton was effusive in his welcome. He had heard everything that Lord Urswick had said the previous evening, he had seen him in liquor, and knew he had an unbridled tongue, but he *was* a lord, and Mr Elton was inclined to be indulgent. He even contrived to leave the young people alone together for a few minutes, reflecting that it was imperative for his daughters to marry, and in view of the parlous state of his finances, the sooner the better. Lord Urswick was charmed with Selina, being predisposed to favour any woman, not positively ugly, who was shorter than he was.

'Are you ever in town, Miss Elton?' he asked her.

'No sir, I was never there in my life. I hope to be invited though, now our friends the Coles are established in Whitechapel. Perhaps I may have to wait a long time,' she ended wistfully.

'Oh, it may not be so long. Perhaps Miss Weston may take you there. Her guardian has a house in St James's Square, you know.' It was said idly, but when he saw Selina's face light up, he wondered if Anna could be persuaded to it.

Soon after, he took his leave, but not before he had pressed Selina's hand to his lips. Confused and delighted she immediately ran upstairs so that she could watch him as far as the corner.

The atmosphere being decidedly cool at home, Bella decided to walk to Donwell, to talk over the previous evening's events with Emma and Georgiana. She found the family in the drawing room, and after spending a little time with her aunt and uncle, she suggested a walk in the grounds with her cousins.

'My mother has been talking to Anna this morning,' said Emma, once they were some distance from the house. 'Anna did not come down to breakfast, so Mama was obliged to send for her.'

'I should have liked to be a mouse in the wainscot during that particular interview,' said Bella, with a playful smile.

'I am sure Anna must be feeling ashamed of herself. It was no conduct for a lady,' said Georgiana. 'I would die rather than face Mama after doing such a thing.'

'I should think Anna was incapable of shame,' said Bella, scornfully. 'Henry is not a bad fellow, but he is easily led. He had to see my father in the library this morning, and came out looking quite white. I think my father's patience is exhausted.'

'And did Anna really race against Henry?' asked Emma, torn between dismay and admiration.

'Oh child, you don't know the half of it! The brazen hussy dressed herself up in breeches, and rode astride. I doubt if she could have beaten Henry otherwise. He is an excellent horseman.'

While Bella and her cousins were in the garden, Anna had returned to her bed-chamber after a disagreeable encounter with Mrs Knightley, who found herself in a perplexing situation. She had no authority over Anna, but felt that she had been entrusted to her care, and that she owed it to the absent Mr Churchill to see whether Anna's conduct could be modified by gentle persuasion. She began by telling Anna how highly she had regarded her parents, making frequent references to the sweetness of Mrs Weston's disposition, and the virtue of her character. Anna only tapped her foot impatiently. Then Mrs Knightley went on to hint that Lord Urswick might not be the most desirable of companions for an unmarried lady. It was all in vain. Anna tightened her lips and stared fixedly at the floor while Mrs Knightley's gentle, pleading tones continued. At last, Mrs Knightley could say no more, and Anna retired, full of indignation. She resolved if possible to return to town, and sat down to write to her guardian accordingly.

Emma and Georgiana returned to the house, Bella having gone home, to find their mother in an agitated state, and it was some time before she regained her composure. She said very little, but enough to make them realise that she had failed in her bid to make Anna more reasonable. Shortly afterwards Anna came down saying she was going to the post office, refusing to leave her letter to be franked by Mr Knightley, or to let a servant take it to the post. Mrs Knightley was anxious to put the morning's unpleasantness behind her, and was eager in her civilities, but Anna looked as though she did not find it easy to forgive.

After completing her business at the post office, Anna made her way to the Vicarage, being unsure of her welcome elsewhere. Selina was delighted to see her, and Anna noticed that everything was in much better order than on her former visit. Mr Elton had just gone out, and Selina was eager to prove herself a good hostess.

'You have just missed Lord Urswick,' she said, smiling coyly. 'He was here not half an hour since.' Anna was surprised, and said so.

'Oh, I met him quite by accident - his horse had gone lame. Papa was at home, so I invited Lord Urswick to take some refreshment. He was much obliged, and said he might take me out in his carriage one day.' She looked at Anna half fearfully, to see what effect this might have on her. Anna sat in silence for some moments, then said:

'You must be aware, Selina, that it would not be proper for you to drive out with Lord Urswick, unchaperoned; but I have an idea. What do you say to forming a party to make a pleasure trip somewhere - perhaps to Box Hill, or some other beauty spot? Lord Urswick's carriage will hold four, and some of the gentlemen could ride.'

'Oh, Miss Weston, what a splendid idea! I should like it of all things. Who will you invite?'

'Let me see,' said Anna considering. 'You and I could go in Lord Urswick's carriage with Emma and Georgiana. Mrs Knightley is in a pet with me and would not make their carriage available, I'm sure, but Henry might persuade his mother to it. Then we could invite Bella and maybe little Anne Walters. I shall call at Hartfield and arrange everything.'

She was as good as her word, and went straight to Hartfield, encountering Henry and Lord Urswick on their way to the stables, to look at the lame horse. Anna told them quickly what she had in mind.

'I think it is a capital idea, Anna,' said Lord Urswick. 'It will get us all out of the way until this unpleasantness blows over. We could call on my aunt at Richmond, and walk by the river. It would make a very pleasant excursion.'

'I am not sure my father would agree to it,' said Henry.

'Ah, that is why I intend to approach your mother first,' said Anna. 'If I am full of apologies, and ask very nicely, she will not be able to refuse me.'

Mrs John Knightley was all complaisance, probably thinking it not a bad idea for her favourite son to be out of his father's way for a little while, and agreed that they could have the use of the carriage. When Bella was approached she at first refused, but after a great deal of persuasion from Henry, and the hint of an invitation to Mr Walters and his brother, she reluctantly agreed. Henry then suggested that he and Bella should call at Donwell Court, while Anna maintained a discreet distance. They duly called upon them within the hour, and the two brothers readily agreed, saying they would bring Anne if she were well enough.

A very different reception awaited Anna when she arrived back at Donwell. Her good humour completely restored, she spoke first to Emma, and was surprised to find her very cool.

'I do not think Mama would allow it,' she said. 'She does not think young people should always be on the gad.'

'Come now, Emma,' said Anna, in a wheedling tone, 'Mrs John Knightley sees no harm in it, and is to lend us her carriage. Bella is going, and Mr Walters. I'm sure that will make you change your mind.'

'Bella must do as she pleases,' cried Emma angrily, 'and as for Mr Walters, what is he to me? You must excuse me, Anna, I cannot - no, I *will* not go,' and brooking no further argument, Emma turned on her heel and went upstairs. Anna had no option but to go into the drawing room, where she found Mrs Knightley and Georgiana. Anna explained her proposal to Mrs Knightley in so respectful a tone, with many apologies for her petulance, and promises of amendment that Mrs Knightley was quite won over.

'You would like to go, I am sure, Georgiana,' said Anna. 'I do hope you will give your permission, ma'am.'

Mrs Knightley looked at Georgiana's eager expression, and agreed, but not without some misgiving. Anna did not mention Emma's refusal, wisely thinking that Georgiana was the one most likely to persuade her to change her mind. A message was sent to Hartfield, and a servant duly dispatched to Richmond with a letter from Lord Urswick to his aunt, to expect them at noon on the morrow.

The sisters went up early to dress for dinner, and it was only then that Georgiana discovered that Emma did not mean to go to Richmond.

'But Emma, you must!' she cried in alarm. 'I could not possibly go by myself.'

'How can you possibly say you will be by yourself, Georgiana?' said Emma, laughing. 'There will be three or four young ladies, besides yourself, not to mention four gentlemen.'

'I know you are angry with Anna for upsetting Mama,' said Georgiana, changing tack, 'but now that *she* has given her permission I cannot see why you should object.'

'Oh, if there were time I could furnish you with several reasons.'

There was a small silence while Emma struggled with the clasp of her necklace.

'Mr Walters is going, Emma. He will be very disappointed not to find you as one of the party.'

'Oh no, Mr Walters has no interest in me!' said Emma, with a hint of bitterness. 'I think he finds Anna much more fascinating.'

Here was the crux of the matter. Emma's heart was sore; she was half in love with James Walters, but after the incident with Anna the previous evening she suspected him of double-dealing.

'Come, Georgiana,' she said, 'there is the dinner gong; we had better go down. I assure you I have no intention of changing my mind.'

Chapter 8

Long before the maid had been in to draw back the curtains Georgiana was up, eager to look her best for her day's excursion. Breakfast was unusually early in honour of the occasion, but Georgiana ate very little, being anxious not to keep her cousins waiting. Emma, too, ate very little, sitting staring at her plate, and wishing she had not been so obdurate. Georgiana had tried once more, timidly, to persuade Emma to change her mind, but had received such a decided negative that she was too discouraged to continue.

Mr Knightley, suspecting the state of affairs, was particularly kind to Emma, and when Georgiana had gone upstairs to fetch her bonnet, he said: 'Emma I must speak with your uncle this morning, but after that I am at your service. Perhaps you would like to go with me to Kingston. I have some business there.'

'Thank you, Papa, but you usually ride to Kingston. I would not want you to order the carriage on my account.'

'Nonsense, child! Your mother is always telling me I do not use the carriage enough. Let us play at 'Ladies and Gentlemen' for once.'

This brought a smile to Emma's face, and she said: 'As it is such a lovely day, perhaps I could walk with you as far as Hartfield, and then I could go on and call on Miss Bates. It is an age since I saw her last.'

'My love,' said her mother, 'surely it is enough to forego your excursion without having to visit Miss Bates. This was a penance I reserved for when I had been truly wicked! (Here she glanced, laughing, at her husband.) '*You* have done nothing wrong, I hope.'

'Mrs Knightley, you should not speak so to your daughter,' said Mr Knightley, in mock reproof. 'Thanks to you she has grown up to be a good girl, who always does her duty.'

'That is true,' said his wife, 'but I rather think it is thanks to *you*, Mr Knightley.'

'Mama, Georgiana and I are very fond of Miss Bates. She has always been so kind to us,' said Emma, not wanting to seem a martyr, though beginning to feel like one as Georgiana came down the stairs looking fresh and eager, in yellow muslin, and a white bonnet, trimmed with daisies.

There was a little bustle as the Knightley carriage arrived, and they all went to the door to see Georgiana off. Bella was accompanied by Anne Walters and her eldest brother, who got down to hand Georgiana in. They exchanged a few words, and Emma saw his expression change. He looked across at her, as though about to speak, then thought better of it and followed Georgiana into the carriage. Lord Urswick's carriage was waiting in the road, and with smiles and waves the whole party set off, Tom Walters, on horseback, bringing up the rear.

Emma turned back into the house, and felt again how foolish she had been to refuse. So much of the day would have been spent on the journey, giving her both the opportunity to avoid Anna and Lord Urswick, and of becoming better acquainted with Mr Walters; and she reflected that if Mr Walters had not found Anna attractive before, there would be ample opportunity for him to be charmed by her before the day was out.

It was the happiest day of Selina Elton's life; to be riding in an open carriage, behind a pair of matching greys; with the paintwork gleaming, the lamps well polished, and best of all, Lord Urswick's crest emblazoned on the door, proclaiming his status to any passer-by; this was Paradise indeed! Anna was also in a very good humour. She was glad to get away from the stultifying atmosphere of Donwell; the weather was perfect, and the vista of harvest fields over the hedges was delightful.

Henry was as merry as a schoolboy given an unexpected half-holiday, and Lord Urswick was gracious to everyone, and particularly civil to Selina.

The party in the second carriage was much quieter. Mr Walters hardly said a word for the first mile or two, and although Bella was disposed to be chatty, she could not be as open and easy with Georgiana and Anne as when they were closeted together in Anne's little parlour. Without Emma, Georgiana could not be perfectly happy, but it was pleasant to be out in the sunshine, which was so warm that the slight breeze from the motion of the carriage was delightful. She kept turning to look back at Tom, who was only a few paces behind, then said to Mr Walters: 'We should have sent word that Emma was not coming, and then your brother would not have needed to ride.'

'Oh, but Tom prefers it,' said Mr Walters. 'Besides, on such a warm day I should think you ladies would like to have plenty of room. It is more . . . elegant,' and he smiled at Anne.

Perhaps Anne was the happiest of them all. She felt that her health was improving with every day that passed, and could not help noticing as she brushed her hair that morning, that it had grown thicker and glossier. She had never been vain, but it was a secret satisfaction to her that, though pale, she no longer looked sickly.

It was a little before noon as they crossed the Thames, and passed through a handsome pair of gates into a long avenue, at the end of which was a fine old house, with a double flight of steps leading up to a noble portico. They entered a wide hall, and looked about them at the profusion of marble and fine paintings. They were then conducted down a long corridor, and shown into a large room, with windows opening down to the ground. From the house, the grounds sloped gently to the river, and were shaded by chestnuts and a fine cedar.

'Oh, Lord Urswick,' said Selina, 'I have never seen anything so beautiful in all my life!'

Before they had time to do more than look about them the door opened, and Lord Urswick's aunt came into the room. Lady Maria Dalton was a tall, thin, formidable-looking woman between forty and fifty, highly rouged, and dressed bizarrely in what the young ladies rightly took to be the latest fashion. Her abundant hair was piled high on her head making her look even taller. She was attended by a small plain woman in black.

'Ah, Roly,' she said, coming forward with outstretched hand, 'How d'ye do? I am glad to see you here - and your friends of course,' she said, looking appraisingly at the young ladies.

Lord Urswick hastened to present his friends to Lady Maria, and Selina, overawed, made such a low curtsey that it was only with difficulty that she could get up at all.

'I see you are admiring that portrait,' said Lady Maria to Mr Walters, whose thoughts were elsewhere, and who started a little at being addressed. 'That is my late husband, Sir Edmund, painted by Romney. It was always considered a very good likeness.'

Mr Walters thought that Sir Edmund could not have been flattered by the portrait, which depicted him as a fat, florid man, who looked as though he enjoyed his claret.

'He was carried off by a fit of apoplexy after a particularly fine dinner,' went on Lady Maria, taking a handkerchief from her sleeve and wiping away a non-existent tear. 'That was five years ago, but I do not believe in repining. I want for nothing and take great pleasure in having young people about me. Life must go on, you know,' as though Mr Walters had contradicted her.

A cold collation had been laid in the dining room for the visitors, and they needed little urging to eat and drink.

'When you feel refreshed I shall show you the house,' said Lady Maria. 'It was built in the reign of Queen Anne, but has had a number of recent improvements.'

The young people would have preferred to go outside immediately, but contained their disappointment, and smiled their thanks. Lord Urswick had seated himself between Anna and Bella, and was making himself agreeable to them. In this setting, with his aunt presiding regally at the further end, he seemed very much aware of his own rank, and was haughty with Selina Elton, almost ignoring her completely. She was aware of what he was at, but instead of maintaining her dignity, she persisted in addressing him.

'Lady Maria is a vastly elegant woman, Lord Urswick,' she said, 'and it is handsome of her to entertain us, being unknown to her before.' Lord Urswick responded with a cool nod. 'I shall not be able to remember half the dishes to tell Papa. Oh, how I wish I were a fine lady and could eat like this every day.' Lord Urswick looked at her in amazement, then turned to Anna and said: 'Perhaps your young friend is not aware that it is an impertinence to presume to praise in this manner.' It was said in an undertone, but was perfectly audible to Selina, who looked overcome with mortification, and to Tom Walters, who was sitting next to her. With a scornful look at Lord Urswick, he kindly drew her attention to himself; and by talking nonsense made her smile unwillingly. Georgiana, who had witnessed the whole episode, honoured him for it.

It was nearly an hour later that they were finally able to go out-of-doors, and walk about the grounds. Lady Maria had conducted them proudly from room to room, pointing out the pictures to be admired and the ancient marbles which Sir Edmund had brought back from the Grand Tour. Georgiana was beginning to feel she could not endure another ancestral portrait, and Anne was looking pale, when Lord Urswick suggested to his aunt that they go out to look at the peacocks.

'Oh, if you are going outside I beg to be excused. The heat will be too much for me,' said Lady Maria languidly. 'Please go anywhere you wish. Dinner will be at half past five,' and she swept off down the long gallery to her own apartments.

It was delightful to walk about in the dappled shade; Lord Urswick led the way with Henry and Anna, Selina trailing a little behind them; then, some yards behind, came Bella, Anne, and Georgiana, closely followed by Mr Walters and his brother. The harsh cries of the peacocks could be heard coming from beyond the kitchen-garden, and Lord Urswick's party went towards the sound, and were soon lost to sight. There was a large fountain on the terrace, which attracted the attention of the second group, and they paused to admire the statue of Neptune with his trident, and dolphins sporting about his feet. Anne rested against the rim, and trailed her hand in the water. This was tempting to the other young ladies, who did likewise. Tom Walters thought it would be amusing to splash his sister, but she, divining his intention, moved out of the way and it was Georgiana who received a handful of water in her face. She started back, momentarily blinded, but before Tom could apologise, or make amends, Mr Walters drew out his pocket handkerchief and offered it to her. She took it gratefully, and wiped her face, laughing, then noticed that something else had come out of his pocket, and was lying on the ground. Georgiana leaned forward to pick it up, and saw that it was a lady's handkerchief, beautifully edged with pansies and lace. It looked familiar, and without thinking, she turned it over, and saw the initials A. W.

'I believe this is yours, sir,' she said, handing it back to him. Mr Walters looked at the handkerchief, and then at her, and reddened.

'It is my sister's,' he said, hastily. 'Here, Anne, you will be needing this.'

Georgiana, confused and angry, finished drying her hands and gave back the crumpled linen to Mr Walters. She had recognised the embroidered handkerchief as belonging to Anna, which was confirmed by the Enscombe crest above the initials. What could this mean? Was there an understanding between Mr Walters and Anna, and if so, what did he mean by paying such marked attention to Emma? He could not have come by the handkerchief by any proper means that she could think of. While Georgiana was pondering these questions, Mr Walters had moved on with his sister and Bella. Tom Walters lingered to make his apologies.

'I am such a clumsy fellow, Miss Knightley,' he said, ruefully. 'I hope I haven't ruined your gown.'

'Oh, no,' said Georgiana, indifferently, 'it will soon dry. So, Mr Walters, you leave for Ireland tomorrow?'

'Yes, we have a long journey ahead of us.'

'Perhaps you should have spent the day preparing for it,' said Georgiana, archly.

'Oh, I could not resist the opportunity of spending one last day with . . . in such pleasant company.' He smiled down at her. 'But why didn't your sister join us? Is she ill?'

'No,' said the candid Georgiana, 'she is never ill. I cannot speak for Emma - you must ask her yourself.'

'Alas, we must make a very early start tomorrow, and will not have the pleasure of calling on you to take our leave. My brother is particularly disappointed not to see Miss Knightley here, as we shall be away some weeks.'

Ahead of them Mr Walters had lingered to speak to Anna, returning from seeing the peacocks, and they were deep in conversation.

'Oh, I think your brother finds himself very well entertained,' said Georgiana, with some spirit, and Tom looked at her in some surprise.

'I beg you pardon, but I do not understand you,' he said.

'I simply meant,' said Georgiana, recollecting herself, 'that your brother could hardly require the presence of another when he is already in such congenial company.'

Tom felt he had said something to offend, but hardly knew what. If only ladies would speak their minds like gentlemen, he thought, he would always know where he stood. He was not one to worry for long, however, and on an impulse, began to run ahead, calling his sister to come and see the peacocks.

After Anne had duly admired the peacocks and spent some time looking at the curious plants in the hot-houses, she felt exhausted and needed to sit down. Tom found her a seat overlooking the river, where she could watch the boats and barges sailing by. Georgiana said she would stay with her while her two brothers went to inspect some fine horses in a paddock just beyond the kitchen garden. There was a broad path leading off along the river-bank under the willows, and Bella suggested to Henry that they take a walk in the shade. Looking round for Selina and Lord Urswick who were nowhere to be seen, Anna joined them and they set off, ducking under the trailing fronds of the willow, and were soon lost to sight.

'Perhaps you would do better to go back into the house,' said Georgiana, looking anxiously at Anne. 'I will ask one of the servants to bring you a cooling drink.'

'No, I thank you,' said Anne, eagerly, 'do not trouble yourself. I am perfectly happy sitting here. This is a sweet spot, Georgiana. There is something so restful about the lapping of the water, and the light and shade playing on the surface, as the willows are stirred by the breeze. Even though I was only a child at the time, I used to long for a place like this when we lived in India. Sometimes I felt I could hardly breathe . . . Oh, look, here are some swans.' They both watched the swans for a little while, then Anne closed her eyes, and leaning back, rested her head against the trunk of the tree.

Georgiana wanted very much to ask Anne about the handkerchief, but hardly knew how to begin. After pondering for a while, she decided to wait until she could talk it over with Emma. The minutes went by and her own eyelids were beginning to droop, when there was a 'Halloa' from the river. Startled, Georgiana opened her eyes and saw a rowing boat drawing towards a landing stage to her left. The boat was being rowed by Lord Urswick, and Selina Elton, smiling triumphantly, was seated opposite him, holding a parasol.

'Give a hand here, Miss Knightley,' called Lord Urswick, and obediently Georgiana ran down to the end of the jetty, and caught the rope he threw to her. She had no idea how to make it secure, and Lord Urswick was shouting 'Tie it round the post!' when Tom Walters, hearing the commotion, and summing up the situation in a moment, came running to her aid. Tom soon had the boat tied up somewhat inexpertly, and gave a hand to Selina as she stood up, wobbling precariously, the little craft bobbing like a cork.

'Oh!' she squealed, 'I am getting my shoes wet!' But with a push from Lord Urswick, and a haul from Tom she found herself safely on the jetty.

'Oh, Mr Walters,' she said, clinging to his arm, 'I feel so strange!'

The obliging Tom helped her to a seat beside his sister, who had viewed the whole proceedings with quiet amusement.

'Lord Urswick says you have to get your sea-legs to feel secure in a boat,' said Selina, puzzled, 'but I told him this was only a river.' She was still trembling.

'Have you been on the river long?' asked Georgiana curiously.

'Oh yes, this hour and more. Lord Urswick knew that there was always a rowing-boat to be found here, and thought it would be great sport to run off while the others weren't looking.'

Georgiana was tempted to point out the impropriety of such behaviour, but reflected that Selina was not *her* sister, and might not take kindly to a hint, however well-intentioned.

Anna, however, had no such scruples. They were all drifting back along the terrace after their various excursions, when Selina ran up to Anna, and, taking her arm, said gaily: 'Oh Miss Weston, you will never guess where I have been!' Anna stood still and listened as Selina told all in a confidential tone, interspersed with giggles, and her expression was one of grave displeasure. Taking Selina aside, and waiting until the others were out of earshot, Anna began to scold her, and it was not long before Selina was sobbing piteously.

It was now the dinner hour, and after that the carriages were brought round, and they took their leave of Lady Maria. It was a subdued drive home; Anna had refused to have Selina in the same carriage as herself, and with scant courtesy, had made her change places with Georgiana. Lord Urswick was annoyed with Anna for being so high-handed, and sat muttering to Henry, who kept yawning. Georgiana was furious at being ordered about by Anna, and refused to speak at all. In the other carriage the atmosphere was little better; Bella chatted amiably to Anne, but pointedly ignored Selina, while Mr Walters looked fagged to death, and scarcely said a word.

Chapter 9

Although Emma still wished she had gone to Richmond, she felt it would do no good to dwell on her disappointment, and resigned herself to spending a tame and quiet day at home. A few minutes before ten o'clock her father reminded her of her promise to walk with him to Hartfield, and once out into the soft air, with the mill stream sparkling on their left, Emma's spirits rose, and she was able to respond cheerfully to her father's remarks. They were welcomed at Hartfield by Mr John Knightley, and the two gentlemen went straight into the library, leaving Emma to seek her aunt in the drawing room. Mrs John Knightley was feeling low-spirited, and Emma spent half an hour with her, helping her sort the strands of wool for her worsted work. John came in just as she was about to take her leave, and seemed surprised to see her there.

'I thought you would have gone to Richmond with the others,' he said. 'However, I am glad to see you do not care for that sort of thing.'

In general, nothing could be further from the truth, for Emma liked an excursion as much as anyone; but she let it pass, feeling unequal to giving any adequate reason for not going.

'Emma is just off to visit Miss Bates,' said Mrs John Knightley. 'Why don't you walk with her, John, if you have no other engagement?'

'Well,' said he, considering, 'I could walk as far as the farrier's with you. That wretched Urswick lamed my horse, and I want Dawkins to come and take a look at him.'

As they walked together across the broad sweep which led out on to the Highbury road, Emma said: 'What a beautiful day for driving in an open carriage.' John looked about him, but there was no carriage in sight.

'Oh, I suppose you are thinking of Richmond,' said he, indifferently, 'but Emma, there is something I want to tell you.' Emma was surprised at his portentous tone.

'You look very serious, John,' she said, looking at him enquiringly. 'It is not bad news, I hope?'

'Not at all, not at all; if my uncle is agreeable, and I have no reason to fear otherwise, it will be very good news indeed.'

'This is most intriguing, John, but do not keep me in suspense. How is my father concerned with this good news?' said Emma.

'Why, at this very moment, I hope he is consenting to my receiving the Donwell living.'

'But how can that be?' cried Emma. 'You are not a clergyman.'

They had just reached the bridge that led to the main street of Highbury, and they paused to look over the parapet at the fast-flowing water.

'If my uncle gives his consent, I shall go immediately to Oxford and prepare for ordination.'

'Of course, even if he does consent, it may be some years before the living becomes vacant,' said Emma, almost feeling that John was anxious to precipitate the Rector's demise.

'Not so!' said John, triumphantly, 'for I have it from Mr Elton that old Mr Otway wishes to retire. His married daughter is settled in Kingston, and would dearly like to have him make his home with her.'

They began to walk on.

'This is all so sudden, I can hardly believe it,' said Emma. 'Is there some other reason why you wish to set up your own establishment? Apart, that is,' she added hastily, 'from an earnest desire to follow a noble calling?'

John looked as if that aspect of a clergyman's life had not occurred to him.

'Well,' he said, smiling complacently, 'a man of five and twenty must marry sooner or later, don't you think so?'

'Indeed, if he has a good income and has found a young lady to love,' said Emma, doubtfully, 'but I never suspected you of cherishing a particular fondness for anyone.'

'It is most important to choose wisely,' said John. 'A clergyman's wife has much to do in the parish, and it is vital that she be of a sober, upright character. As to love . . . that will come. I flatter myself I am not altogether repulsive to the fair sex.' (Emma tried hard not to smile.) 'However, we will talk of this again. There is Miss Bates, just coming out of Ford's. If you make haste, Emma, you will catch up with her. Poor soul, she walks very slowly these days!' and with a 'Good day to you,' he turned in at the farrier's.

Emma spent a pleasant hour with Miss Bates, who was delighted to see her. After enquiring after Emma's parents and sister, Miss Bates said, with an arch look: 'A little bird told me that a certain gentleman will be going away soon.'

Emma blushed, thinking that she meant Mr Walters, but Miss Bates went on: 'Yes, Mr Elton called here only yesterday, and said he thought Mr John Knightley might be going to be ordained. There! I was never more surprised in my life! Not but what he would make a very fine parson, but Rector of Donwell . . . he is full young.' She paused for breath, and Emma put in quickly:

'My cousin mentioned it to me in confidence, Miss Bates. I do not think he would wish it to be generally known until the matter is settled.'

'Oh, my dear,' said Miss Bates, 'I shall not say a word! Mr Elton swore me to secrecy, but I thought it would be allowable to mention it to you, so close to him as you are.'

'Indeed, I think very highly of my cousin, John, but . . .' began Emma.

'That is just what I was going to say, my dear. I thought when I saw you together this morning that you make a lovely couple.'

Emma was both amused and horrified that Miss Bates should connect her with her cousin in this way, but she thought that to argue about it would serve only to fix the idea more firmly into Miss Bates's mind. Miss Bates was already off on another tack.

'I understand that a certain noble gentleman is paying marked attention to Miss Selina Elton,' she said, with a happy smile. 'She is a very pretty girl, and matches of greater disparity have taken place.'

'Forgive me, ma'am, but there I think you are mistaken,' said Emma.

'But I had it from Mr Elton,' said Miss Bates, eagerly. 'At least, he did not say so outright, but he dropped a hint, and looked pleased. Her driving in his carriage is a very marked attention, you know.'

Emma, exerting herself to change the subject, asked after the kitten, which was brought in from the kitchen to prove it had grown. After taking some refreshment and hearing all the rest of the news, Emma took her leave, Miss Bates following her to the gate and showering her with thanks. Outside the pastry-cook's shop she met her father, who was just coming to fetch her home. He turned back with her, smiling and greeting his neighbours the while. They crossed the bridge and, after passing Hartfield, Mr Knightley broached the subject uppermost in his mind and asked Emma if John had told her his news.

'Indeed he did, Papa, and I was never more astonished in my life.'

'Do you not think, then, that he will make a good clergyman?' asked her father.

'Oh, he will be no worse than many another, but I cannot help feeling he views it as an easy, comfortable life.'

'And is that so very bad?' said Mr Knightley, with a teasing smile.

'Papa, you know very well there should be something more; a desire to help the unfortunate, a zeal for souls, even,' said Emma eagerly.

'Come, we are getting into deep waters here. I think John is a sensible, honest man, with high principles, who will do his duty. We cannot ask for more. In short, I have given my consent. I must therefore defer my business in Kingston, and go to see Mr Otway this afternoon, otherwise it will be all over the village, and I would not have him hear it from anyone but myself.'

'I fear it may already be too late, Papa,' said Emma. 'Miss Bates was full of it just now. Mr Elton told her.'

Mr Knightley bit his lip in annoyance. 'In that case I must go to Mr Otway at once. Will you tell your Mama I shall be late?' and leaving Emma at the entrance to Donwell Abbey, he strode off down the lane to the Rector's house.

It was late when Georgiana arrived home from Richmond, and it was not until eleven o'clock the following morning that she had an opportunity for a long talk with Emma. The day was overcast and threatening thunder; Mr Knightley, fearing for his grain which was ripening fast, had ridden over to Home Farm to consult with his bailiff. Mrs Knightley was also absent, having gone to call on her sister, who was unwell.

'They have chosen a bad day for their journey,' said Emma, looking out of the window at the darkening sky.

'Papa and Mama?' said Georgiana, in surprise. 'Oh no, you were thinking of Mr Walters and his brother. I hope the rain holds off.'

'Yes, Georgiana, I was thinking of Mr Walters, but only because it looks as if it might be stormy. I never think of him for any other reason, I assure you.'

Emma was not in the habit of telling untruths, but in this case she had convinced herself she was telling the truth.

'I think you may be right not to trust him, Emma,' said Georgiana, seriously. 'I hardly know how to tell you this, but something very strange happened yesterday,' and she related the circumstances of the dropped handkerchief.

'If he said it was his sister's, then it must be so; her initials are the same as Anna's,' said Emma, wanting to defend Mr Walters to Georgiana, though she had spent the past few days censuring him in her heart.

'That is true,' said Georgiana, 'but the handkerchief was so distinctive. I remember when Anna first came here you admired one of hers that had a border of cornflowers under the lace. This one was just like it, only it was worked with tiny pansies, and when I turned it over it had the Enscombe crest above the initials.'

'Perhaps Anna gave Anne the handkerchief,' said Emma. 'She has always been very generous with her possessions. She pressed me to accept a work-box when I happened to admire it, and it was very difficult to refuse it.'

'Then why did Mr Walters redden and look conscious when I picked it up?' said Georgiana.

'There could be a number of reasons,' said Emma laughing. 'Most gentlemen do not carry pretty little pocket handkerchiefs of that sort!'

It was still a mystery, but Emma, far from feeling greater mistrust, felt sure there must be a rational explanation, and scolded herself for making so much of it. She remembered the look on Mr Walters' face when he realised she was not going to Richmond. There was real disappointment in his expression. Even Georgiana's opinion, that Mr Walters had not enjoyed his day out, was balm to her soul.

Georgiana then told Emma about Selina Elton and Lord Urswick, the giggling and flirting, finishing with: 'They were gone an hour or more upon the river.'

'I fear he is trifling with her,' said Emma, 'and destroying her good name into the bargain. I have never liked Mrs Elton, but I do her the justice to say this: Selina would never have dared to behave in such a light and foolish fashion if her Mama had been at home. Mr Elton does not seem to notice anything she does.'

Anna had been out all morning, but did not say where she had been. The dark clouds had passed over, and that afternoon the two sisters decided to call on Anne Walters. It was a relief to go to Donwell Court without being suspected of pursuing the young men, which had been the substance of one or two ill-natured remarks from Selina Elton. Mrs Walters made them very welcome, and they were shown, as usual, into Anne's little parlour.

'I am so pleased to see you both,' she said, 'for it is so dull without my brothers. I thought the morning would never end. They were away very early this morning, or they would have been sure to call on you. James made a great point of it, so I hope you will excuse him. Shall I send him your good wishes when I write, Emma?'

Emma smiled and said what was proper, and with raised spirits chatted and laughed. Anne and Georgiana re-lived the whole of the previous day for Emma's entertainment, and she was greatly amused.

'Oh, I almost forgot,' said Emma; 'such a piece of news about our cousin, John!' and she told them what she had heard the previous day.

'I think Mr John Knightley will make a splendid clergyman,' said Anne. 'He has such a deep, sonorous voice which is just suited to delivering sermons; and he has such a kind heart.'

Emma and Georgiana cast round hastily for some remembrance of his kind heart, but could not think of any.

'Whenever I hear his 'deep, sonorous voice',' said Emma, laughing, 'he is usually shouting: 'Get out of it, you young devils!' at Frank and Charles! My father says he is to leave for Oxford next week, which will sadly deplete our circle of acquaintance.'

'I do not think Anna will stay much longer, either,' said Georgiana. 'She told me, in the carriage coming home, that she has written to her guardian to ask if she may return to London. Then, of course Lord Urswick will go too, and maybe Henry. We shall be very dull without them.'

'We never used to find our lives dull,' said Emma, considering, 'but so much has happened in the past few months; so many new acquaintance, so much coming and going; I confess, I find it a little unsettling.'

'I have grown to love Highbury, and Donwell, and everyone in them,' said Anne. 'I am so happy Papa chose to settle here. I could never be dull when I have two such good friends to entertain me,' and she clasped their hands affectionately.

Mr Knightley was very happy to have the power to bestow the Donwell living upon his nephew, John. He had a very cordial interview with Mr Otway, a widower of some seventy years old, who had for some time desired to accept his daughter's invitation. He agreed to vacate the living at Mr Knightley's convenience, and happily conducted him through the large Parsonage, which was in need of some improvement. On his way home, Mr Knightley thought with rather less pleasure of his eldest nephew, Henry, who had been the principal subject of his interview with Henry's father. How Mr Knightley wished he could leave Donwell in more fitting hands, but, as this was impossible, he determined to try to improve Henry's character, and make him more aware of the serious duties he would one day undertake.

He had proposed to Mr John Knightley that Henry should spend some time with the Donwell bailiff, learning about the management of the estate, and with Mr Martin of Abbey Mill Farm, to acquire some knowledge at first-hand of crop management and animal husbandry. It was an unusual step to take, but Mr John Knightley thoroughly approved the measure, being convinced that a life of luxury and idleness was ruining his son. The following evening he requested a private word with Henry, who joined him after dinner, full of suspense. When he told Henry of his uncle's proposals, he was angry and indignant.

'What! Live on a farm, and herd sheep, or feed pigs? That is no occupation for a gentleman, Father; you cannot require it of me. It is too much! Perhaps my uncle thinks I should go with Mrs Martin to the dairy and learn to make butter and cheese.'

'I believe Mrs Martin has a dairy-maid to perform that office,' said Mr John Knightley, dryly. 'Henry, your uncle wishes you to be a good landlord, whenever you come into your inheritance. He would like you to ride out with him and his bailiff to oversee improvements and understand the source of your revenues. As for Abbey Mill Farm, your uncle does not expect you to soil your hands, not that your brothers seem to mind. No, if you are to understand what it is to be a farmer, you will be quick to see when matters go awry and have the ability to set them to rights. Your uncle knows all the minutest concerns of the estate, down to which apples sell best at market. He also knows each of his tenants by name and interests himself in all their concerns. If you turn out to be half as good a man as he is, I will be satisfied.'

Henry realised that further argument was useless, and at a sign from his father he turned to go.

'One more thing,' said his father, as he turned the door handle. 'You may choose not to oblige me in this - you are of age, after all - but I warn you that I intend to reduce your allowance by half until I see some improvement in your conduct. You may go.'

Henry's only response was to bang the door. In the hallway he found Lord Urswick hovering, anxious to know the outcome.

'It is even worse than I thought, Urswick,' said Henry. 'I must get some air - are you coming?'

They went out of the house and turned towards Donwell, Henry not having any clear idea of where he was going. For a while he strode ahead so fast, lashing at the nettles with his stick, that Lord Urswick had difficulty in keeping pace with him. At last he slowed down, and leaning on a stile, he looked across the fields sloping down to the river, to the distant hills. It was a pleasant prospect, and Henry began to think of the value of his inheritance; more than a thousand acres of good arable and pasture land, fine timber and good tenants.

'It's no good, Urswick,' he said slowly. 'I'll have to obey my father in the end,' and he told his friend of the arrangements that had been made for him. Lord Urswick was full of indignation, and urged Henry to go back and tell his father to go to the devil, but Henry thought that might not be wise.

'Well, if you are going to be occupied all the time,' said Lord Urswick, 'there is little point in my staying here. Anna seems to be suffering from *ennui*, and wishes to return to London. Perhaps I shall stay for another week or so, until she has obtained permission from her guardian, then I shall have the pleasure of conveying her thither. I shall persuade her to bring the fair Selina - I have not done with that little minx as yet.'

'I should be careful there if I were you, Urswick,' said Henry. 'She seems an empty-headed little thing, but she has ambition. Take care you are not lured into matrimony.'

'What? Marry a chit of a village girl? I think not, my boy. She amuses me, that's all, and in London she might amuse me still more.'

They had reached the entrance to Donwell Abbey, and Henry stood for a moment, wondering whether to call on his uncle or not. He had regained his good humour, and thought his punishment (as he saw it) might be shorter if he accepted it with a willing spirit. He was saved the trouble of going down to the house by the appearance of his uncle, who was taking a stroll in the evening air. He greeted them cordially, and invited them into the house, but they civilly declined, Henry begging the favour of a private word. Lord Urswick said he would start back to Hartfield, and they were left alone.

'Have you spoken with your father?' asked Mr Knightley.

'I have, sir. I confess I did not like it much at first, but I know you mean to do me good, and I am grateful to you.'

Mr Knightley was privately astonished that Henry should accept his proposals so meekly, but merely said: 'Well done, my boy. Come over early on Monday, and we will ride out together. There are a couple of cottages in Lower Farm Lane which have fallen into disrepair. One has been untenanted for over a year, and the old man in the other may have to move into the almshouse soon as he is so frail. I am minded to pull them down; perhaps you could favour me with your opinion,' and with a friendly handshake he left Henry to hurry away after his friend.

A week went by, Anna had still had no word from her guardian, and Lord Urswick was showing no sign of returning to London without her. John had arranged to leave for Oxford on the Friday of that week, and in honour of the occasion, he and his family had been invited to dine at Donwell Court. Mr and Mrs Knightley and their daughters had also been invited. The engagement was for Wednesday, and the day was still very warm at five o'clock, as both carriages turned in at the gates of Donwell Court.

They were shown into the large drawing room, which had been handsomely fitted up by Colonel Walters and his lady, and were given a warm welcome. Anne claimed Emma and Georgiana, and Bella quickly joined them. Anna seemed to be trying to be particularly agreeable to her hostess and the other ladies, who were smiling graciously. John meanwhile engaged his uncle in serious conversation. Henry and Lord Urswick, not usually awkward in company, had very little to say.

'We had the pleasure of hearing from James this morning,' said Anne. 'He was happy to tell us that the fires were caused by one of the estate workers. The man had no political motive, but wished to take revenge for being dismissed from his post for dishonesty. He has been handed over to the authorities and all is calm. The overseer there is an honest, reliable man, and my brother thinks that matters may be safely left in his hands.'

'Does this mean your brothers will be coming home sooner than expected?' asked Emma, eagerly.

'He didn't mention coming home just yet, but it does seem likely. He asks to be remembered to you, Emma,' said Anne with a smile. Emma could not help smiling with pleasure, and Bella looked a little piqued.

'They have been gone less than a fortnight,' she said, 'and there must be a great deal to do. You must learn to do without the attentions of Mr Walters a little longer, Emma.' It was said in playful fashion, but Emma heard the hint of jealousy in her tone, and was surprised. Usually she and Bella were the best of friends.

Dinner was announced, and they all went into the dining room. Emma found herself seated next to her cousin, John, who was particularly assiduous in his attentions. Emma, remembering what Miss Bates had said, felt uneasy; she had a great affection for all her Knightley cousins, particularly so since she had no brothers of her own, but it was precisely this that made her feel, even if her affections had not been engaged elsewhere, that John could never be more to her than a brother. She found she was evaluating everything he said, and was hoping for an opportunity to put some distance between them. It came at last. She had made some trivial observation which John seized upon, and, leaning towards her confidentially he said: 'Exactly! Emma, you and I are alike in every particular, but then, we always were the best of friends, weren't we?'

'Indeed, John,' said Emma, moving a little away from him, 'I have always loved you like a brother,' and catching her father's eye, she asked him some question about the harvest.

Anna, Henry and Lord Urswick were behaving very decorously hoping not to incur the displeasure of their elders. Mr John Knightley spoke approvingly to Colonel Walters of his son's initiation into estate management.

'I had always fancied it was your son, George, who was interested in the estate,' said Colonel Walters. 'I often see him about the district in the company of young Mr Martin, of Abbey Mill Farm.'

'Yes, I could never interest George in the law, or any other profession. He is a fellow who must always be out-of-doors. Rob Martin is a steady, reliable companion - I have no fears for him while he is with Rob Martin. Robert has been educated, you know, and is quite the gentleman; and he will inherit a very pretty property in Abbey Mill Farm. One of my brother's tenants, Mr Cox of Upper Farm, is getting old and has no one to come after him. George is hoping his uncle will give him the tenancy when it becomes available.'

'You are fortunate in having so many fine sons, sir,' said Colonel Walters. 'What a blessing it is to have them so well provided for.'

After tea and coffee were served there was music, then someone suggested dancing, and Mrs Walters offered to play. Emma was immediately engaged by John, and they led off, followed by Bella and Lord Urswick, and Anna with Henry. To make up the set, Anne stood up with Georgiana. Emma concentrated on her dancing, and went down the set without a word. Anne could only manage one dance, and went to sit by her mother, so her father offered his hand to Anna, who was glad to stand up with such a fine, military figure. Henry danced with Georgiana, and Emma, who had walked away to speak to her mother, found that she would have to stand up with John again. Notwithstanding any other reason, it was a penance for Emma to dance with John, for he did it very badly, casting off left when he should have gone right, and stepping on her toes. After the second dance she was applied to by Lord Urswick, and made her escape from John, who, unabashed, took an opportunity to stand close to her as they waited for the carriages to be brought round, saying: 'I shall call on you tomorrow.' He took her hand as though meaning to kiss it, but she snatched it angrily away, and went and stood by her father.

John called at Donwell the following morning to take his leave, intending to set out for Oxford on Friday. He met with a very cordial reception from his aunt and uncle, but Emma would say nothing to him beyond the merest civilities.

Georgiana had torn her gown the previous evening, and as Anna had offered her the services of Marie, who was an expert needlewoman, they soon left the room to seek her out. John was asking his uncle about the harvest, which developed into a talk about the weather in general, and he finished by complimenting his aunt on the garden, which was looking particularly fine.

'Those new rose bushes which were planted only last autumn are doing particularly well,' said Mrs Knightley. 'They are on a sheltered bank near the beginning of the avenue,' and on John's expressing an interest, she went on: 'Emma you were cutting some of those lovely dark red ones only yesterday. Perhaps you would be kind enough to show them to John.'

There was nothing Emma could do but obey, so they walked out of the house and across the lawn.

'I was hoping to speak to you, Emma,' said John, as soon as they were well away from the house, 'and I am sure that what I am going to say will come as no surprise.'

Emma, wanting to run away, nevertheless felt that she should hear him out.

'You and I have always been close since you were quite a little thing, and now my future is decided there is nothing to stand in our way. You must know I love you dearly, and you are ideally suited to being the wife of a clergyman . . .'

'Let me be quite clear about this, John,' Emma interrupted him eagerly. 'Are you asking me to be your wife?'

'Of course. Come, do not be 'missish' and pretend to be surprised.'

'I am not just surprised, I am astonished!' cried Emma. 'John, you are my cousin!'

'To marry a cousin is within the degrees of kindred permitted by the Church of England,' said John in a pompous tone. 'If Mother Church does not object, why should you?'

'I cannot marry you, John,' said Emma, trying to keep from sounding impatient. 'I do not mean to be unkind, and I thank you for thinking of me, but I do not love you.'

'Not love me!' cried John, indignantly. 'Why, only last evening you said you loved me, which is what prompted me to try for your hand before I go away. I fear you are trifling with me, Emma,' and he directed at her a look of approach.

Emma remembering what she had said to John, and feeling unequal to going over the whole matter again, suddenly burst out laughing.

'You see!' cried John, in an injured tone, 'You *are* trifling with me. I expected better from you, Emma.' Emma was sorry and tried to put matters right.

'My dear John,' she said, persuasively, 'you are right when you say we have always been friends, but you must not confuse that friendship with love. I hope this will not spoil our friendship, but I really cannot marry you. You are too noble, I am sure, to be angry with me for what I cannot help.'

John still looked resentful, but said nothing for the moment, and they walked on towards the bank of roses.

'Perhaps if I spoke to your father,' he said, thoughtfully. 'I am sure he could persuade you that it would be in your best interests to accept me.'

'Now I have done!' cried Emma, losing her temper. 'It is most disagreeable to me to have you persist in this ill-bred fashion. Do not delude yourself that I will ever change my mind,' and she turned and began to run back to the house. Her mother saw her as she hurried into the hall, and said in some surprise:

'Where is John? I thought he would have come back to the house with you.'

Emma made what excuse she could, and wanting to be alone, went upstairs to her bed-room.

John set off for Oxford the following morning without speaking to his uncle, much to Emma's relief. He was angry and resentful, but having had no real feelings for Emma, it was his pride that was hurt. Emma hoped that during his absence he would come to see reason, and it would be as though nothing had happened when he returned.

Chapter 10

A week went by, the harvest was being gathered in, and Anna still had no word from her guardian. She guessed that he had gone from France into Italy, and was beginning to despair of ever hearing from him, when the longed-for letter arrived. He wrote from Florence, and at first she was a little disappointed to find he was full of his own concerns. It was evident he had forgotten his reason for sending her into Surrey in the first place, for he gave Anna permission to return to London, providing she took with her some female companion. He sent his compliments to Mr and Mrs Knightley, and ended by saying it would only be three or four weeks before he would be home again, and he begged that she would 'stay out of mischief' until then.

The yielding, indolent tone was just what Anna had hoped for, and she took the letter and showed it to Mrs Knightley. That good lady was a little perplexed, and unsure of the propriety of Anna's living alone.

'But ma'am,' said Anna, 'I shall hardly be alone. In our London house there is a butler, a housekeeper, two footmen . . .'

'Anna,' said Mrs Knightley, with some asperity, 'I beg that you will not be satirical. You must engage some well-bred woman, not young, to return with you to London.'

'Oh, if it is necessary,' said Anna carelessly, 'I shall take steps to find someone in London, but what do you say to Selina Elton as a companion, ma'am?'

'I should say she is most unsuitable,' cried Mrs Knightley. 'Forgive me, Anna, I never thought it wise in you to encourage that girl.'

'My guardian would not be so nice,' said Anna, haughtily. 'Selina is a gentlewoman, and I am sure she would be glad to get away from home for a while. I intend to call on her father this morning. If he does not object, ma'am, I shall return to London by the end of the week, and take Selina with me.'

Anna met with no opposition from Mr Elton; indeed, she thought he seemed ready to bundle Selina out of the house at that very moment. He was delighted, and his broad face was wreathed in smiles.

'Selina, my dear,' he said, 'thank Miss Weston for your great good fortune. As a companion you will go everywhere with Miss Weston, and do whatever she requires of you.'

'Oh, I will, Papa, I will!' cried Selina, in a very transport of joy.

'I expect you would like a private word with my daughter, Miss Weston,' said Mr Elton. 'If you will excuse me, I shall go to my study,' and pausing only to pat Selina fondly on the shoulder, he left the room.

'Selina, I must make haste and call on Lord Urswick. I am sure he will make no difficulty about your accompanying me in his carriage, but I must just say this: I expect you to conduct yourself at all times as a gentlewoman should.'

'Of course, Miss Weston, I should not dream of doing otherwise,' said Selina, eagerly.

Anna put up a restraining hand: 'Please allow me to continue. We will not mention your going off with Lord Urswick in that disgraceful way, but there is something else. I regret to say that I have noticed in you a love of finery. As my companion this is not appropriate; you must dress more quietly. I beg therefore, that you will remove all the lace from your gowns, and bring with you only the plainest.'

Poor Selina began to look alarmed.

'If you begin immediately, you will have ample time to prepare properly. Marie is good with her needle - I shall send her to you.'

Selina was very much in awe of Anna's maid, but as she was a poor needlewoman herself, she had no option but to agree.

It would be mortifying to lose the trimmings on her best gowns, but Selina would have been willing to dress in sackcloth for the opportunity of going to London.

Selina had so lopped and cropped her gowns, and removed the trimmings from her bonnets, that she looked like a little Puritan as she stepped into Lord Urswick's carriage one morning in early September. Anna, impatient to be off, was short to the point of rudeness with both father and daughter, and their leave-taking was consequently brief. Mr Elton gave scant thought to his younger daughter, or to the dubious protection afforded by Miss Weston, as he re-entered the Vicarage. He was eager to open a letter from his wife, which had just at that moment been put into his hand. It was some time since she had written, and he read it with curiosity mixed with dread, for some of her letters had not been kind. The letter opened very cordially:

My dear Mr E.,

Such good news about Selina! It has long been my wish that my daughters should move in a more superior society than that afforded by Highbury. Please give her my best love, and tell her most particularly to write to me soon.

You will wonder, my love, what can have detained us so long in Bath. My letters have been very short, but I know my caro sposo will forgive me when he hears my news. Our dearest Augusta is going to be married! There, are you not astonished? But you will wish to know how it came about.

You must remember I told you in my last letter that we had met with your old friend, Mr Craig, who is Vicar of Upton Prior. He came to Bath for his health some time ago, and was captivated by Augusta straight away. Upton Prior is but a short distance from Bath, and we have since

visited him there on several occasions. I enclose a note from him, asking
your blessing, which I am sure you will not withhold.

Once we have purchased Augusta's wedding clothes, we shall be home
within the week. I cannot tell you, my dear husband, how I long to see you
again, now the late unpleasantness has passed.

                    Your loving wife,

                              Augusta Elton

Mr Elton stood up, walked about, and sat down again several
times before he could take in what his wife had told him. The
Mr Craig in question had been up at Oxford with Mr Elton
and was, perhaps, a year younger. His wife had died some eight
months earlier from a lingering illness, leaving him with a son
of ten, and a daughter of fourteen years. He was a respectable,
well-to-do man, but Mr Elton was concerned that his beloved
elder daughter should be married to a man old enough to be
her father. After some deliberation, he sat down to write his
consent to the match, consoling himself with the thought that
he could better ascertain Augusta's feelings in the matter once
she was safely home.

Henry Knightley, much to his surprise, was enjoying the regime
imposed upon him by his father and uncle. He rose early, and
took his exercise by riding over to the Home Farm, where he
joined the bailiff in his place of business, or rode out with
him about the estate. He sometimes visited Abbey Mill Farm
informally, and went out shooting with his brother, George,
and Rob Martin, whom he found surprisingly conversible. With
all the fresh air, he had to struggle to keep his eyes open after
ten in the evening, and was glad to go to his bed at what once
he would have termed an unconscionably early hour.

His mother was glad to speed Lord Urswick's departure,
being much occupied with preparing her two youngest sons

for the ordeal that awaited them - namely, to go out into the world to seek their fortune. Bella and the maids, together with Mrs John Knightley herself, were to be found from early until late sewing shirts, or fine-stitching linen, in preparation for their imminent departure. Charles, who was now fourteen, was to be taken up to London by his father on the fifth of September, and Frank was to leave the following day, on the Mail coach to Portsmouth.

About a week after the departure of Lord Urswick and Anna, Henry met with Mr Elton in the lanes. Mr Elton, smiling and affable, hurried through the usual civilities as though having something of importance to impart.

'I am sure you will be interested to hear, my dear sir,' he said, 'that Mrs Elton and Augusta are coming home three days hence, on Monday to be precise.'

Henry murmured something civil.

'Yes,' went on Mr Elton, 'everyone in Highbury will be surprised when they hear the banns being called for the first time on Sunday sennight.'

'Banns, sir? I do not understand you,' said Henry. 'Pray, whose banns are these?'

'Why, my daughter, Augusta, is the lady in the case. She has met a most respectable gentleman - old family friend - a widower, you know, and a clergyman; I knew him at Oxford.'

'Allow me to congratulate you, sir,' said Henry, feeling a slight pang. He had always had a liking - not mentioned at home - for Augusta Elton. 'I hope your daughter will be very happy.'

As Henry was walking his horse round to the stables at Hartfield, he met his two cousins who had been spending the morning with Bella.

'It is not often I have some news to impart . . .' he said gaily, but was interrupted by Georgiana.

'We know what you are going to say, Henry; Bella had it from Miss Bates. Augusta Elton is coming home to be married to an old man.'

'Oh come, Georgiana,' protested Emma, 'a man of three or four and forty can hardly be called 'old'. At that reckoning our dear Papa must be in his dotage!'

'Would *you* marry a man of that age?' retorted Georgiana, 'and a clergyman, too, which makes it worse. It would be like being married to Mr Elton, and I cannot imagine a worse fate than that!'

Emma could not help laughing, but Henry looked thoughtful.

'We always thought she had a fondness for you, Henry,' said Emma with a saucy look at her cousin, 'but perhaps she grew tired of waiting.' Henry looked disconcerted, but only said quietly:

'It seems sad for a girl of nineteen to throw herself away in this manner, but with the family fortune all to pieces she may have felt obliged to accept him.'

Emma nudged Georgiana, who said: 'It is not too late, Henry.'

'Too late?' said Henry, in some surprise. 'Oh, I see what you mean, but I assure you I never had a thought in that direction,' and taking his leave he walked on, past the offices to the stables.

Mrs Elton lost no time in calling at Donwell Abbey with Augusta, and seemed to Mrs Knightley to be more insufferable now than she had been three months earlier. Augusta looked tired and pale, and seemed pathetically grateful for the kind remarks of Emma and Georgiana.

'Where shall you live after you are married?' asked Emma.

'Why, at Upton Prior, of course; where else should she live?' cried Mrs Elton, before Augusta had time to answer.

'I'm sorry, ma'am,' said Emma, quickly, 'I had not heard all the details of the match.' Mrs Elton smiled graciously.

'Mrs Knightley,' she went on, 'it is such a pretty Parsonage, new-built only thirty years ago. Of course it grew a little shabby while Mrs Craig was ill, but all that is now in hand. Mr Craig has given Augusta *carte blanche* to choose the wallpaper, and he is fitting up a pretty little parlour for her use.'

'It must be very gratifying to you, Mrs Elton,' said Mrs Knightley, 'to have your elder daughter so well settled. What a pity Upton Prior is at such a distance.'

'Oh, we say nothing of that!' cried Mrs Elton. 'I shall be a very frequent visitor to that household, I can tell you.'

'Is there any news of Selina, ma'am?' asked Georgiana.

'Ah now, there I cannot comment, but we have our hopes. I understand a certain gentleman is charmed by her.'

'I expect she will come home soon, to attend Augusta at her wedding,' said Emma.

Mrs Elton was momentarily disconcerted. 'As to that, I cannot say. Selina is such a *close* friend of Miss Weston's that I doubt if she can be spared. In any case, there is no occasion for Augusta to have a bridesmaid. We do not believe in pomp and finery. The wedding is to be a very quiet affair, in view of Mr Craig's situation, but he is so enamoured of our dear Augusta that he wishes the nuptials to take place as soon as possible.'

Augusta looked even paler than before, and Emma asked her if she were quite well.

'Oh yes, I thank you,' she said, with a wan smile. 'I confess I am a little tired. It was a long journey from Bath, and there has been so much to do since then.'

'And is your father to perform the ceremony?' asked Emma.

'No, Papa is anxious to give me away, so Mr Otway is coming over to Highbury as a favour to marry us.'

'And are you going away after the wedding?' said Georgiana.

'Mr Craig says he cannot leave his children for very long, so as soon as we are wed, we must travel back to Upton Prior. Would it be presumptuous of me to ask you to write, Miss Knightley?'

Emma felt so sorry for her that she readily agreed.

After Mrs Elton and her daughter had taken their leave, Emma said to her mother: 'What do you think of this match, Mama? I cannot help feeling sorry for Augusta.'

'The poor girl does not look very happy,' said Mrs Knightley. 'I suspect she has been hurried into it by her mother, who sees only the size of the Parsonage and the occupant's fortune.'

'But if he loves her, Mama . . .?' said Georgiana.

'I should think convenience has more to do with it than love. Here is a man, no longer young, who needs a housekeeper and a mother for his children.' Mrs Knightley looked fondly at her girls. 'My dears,' she said, 'do anything rather than marry without love. Even where there is love, marriage is not a bed of roses, but to live on such intimate terms with someone you do not love would be insupportable.'

The banns had been called twice, and the Highbury gossips were wondering why the bridegroom had not appeared, when at last he arrived. Mr Elton had arranged for him to be lodged at the Crown, and a small band of loiterers watched as his box was carried in. The following day, a Sunday, a stout gentleman between forty and fifty was seen to enter the Vicarage pew, accompanied by Mrs Elton and Augusta. An old woman who was very deaf, and consequently spoke more loudly than was proper in a church, was heard to say:

'That's never 'im! 'E looks too old to be a bridegroom.'

There was a ripple of laughter, hastily stifled, and after the service was over, (the bridegroom's age being no just cause or impediment), a number of villagers found pressing reasons to linger in the churchyard, to get a better look.

Augusta, as pale as a lily, walked out with her intended husband, and paused to receive the good wishes of the neighbours. Mr Craig seemed very affable and pleasant, and regarded Augusta fondly. Mrs Elton smiled and bowed most regally, and took Mr Craig's arm, as he escorted them home.

The wedding, which took place on the following Friday, was a very quiet affair. It was the first of October, and the morning was chill and misty. The bride in a new pelisse over a silk gown, walked to church on her father's arm, the offer of the Knightley carriage having been refused. The bridal party was small; besides Mr and Mrs Elton there was Miss Bates, in her new bonnet and Kashmir shawl, Dr and Mrs Perry, and old Mr Cox, the lawyer. After the wedding breakfast, it was time for the happy couple to set off on their long journey back to Upton Prior.

'I wish Selina had been here, Mama,' said Augusta, as she kissed her parents.

'I know, my love, but it is for the best. We must not stand in her way. She is far more likely to meet with a suitable husband where she is, than if she stayed here in Highbury,' and with a 'God bless you!' they took their leave.

Henry Knightley felt that he had been working so hard, and behaving so nicely, that he deserved a reward. He duly applied to his father for leave to visit his friend, Urswick, for a few days. Mr John Knightley, who had been impressed with his diligence, gave his permission, with a stern warning to be back after the allotted period. The day after Augusta Elton's wedding, therefore, found Henry setting off for London. Emma and

Georgiana, meanwhile, had heard from Anne that her brothers would soon be home, and lived in daily expectation of a visit. Georgiana was the more eager of the two, Emma still doubting Mr Walters' intentions.

The longed-for visit came, and gave very little pleasure. Emma, glad that both her mother and her father were at home, scarcely looked up as the two young men entered the drawing room, and it was Georgiana who went forward eagerly to offer her hand. Mr and Mrs Knightley were at pains to make them welcome, but there seemed to be some awkwardness. Emma, thinking that it might be her fault for being less than cordial, put down her sewing and tried to interest herself in the conversation. Mr Walters, always quiet and reluctant to put himself forward, nevertheless managed to find a seat close to Emma, and they exchanged a few words. It was obvious to Emma that he was uncommonly pleased to see her again, but Tom Walters, on the other hand, seemed determined to look anywhere but at Georgiana, and was not his usual lively, cheerful self. Emma sat regarding Tom for some minutes in silence, and then said to Mr Walters:

'Did something occur while you were in Ireland to distress your brother? He does not seem as bright as usual.' Mr Walters coloured deeply, and seemed to be struggling to think of something to say.

'We are both tired after our journey,' he said at last. Emma thought this was no explanation, but was too well-bred to press the point.

Georgiana had made several attempts to engage Tom in conversation, but his replies were so short, and his confusion so plain, that she stopped speaking altogether, her lips tremulous.

The brothers stayed for only a very short time, saying in excuse that they had not yet called upon their other neighbours.

'My sister says she hopes you will call upon her again soon,' said Mr Walters to Emma, taking her hand and pressing it warmly. Emma could not help feeling gratified, but a glance at her sister made her realise that she was experiencing very different emotions.

As soon as the visitors were gone, Emma suggested a walk to Georgiana, and with a warning from their mother not to stay out too long in the wind, they were soon making their way along the gravel walk through the shrubbery.

'I thought you had made up your mind not to trust Mr Walters, Emma,' said Georgiana in a reproachful tone; 'but I saw him take your hand, and you smiled up into his face as though you liked it.'

Emma wrapped her shawl more tightly about her. 'I always try to be civil to visitors,' she began, but Georgiana gave her such a look that she went on hastily: 'No, you are right; I am being less than candid. It was not just civility - oh Georgiana, I do like him. I like him more than any man I have ever met, and I am sure he likes me.'

'I wonder whether we are good judges of character,' said Georgiana, after a while. 'There was a time when I thought Tom Walters had a decided preference for me, but after seeing him this morning I hardly know what to think.'

'Remember,' said Emma, 'we have not been acquainted with them for very long. Perhaps Tom is just a flirt, who takes up with a girl and then draws back, though I wouldn't wish to think ill of any member of that family.'

'Oh Emma, he would not even look at me,' said Georgiana. 'What have I done to deserve such treatment?' and she burst into tears.

Emma tried to soothe her, but having witnessed Tom's altered behaviour, she could not give Georgiana the assurance she was seeking.

That afternoon they called on Bella who seemed in very good spirits.

'Mrs Walters has just been here with invitations to a ball,' she said.

'Mr Walters and Tom called on us this morning, but they never mentioned it,' said Emma.

'I think it has only just been decided,' said Bella. 'Mrs Walters wanted to give a ball for them, to welcome them home, but decided the drawing room at Donwell Court was too small. Then Mr Elton suggested the Crown, which Mrs Walters thinks will be very suitable, as long as she can decorate the rooms with flowers.'

'There used to be regular assemblies at the Crown some years ago, I remember,' said Emma. 'I was sad that we were too young to go, but Mama had a notion it was rather shabby.'

'The gentlemen's Whist Club meets there regularly,' said Bella, 'and my father says the Assembly Rooms were newly decorated two years ago.'

'Will Henry be home for the ball?' asked Georgiana.

'Oh yes; let me see . . . today is Wednesday, and his visit was only meant to last until tomorrow. I have sent him a line, telling him of the ball, and that Mrs Walters is eager that he should come, and bring his friends. He may wish to delay his return so that he can travel back with them. The ball is to be on Friday sennight.'

Emma and Georgiana returned home to find that Mrs Walters had called in their absence and left invitations for them all. Emma was delighted, but said as little as possible to Georgiana, who had not been restored by this to her usual good humour.

On Thursday morning Emma decided to visit Anne Walters. Georgiana, pleading a headache, would not go with her, but it was such a short walk to Donwell Court that Emma did not mind going alone. Before she was shown into the drawing room there was a little bustle, and she was kept waiting until Mrs Walters herself came out, looking anxious.

'Your sister is not unwell I hope, Miss Knightley,' she said as she ushered her in.

'Thank you, no; she has a headache, ma'am; nothing to signify.'

Colonel Walters was standing by the fire, looking grave, but Mr Walters came forward with a welcome that was cordial. Tom Walters was nowhere to be seen.

'Anne has been longing to see you,' said Mr Walters.

'Oh yes, Emma, I wanted to talk to you about the ball, but that can wait until later.'

The servant came in with some refreshment, and everyone was quiet; Emma could not account for the air of constraint she detected. Colonel Walters soon excused himself, and Emma made some slight enquiry for Tom.

'You have just missed him,' said his mother, 'he has gone out riding. To be frank with you, Miss Knightley, he and his father have had a little disagreement.'

'I am sorry for it,' said Emma, curious to know what had happened. Mrs Walters was looking grave.

'You should tell Emma what they were quarrelling about, Mama,' said Anne, gently. 'Everyone will know soon enough.'

'You are right, child, we will have no secrets from Miss Knightley. In short,' she said, turning to Emma, 'we must ask for your congratulations. Our son, Tom, is engaged to be married.' Emma must have looked shocked, for she hurried on: 'The young lady, Miss Dixon, lives in Ireland. In fact, her father's estate lies only three miles from our own. The family are well known to us. Miss Dixon's mother is the daughter of

Colonel Campbell, who commanded the regiment when my husband was a subaltern.'

'So it is a very desirable match, ma'am,' said Emma, struggling for composure.

'Indeed, she is a pleasant enough young woman; I know no harm of her.' (Emma thought this was an odd way to speak of her son's affianced bride.) 'We were just a little put out, this is between ourselves, Miss Knightley, at the speed of it all. Tom met Sophia last summer when we were all in Ireland, and danced with her once or twice. We had no reason to think he had singled her out. Perhaps you, James, can throw some light on the situation.'

'Believe me, I wish I could,' said he. 'The Dixons were very kind to us while we were over there. Tom saw them almost every day, while I was occupied with estate business. Sophia is an only child, and I suppose they were thrown together.'

'And has Mr Dixon given his consent?' asked Emma.

'I think he was surprised, but yes; they are very fond of Tom,' said Mr Walters. 'They would not part with their one ewe lamb unless they were sure she was going to be happy; she is only seventeen. They have, however, insisted on a year's engagement. If they can bear the separation, and are of the same mind, they are to be married next summer.'

Emma's heart was sore for her sister, and she longed to be home. When Anne invited her to go and sit with her in the parlour, Emma made an excuse which sounded feeble even to her own ears. Anne was quick to assess her feelings and kissed her, asking her to come again soon, and to bring Georgiana. Mr Walters was on his feet in a moment, and offered to walk with Emma to Donwell Abbey.

'I know how you must be feeling, Miss Knightley,' he said, as they went out of the gates into the lane. 'My brother is a great blockhead!' and he took her arm in his own. 'It will be hard for you to tell your sister.' A tear ran down Emma's cheek.

'Is Miss Dixon very beautiful?' she asked.

'At the risk of being disloyal to my brother, I should say 'not at all'. Compared with your sister she is as a candle to sunshine. Just between ourselves, Miss Knightley, I am not sure he loves her. They were thrown so much together, I think he was drawn on to make a declaration, and could not take it back. The Dixons live such a very quiet, retired life, that Sophia was almost bound to fall in love with the first man, not positively ugly or charmless, who took an interest in her.'

'She does love him then?' said Emma.

'Oh yes, she is wild for him. Poor Tom! I think he finds the whole situation bewildering. I wish we had been able to come away sooner, but business kept me in Ireland longer than I would have wished, and not only for Tom's sake.'

Emma was confused; on the one hand she was deeply concerned for her sister, but she could not help feeling delight at her own situation, walking along with Mr Walters, her arm pressed close to his side. The walk was all too short, and even though he escorted her down the long avenue right to her door, they had been alone together only ten or fifteen minutes.

Emma found Georgiana playing the pianoforte in the drawing room. She was alone, and Emma thought she had better tell her the unwelcome news straight away, though her heart shrank from doing so. Georgiana, sensing something was wrong, stopped playing and said: 'What is it, Emma? Why do you look at me like that?'

'Georgiana, I have some bad news for you. Tom Walters is engaged.'

'Impossible! You are teasing me,' said Georgiana, uncertain whether to laugh or not.

'No, my love, you know I would not jest about such a thing,' said Emma. 'I have just heard it from his mother, and Mr Walters confirms the story,' and leading Georgiana to the sofa, she gently told her the whole story. Georgiana went very pale, but she did not weep.

'I cannot understand it, Emma,' said Georgiana in disbelief. 'He has been paying me such very marked attentions - I have not told you the half of it. Has he been engaged all this time? And if his parents are displeased, why are they giving this ball?'

'I think they are only angry with him for being so precipitate,' said Emma. 'They like Miss Dixon well enough, but they had no idea he was in love with her, or had contemplated marriage. As to the ball, from something his father said I gather that he had concealed his engagement from them until after his mother had issued invitations to half of Highbury.' Georgiana looked indignant.

'Then he is a trifling, worthless fellow, and I shall have nothing more to do with him,' she said strongly.

'I admire your spirit, Georgiana,' said Emma, smiling, 'but our families are so much together that it would be impossible to avoid him.'

'I shan't go to the ball,' said Georgiana, getting up suddenly. Not knowing what she was doing, she went to the pianoforte and began rearranging her music.

'Leave it for a little while,' said Emma, soothingly. 'It is not necessary to make any decision now.'

'I really thought he liked me,' said Georgiana, brushing away a tear.

'If I tell you something, will you promise not to raise your hopes?' said Emma. 'You know now he is engaged you must not think of him.' Georgiana gave an eager assurance, and Emma went on: 'Mr Walters thinks he may not have intended to propose to Sophia, and hinted that he may now be regretting it. He said you are far more beautiful than she is.'

'Well really!' said Georgiana, banging the lid of the pianoforte. 'That makes it worse. How could he propose to her if he really prefers me? Is he without any sense? Is he spineless? I know you mean well, Emma, but what you have told me makes me despise myself for ever being taken in.'

Georgiana's feelings were deeply wounded, and she was very angry with Tom Walters, which may have caused her to vent some of that anger on her hapless sister.

'You seem to be on very good terms with Mr James Walters all of a sudden,' she said. 'Have you forgotten that only a few weeks ago he was paying court to Anna, and most improperly cherishing her handkerchief?'

'I admit that the circumstances of that incident are against him,' said Emma, 'but he seems so upright and honourable, I cannot believe him capable of double-dealing.'

'Yet his brother has proved to be so,' said Georgiana, unkindly, 'and these things generally run in families.'

Emma felt the injustice of such a remark, but wisely decided that nothing could be gained by further discussion, and left the room, while Georgiana went back to the pianoforte, and struck up the opening chords of her favourite song from *The Stranger:* 'I have a silent sorrow here'.

A few days went by, and Georgiana had no opportunity to show Tom Walters how little she cared for him. On Sunday it was inevitable that the two families would meet at Morning Service, and she prepared for church with some trepidation. There was still a little coolness between the sisters; Georgiana's pride would not let her apologise for her unjust remarks, and Emma was afraid to say anything in case it irritated her sister further. The Abbey pew was at the very front of the church, just below the pulpit, and without turning round it was impossible for Georgiana to know whether Tom Walters was there or not. At one point she fancied she heard the Colonel's deep tones ringing out in a rousing hymn, but that was all.

At last the service was over, and they came out into the October sunshine, the beeches in the churchyard a blaze of autumnal colour. Colonel Walters was talking to Mr Otway, but Mrs Walters and Anne were waiting to greet them. Georgiana was lagging a little behind, fearing to look up and encounter Tom, and Anne stepped forward eagerly, holding out her hand.

'My brothers would not wait for the carriage,' she said. 'It is such a fine day they insisted on walking home.'

Georgiana felt obscurely cheated.

'Will you both come over tomorrow?' asked Anne. 'I have never been to a ball before, and I am not sure what to wear. I hope you will advise me.'

Georgiana looked down at her shoes, then said: 'I er . . . promised Bella I would spend the day at Hartfield tomorrow.' Anne understood the situation, and did not press her.

'I will come anyway, if you think my advice will be of use,' said Emma, and they parted with smiles and handshakes. Georgiana began to feel a little ashamed of her ill humour, and was tempted to change her mind. She looked back, but Anne was already getting into her father's carriage, and the moment was lost.

On Monday morning Emma walked over to Donwell Court alone, Georgiana having gone to Hartfield in the carriage with Mrs Knightley. As soon as she arrived, Anne bore her off to her dressing room, to go over the finer points of dress for the ball. Emma was amused and entertained as Anne showed her the gown she was to wear, and a variety of shawls, kerchiefs and necklaces which might enhance her appearance. As Anne was returning one pretty scarf to its drawer, she took out a small package and held it out to Emma, saying: 'I was so grateful to Miss Weston for giving me these; they are so pretty.'

Emma took the package curiously, and unwrapped the tissue paper. Inside were a dozen handkerchiefs of the finest lawn, richly embroidered and trimmed with lace.

'Anna gave these to you?' said Emma inquiringly. 'I was not aware that you and she were on such terms.'

'Oh, I hardly know Miss Weston at all,' said Anne. 'These were really a gift for my brother James . . .' then seeing Emma's almost comical look of dismay, she laughed and went on quickly: 'I must be more precise. Do you remember that Miss Weston persuaded James, rather against his will, to exercise her horse?' Emma nodded. 'She was most grateful to him, and was minded to make him a gift of a saddle. As you can imagine, James was horrified, and swore he would take nothing. She would not let the matter rest, however, and plagued him so much about it that she wearied him. In the end he said he would accept a small token gift for me, and so she sent me these pretty handkerchiefs. Even then, James was angry and said it was too much, but Miss Weston would have been offended if he had tried to return them.'

Emma smiled with relief, and said: 'It is fortunate that you share the same initials.'

'Yes, isn't that strange?' said Anne, examining the tiny stitches in the flower borders, and sighing as she went on: 'I wish I were a good needlewoman, but such fine work hurts my eyes.' After a pause, as she folded them away with a few sprigs of lavender, she said: 'I nearly lost the one with the pansies - that would have been such a pity. It was on the day of our visit to Richmond, you remember, Emma - oh no, you did not come. Well, just as we were leaving home, James pricked his finger on a thorn bush, and I offered him my handkerchief, only then the carriage arrived, and he forgot to give it back to me. Then, later on, the careless fellow dropped it, and it was only thanks to your sister that I got it back.'

Emma was more relieved than she could say. Anne was so open and artless there could be no doubt of her word. She felt guilty for ever doubting Mr Walters, but her opinion of Anna was not improved. It was just like her to press an unwanted gift upon a gentleman, even though she knew it would be quite improper to do so. Anna seemed to take a delight in flouting convention and causing embarrassment to anyone upon whom her fancy rested.

'I have never perfectly understood your connexion with Miss Weston,' went on Anne. 'Is she a relation?'

'When we were young, we looked upon Anna almost as a sister,' said Emma. 'I don't remember Mrs Weston, but Mama always speaks of her so fondly. Poor Anna was only four when she died, and Mr Weston used to bring her to Donwell almost every day. She learnt her lessons with us, and as her Papa was away on business quite often, she used to live with us for weeks on end. She was always shy and timid then. After she went to live with the Churchills of course we saw her very little. Now she is like a stranger, and her society ways make me feel like a little country mouse.'

'Oh, you are very far from being that,' said Anne. 'My brother thinks you are very beautiful; he speaks of you all the time. You must have guessed how highly he esteems you; in short, I hope one day we may be sisters.' Emma clasped her hand affectionately, but could say nothing.

A little later there was a tap on the door, and Mr Walters put his head round.

'Miss Knightley, I am glad you are still here. I wanted to engage you for the two first dances.'

'Go away, James!' cried Anne. 'A lady's boudoir is no place for a gentleman.'

'I beg your pardon, ma'am,' said he, laughing, then looking at Emma he said: 'You mustn't forget, Miss Knightley - the two first dances.'

'I should be honoured, sir,' said Emma, and in a moment he was gone.

At Hartfield, Georgiana was walking with Bella in the grounds. Henry had arrived home the previous evening, and came out to join them. It was obvious to Georgiana that Bella had told Henry of Tom Walters' engagement, for he was particularly kind to her, and before the morning was over he had made Georgiana promise to dance the two first dances with him.

'Did you enjoy your visit to London?' she asked him, as they were driven indoors by a flurry of rain.

'Yes, quite well, I thank you. Urswick has promised to come down on Wednesday and bring Anna and Selina with him. I have just delivered Anna's note to your mother, to say she will be staying at the Vicarage.'

'At the Vicarage!' exclaimed Bella. 'What game is she playing now?'

'You do well to call it a game,' said Henry. 'She puts me in mind of Marie-Antoinette, playing at being a shepherdess or a milkmaid. I could see Aunt Emma was not very pleased.'

'And will Lord Urswick be staying with us?' asked Bella.

'I had to invite him, of course,' said Henry, 'but he is to put up at the Crown - keeping out of my father's way, I shouldn't wonder.'

'John is coming home tomorrow,' said Bella. 'I wonder if he will think it proper for a clergyman to dance.'

John came home on Wednesday as promised and went immediately to see his uncle. That evening Mr Knightley announced to his family that John was to preach his first sermon at Donwell church on the coming Sunday. After presenting him to his future congregation, Mr Otway was to leave a week later for Kingston, and a happy retirement.

'Will John move into the Parsonage straight away, Papa?' said Georgiana.

'He will live at home until the repairs and refurbishments are carried out. Perhaps in a month or six weeks, and certainly before Christmas we shall see John fully established as Rector of Donwell.'

Emma listened with great interest tinged with relief, for she had been from home when John called. She did not relish the prospect of meeting him for the first time since his proposal of marriage. Emma had not mentioned it to anyone, and fervently hoped that John would likewise forbear. She knew she could not avoid him at the ball, but thought that they could not do better than meet in a crowd.

Tidings of Anna's arrival at the Vicarage reached them the next morning, followed by Anna in person, attended by Selina. Anna was her usual high-spirited self with the Knightleys, and capricious and exacting with Selina. It was all 'do not sit there', and 'fetch me my reticule,' until Emma felt heartily sorry for the poor girl, and drew her a little aside.

'How pleased your mother must be to see you, Selina,' she said.

'Yes, Mama feels the loss of Augusta sorely. She says I look thin and fagged - and she does not like the arrangement of my hair; she says it is too severe. What do you think, Miss Knightley?'

'Perhaps it is a little severe - you used not to wear it like that, I think.'

'I thought I might have it curled for the ball,' went on Selina.

'I think that would look charming,' said Emma warmly, when she was interrupted by Anna.

'I beg you will not encourage that child to be vain, Emma,' she said imperiously. 'I have told her I prefer her hair drawn back simply, the way it is now.'

'Oh Anna, we all like to look our best for a ball,' said Emma, with a hint of scorn in her voice. 'Selina must be guided by her own taste, or that of her mother - it is not for anyone else to express a preference.'

Anna was not accustomed to being spoken to thus, and went red with anger.

'Miss Weston is to dance the two first dances with Lord Urswick, but he has engaged me for the next two,' whispered Selina, with a complacent smile. 'I am sure he would like to see me with curls.'

Anna had turned away to speak to Mrs Knightley, and Emma heard her mention Mr Churchill.

'Oh, that is splendid news!' said Mrs Knightley. 'Did you hear that, girls? Mr Churchill is coming to Highbury for the ball. Anna says he returned to London unexpectedly a few days ago, and Henry extended the invitation to him, conditional on its being confirmed by a letter from Mrs Walters. Of course, Colonel and Mrs Walters were delighted, especially since Frank is so well known to them by repute, being acquainted with the Dixons.'

Mr Churchill's wife, Jane Fairfax, had been Colonel Campbell's ward, and almost a sister to Mrs Dixon. Mr Churchill and Anna had visited them in Ireland once, but Mr Dixon came to London quite often, and was a frequent visitor in St James's Square. Emma thought she would be glad to see Mr Churchill again, and wondered how Anna would conduct herself in his presence.

Many a young lady went to bed that night, her head full of happy dreams, and her hair full of curl papers. All the younger Otways and Coxes were to be there; the Perrys, the Martins, and the Hugheses, with cousins, and second cousins once removed not excluded. Selina Elton, having decided on curls in defiance of Miss Weston, slept very badly indeed, but felt it was all worthwhile when she saw how pretty she looked when the hair was combed out.

Emma was longing to see Mr Walters again, now that he had been cleared of all suspicion, and went up to dress with great eagerness. Georgiana's feelings were very different. All her dreams had been shattered, and she meant to punish Tom Walters if she could. It was a faint comfort to her to be secure of the two first dances, though they were only with her cousin. Henry would, after all, be the handsomest man in the room.

It was a cold, crisp evening, with a hint of frost and a full moon, as the carriage left Donwell to drive to the Crown. Even Mrs Knightley had dressed with unusual care; she might be nearly two and forty, but she did not want Mr Frank Churchill, who had hardly changed at all, to see no resemblance in her to the lovely girl he had danced with all those years ago. Mrs Knightley thought back to their first meeting and remembered how attractive he had seemed; then scolding herself for being sentimental, she reflected that she had fortunately survived with her heart intact, in view of the fact that Frank Churchill had been secretly engaged to Jane Fairfax all along. Not that she could ever have preferred him to her own dear Mr Knightley, but his visit had put a spring in her step. He was staying this time at Hartfield, and was going to bring some of their party in his carriage.

The Assembly Rooms were so brightly lit that Emma was dazzled as she walked in. Colonel and Mrs Walters were standing by the fire, with Mr Walters and Anne, whose cheeks were glowing with excitement. Many of the hot-house flowers had been sent from Donwell and were filling the room with their perfume, and Mrs Walters was eager to thank Mr Knightley.

Georgiana looked around for Tom, who was talking to the musicians in an attempt to keep out of the way. On seeing her, he looked conscious, but with a determined effort he came across and shook hands with her. They were standing a little apart from the main group, and Georgiana took the opportunity to say coldly: 'I believe I am to congratulate you on your engagement, Mr Walters.'

'You are too kind - yes, Sophia has made me the happiest of men,' he said, looking anything but happy.

'I expect you will be celebrating your last days of freedom by dancing with as many pretty girls as possible,' said Georgiana, meaning to wound.

'Why yes, and if you are not already engaged, I shall be happy to dance with you,' he said, impudently. 'Perhaps you will keep the two last before supper?'

Georgiana gave him a look which should have turned him to stone, and went to join her sister.

They had not been the first to arrive, and more families were flocking in as they spoke. The John Knightleys came next, with Henry and Bella. John and George were to follow with Mr Churchill. Bella joined her cousins.

'How do you think the Eltons are getting here?' she asked.

'They will walk, I suppose,' said Georgiana. 'Oh wait, that would not do for Anna . . .'

'They are to be conveyed in Lord Urswick's carriage,' said Bella. 'I met Selina Elton in Ford's this afternoon, and she couldn't wait to tell me.'

'This is a very marked attention,' said Emma, 'but it must be on Anna's account. She is staying at the Vicarage, you know.'

'Yes, but Lord Urswick is staying here and so does not need the carriage himself.'

'Has he come down yet?' asked Georgiana, looking about her.

'Oh no,' said Bella, laughing. 'I expect he will make an entrance after everybody else has arrived.'

At that moment the Eltons arrived. Mrs Elton's voice could be heard even before the door was opened.

'So very kind,' she was saying to Mrs Perry. 'Only fancy, Lord Urswick sent his carriage for us. Such a very great attention, ma'am. I never was more honoured - his crest is very handsome - and the matching greys!'

'It is not so very wonderful, ma'am,' said Anna coolly. 'I have never walked to a ball in my life.'

Selina Elton came in behind the other two, followed by her father. She looked like her old self, in silk adorned with rather too much lace, and wearing her mother's pearls. Anna was dressed like a princess, with jewels sparkling in her dark hair. After being greeted by her hosts, she turned to speak to the Knightleys.

'Is Frank not here yet? He offered to send his carriage for us, but Lord Urswick had already offered his.'

'Here he is now,' said Mrs Knightley, as Mr Churchill entered the room with John and George Knightley, looking unusually elegant in their evening clothes. Mr Churchill caused quite a stir among the young ladies who had never seen him before, and one or two wondered out loud whether he meant to dance. They all joined the party near the fire, and John turned to his cousins.

'You must dance with me, Georgiana,' he said, pointedly ignoring Emma. 'Any two but the first. I am already engaged for those two,' and he smiled in a self-congratulatory manner. Emma looked enquiringly at Bella, who said in a whisper: 'He went over to Donwell Court this afternoon on purpose to ask little Anne. Wasn't that kind of him?'

'And who is your partner to be for the two first dances, Bella?' asked Georgiana.

'Mr Tom Walters has been kind enough to ask me; I hope you will not mind it, Georgiana.'

'Mr Tom Walters is nothing to me,' said Georgiana, carelessly. 'I'm sure I have the best partner in the room.'

The orchestra was beginning to tune up, gentlemen were going in search of their partners, and Lord Urswick had still not appeared. Anna could be seen, tapping her foot angrily, as the couples made up the sets, led by Anne Walters and John. There was a hasty discussion between Mrs Walters and her husband, then Colonel Walters went over to Anna and said: 'I see your partner has been delayed, ma'am; will you do me the honour of standing up with me?'

All the older men, including Mr Knightley, could now safely go off to their cards, but Mr Churchill did not go with them. Going over to Mrs Knightley he said: 'It does not seem like twenty years since you and I danced in this very ballroom.'

'Indeed it does not.'

'You look just as you did then,' he said, gallantly.

'Oh come, Mr Churchill, this will not do! I am no lady of the *beau monde* - you need not flatter me.'

'But I mean it,' he said. 'Your daughter there is the very image of your former self, but you could be her older sister.'

Mrs Knightley scolded herself for blushing, but eased her conscience by telling herself he was always something of a rattle.

'Do you mean to dance, Mrs Knightley?' he went on, smiling. 'I see you have no card.'

'At my age it would hardly be proper,' she said, 'but I confess I am tempted. I dearly love dancing.'

'Then perhaps you will dance with me a little later on,' he said, leaving her with a variety of feelings, necessitating the vigorous use of her fan.

Emma thought she had never been so happy, and even Georgiana was laughing and chatting with Henry enough to give at least the illusion of happiness. The dances were over far too soon, and the ladies were escorted back to their places. At that moment Lord Urswick came in, and looked about for Anna. She had returned to a place near the Eltons, who were sitting with the chaperones, and was standing a little way off, talking to Selina, when they were approached by Robert Martin. He asked Selina to dance, but with a haughty toss of the head she told him her dance card was full. As he was turning away, looking mortified, Anna saw Lord Urswick coming towards her, and to spite him she said: 'I will dance with you, Rob, if you will ask me.'

Poor Robert had no option but to go with her down the room, where a new set was forming. Mrs Elton's attention was caught by this and she said loudly: 'Those Martins are always giving themselves airs. How could a clod-hopper like Robert Martin dare to solicit a dance from Miss Weston?'

'I know, my love,' said her husband, 'it is very shocking, but you cannot always choose your company in a ballroom.'

Mrs Martin was seated quite near the Eltons, and for the moment was alone; her elder daughter was dancing, and her husband had gone to play cards. When she heard Mrs Elton's ill-judged remarks, she coloured deeply and stood up, as if to move away, when she was joined by Mrs Knightley, who had also been near enough to hear.

'Well, Harriet,' she said brightly, 'this is just like old times. Who would have thought as we flew down the set that one day we would be sober matrons?'

'Oh dear, yes,' said Mrs Martin, 'the years have flown by. I never thought to see myself the mother of six children - there is dear Henrietta, dancing with John Cox; how tall she is.' Turning to Mrs Knightley with something like her old eagerness, she said: 'Oh Mrs Knightley, you do not look like a sober matron. When I saw you talking to Mr Churchill I thought you should be dancing with the rest.'

Mrs Knightley made an eager gesture as if to disclaim the compliment, and steering the conversation back into safer waters, said: 'you must be very proud of your fine family, Harriet; two pretty daughters and four fine sons; I quite envy you.'

'They are all good children,' said Mrs Martin, complacently, 'but I confess Robert is my favourite. He is such a good, steady young man, and so kind to his brothers and sisters. Poor little Jane was fretting because she is too young yet to go to a ball, and Rob went to Ford's himself to buy her some ribbons to console her, and said he would teach her to dance himself.'

At that moment they were joined by Mrs John Knightley, who added her praises of Robert to those of her sister, until Mrs Martin turned quite pink with pleasure.

It was now time for the supper-dance, and Georgiana was accosted by Tom Walters to claim his dance. She happened to be standing by his mother, and feeling all the awkwardness of a refusal, silently took his hand, and suffered herself to be led on to the dance floor. She was determined to maintain her silence, and trod the measure with a solemn face.

'Come, Miss Georgiana,' said her partner after a while, 'we must say something; it will look odd if we do not talk at all.

You could not look more severe if I were a poacher up before the bench, and you were a hanging judge. With your colour hair, I do not think a black cap would be very becoming. There! Do I detect the hint of a smile?'

'You are very amusing, sir,' she said, 'but it would become you to cultivate a more sober manner now you are engaged.'

'I must wait a twelvemonth to be wed; would you have me live like a monk? If so, I shall dress in a white habit, and flit about the ruins of Donwell.'

Georgiana could not help smiling, and intrigued by the mention of the ruins of the first Donwell Abbey, said: 'I never heard tell that our ruins are haunted, though they look eerie enough by moonlight.'

By the time the dances were over they were in a better humour with each other. Georgiana found that it was very hard to dislike Tom Walters, and resolved to give up the struggle. Although he had wounded her pride, she reflected that he might one day be her brother by marriage, and she could not ruin Emma's happiness by causing any coolness between them.

As they went into supper, Emma noticed that Anne Walters was looking pale and tired.

'Mama says I may not dance any more,' she said sadly, 'but I am sure that once I have eaten I shall feel better.'

Lord Urswick had seated himself next to Selina Elton, and she was whispering to him from behind her fan, her mother looking on complacently. Anna was seated some way off from Emma, next to James Walters. He grimaced slightly when he caught Emma's eye, and she smiled in return, understanding him to mean that he did not like his situation. Mr Churchill was sitting with Bella, and Emma was surprised to see how animated she was; Georgiana was with Henry, who was being very solicitous for her welfare. Emma herself was between her father and Mr Elton, and she had very little to say to the latter, beyond the merest civilities of the table.

'It is such a comfort, ma'am, to have a daughter so well married,' Mrs Elton was saying, across the table to Mrs John Knightley.

'Yes, you must be very happy,' said she, 'though I could not bear the thought of Bella's being settled at such a great distance from me.'

'I don't expect there is much prospect of that happening in the near future,' said Mrs Elton, looking with no very friendly eye at Bella, who was laughing with Mr Churchill.

'No, and I am glad of it,' said her fond Mama. 'If Bella were to marry for love of course we would be pleased, but otherwise I see no occasion for her going from home. She will be well provided for.' Mrs John Knightley spoke candidly, but meant no reflection on Mrs Elton's reduced circumstances. That lady, however, bridled angrily.

'Love or no love, I am sure she would not pass up the chance of a husband with a large estate - in the north of England, say.'

Mrs John Knightley looked at her in astonishment.

'I do not perfectly understand you,' she said. 'As far as I am aware, Bella has never exchanged two words with Lord Urswick.' Mrs Elton saw her mistake, and said hastily: 'Oh, as to that - I think Lord Urswick's attentions are being paid in quite another quarter,' and she smiled fondly at Selina.

Emma was not the only one to hear this exchange; Anna, sitting some distance away, had heard enough to regard Mrs Elton fixedly with a look of contempt.

Emma forced herself to address Mrs Elton. 'Will Anna be staying in Highbury for long, ma'am?' she asked.

'Unfortunately, Lord Urswick is obliged to return to town tomorrow, and Miss Weston is to go with him.'

'And Selina - does she go too?' asked Emma, her curiosity getting the better of her.

'Oh, Miss Weston cannot bear to part with her. I am sure she will be invited to accompany her.'

After supper, as the dancers were forming new sets, Emma witnessed an exchange between Anna and Lord Urswick. She was not within earshot, but it was evident that Anna was very angry. After a few moments, during which Anna seemed to be doing all the talking, Lord Urswick turned on his heel, went straight to Selina Elton, and led her on to the floor.

'But sir,' she protested feebly, 'I was to dance this one with Mr John Cox.'

'Mr John Cox can go to the devil,' said Lord Urswick civilly. 'I have a fancy to dance with you again.' Selina was all blushes and smiles, and looked about her in triumph, especially at the discomfited John Cox.

Anna stood surveying the scene for a few moments, then went up to Mrs Elton.

'I have a headache, ma'am, and would like to leave,' she said abruptly.

'Oh, but Miss Weston, how is that to be done? We came in Lord Urswick's carriage, and he is occupied at present. I dare not disturb him - it would look so strange.'

Mrs Elton had no intention of leaving the ball while Selina was dancing with Lord Urswick, and might dance again. Anna turned to Mrs John Knightley, who was seated nearby.

'You will go home soon, I am sure, ma'am,' she said.

'I am very tired, certainly, but we must stay for Bella,' said that good lady.

Mr Churchill had been standing nearby, assessing the situation, and drew Anna aside. 'You cannot just walk out, Anna!' he said with some force. 'It would be very rude and might break up the party.'

'Would you have me stay and suffer?' said Anna in what she hoped was a pathetic tone.

'Oh, you poor dear!' said Mrs John Knightley. 'I know what it is to have a bad headache. I would gladly take you now, but what of Bella?'

'If that is your only difficulty, Mrs Knightley, allow me to be of service. Bella shall ride home in my carriage,' said Mr Churchill.

'But there will not be room for my sons,' said Mrs John Knightley.

'Hartfield is only across the road, ma'am. Surely they can walk,' said Anna, and Mrs John Knightley, eager to be civil, prepared to leave. Her husband, who had been dozing for the past half hour, rose with alacrity and offered Miss Weston his arm.

Mr Churchill lost no time in acquainting Bella with the circumstances. She was by no means displeased at the prospect, especially as Mr Churchill was wishing to dance with her a second time.

'I suppose I should have escorted Anna myself,' he said, 'but I was enjoying the company too much to leave,' and he looked at her intently.

It was a little before midnight when Mr Churchill finally asked Mrs Knightley to dance. Mr Knightley was sitting with his wife, and stood up as Mr Churchill approached. Mrs Knightley looked at her husband half fearfully as the request was made. Mr Knightley smiled down at her.

'I was not aware you wished to dance, Emma,' he said, 'or I would have asked you before this.' Then turning to Mr Churchill he said: 'I am sure you will forgive me, sir, for wishing to dance with my own wife, so beautiful as she is,' and he took her hand and led her on to the floor.

Chapter 11

The morning after the ball Emma and Georgiana rose late, and had scarcely had time to eat their breakfast when a visitor was announced. It was Mr Churchill, come to return Mrs Knightley's glove, which she had dropped as she was leaving the ballroom. He brought with him the news that Anna and Lord Urswick had already departed for London, and that Selina Elton had been left behind. Mr Churchill himself had been pressed by Mrs John Knightley to prolong his visit, so as to hear John preach his first sermon on the coming Sunday, and he had agreed with pleasure.

'Country air always agrees with me,' he said, 'and I thought I might get some shooting while I am down here.'

Mr Knightley said that his woods and coverts were at Mr Churchill's disposal, and he departed, a happy man, to pay calls on his other friends in Highbury.

Half an hour later Mr Walters and his brother were shown into the drawing room. Mrs Knightley was very gracious to them both, and praised their dancing, before leaving the young people together.

'Tom was out riding at seven o'clock this morning,' said Mr Walters, 'while I was still in my bed. Lord Urswick's carriage was just being wheeled out as he passed the Crown, so I expect his party are on their way back to town by now.'

'So Mr Churchill just told us,' said Emma, 'but did you know that Selina had been left behind?'

'Miss Selina Elton was flirting outrageously with Lord Urswick last evening,' said Tom. 'Perhaps Miss Weston was jealous. I remember now, I heard her berating him.'

This idea was new to Emma. She was aware that Anna and Lord Urswick were old friends, but it had not occurred to her that Anna might be in love with him. Lord Urswick, for his part, seemed to treat Anna in the same way as he treated Henry; he was jovial and hearty, but betrayed no symptoms of love.

Georgiana had taken little part in this conversation, and sat near the fire, idly turning the pages of a book.

'Miss Georgiana,' said Tom Walters, 'if you have not taken your walk yet, would you and your sister be so kind as to show us the abbey ruins?'

'Oh,' said Georgiana, without looking up, 'there is nothing to see. I have no eye for the picturesque.'

'Georgiana, that is not true!' cried Emma. 'How often have you said to me that you wished you could draw, when we have been walking about the ruins. Come, it is a fine day - we must walk somewhere; will you go with us?'

'Very well,' said Georgiana, with a great show of reluctance, 'but I will not be able to walk far; my feet still ache from dancing.'

The young ladies fetched their bonnets and shawls, and led the way out of the house. By turning left and passing the stables they were soon in a sheltered woodland walk, which led downhill for a furlong, then curved round to the left and ended in a green-sward. Upon this level ground stood a few grey stone walls, and a high arched window, the whole being bordered by a stream.

'This is a tranquil spot,' said Mr Walters, looking about him. 'I have never been this side of the abbey before.'

'Yes we have a fine view of the house from here,' said Emma. 'The principal part, facing the avenue on the north side, was built in the last century, but that wing there, facing west, was the original refectory.' She pointed to some broken columns: 'These were the cloisters, and this was the chapel.'

Tom Walters was clambering over some fallen masonry. 'See this little basin in the wall,' he said, his interest quickening, 'I think it was called a piscina. How strange a life it must have been!'

'I should not have thought such a life would have any attraction for *you*,' said Georgiana.

'What is the refectory used for now?' asked Mr Walters.

'Oh, it has had a variety of uses,' said Emma. 'In former times it was a granary, but my grandfather had a sprung floor put in for dancing, and now it is a store-room.'

'How I wish we could have a ball here at Donwell,' said Georgiana. 'I shall ask Papa if we may - it would only be the moving out of supernumerary chairs and tables. What do you think, Emma?'

'I think it would involve a great deal more work than you have thought of, Georgiana,' said she. 'However, it would do no harm to go and look.'

The four young people duly turned back towards the house, crossing the green-sward and ascending some steps cut into the steep bank. The door to the refectory was locked, and those windows that were not shuttered were too high to give a view of the interior.

'If we go back into the house we can gain access from there,' said Georgiana, heading east across the terrace, and startling her mother, who was sitting at the morning-room window. A gravel walk brought them round to the front entrance, where they encountered Mr Knightley. He looked a little surprised to see them, and Georgiana quickly explained their errand.

'I thought this might happen,' he said wryly. 'Now there has been one ball, you will be wanting to dance every day of the week. Well, well; no time like the present. Let us go and see what can be done with the old Abbot's hall, which is what we used to call it as children.'

The housekeeper was applied to for the keys, and Mr Knightley led the way down a long corridor.

'Here we are,' he said, trying first one key and then another, before hitting upon the right one. He then threw open the door, which creaked obligingly, and gestured to his daughters to precede him into the gloom.

The hall proved to be a lofty, pleasant room, once the shutters were opened. True, it was a little dusty and needed airing, but the tattered hangings and mouldering carpets of Tom Walters' fancy were absent. Where once it had lain open to the rafters there was now a plastered ceiling, and the room itself was more than sixty feet long. At the gable end was a large gothic window, and beneath it an oak door, which Mr Knightley unbarred. They went through it eagerly and found themselves on the very terrace they had crossed, looking south to the ruined chapel and the wooded hills beyond. After admiring the view, they went back into the refectory.

'We used to play in here when the weather was too wet or cold to play out-of-doors,' said Georgiana. 'Do you remember, Emma?'

'Of course. Anna always liked to be in here. She used to admire herself dancing before those large looking glasses.'

The two brothers looked at each other as if this came as no surprise.

'Papa, it would not take long to set all to rights, would it?' said Georgiana, in a wheedling tone.

'Well, well; we shall see,' said her father. 'I must talk it over with your mother; and now, if you have seen all there is to be seen, I must return these keys to Mrs Blake.'

Sunday came, and both Knightley families with Mr Churchill were in church to hear John preach his first sermon. It was an anxious time for his mother, who sat clutching her smelling-salts and expecting to be overcome. John acquitted himself very creditably, and the whole family rose for the final hymn with sighs of relief. Emma made a point of offering John her congratulations, as they lingered in the church porch, and they were received graciously enough. Emma hoped that all would now be as before. Colonel Walters also came forward with his congratulations; his sons were with him, but Emma only had time to bid Mr Walters a shy 'good morning' before being hurried away to a family celebration at Donwell.

Mr Churchill announced that he was to stay until Friday, and everyone expressed their delight. The young people looked upon him as quite one of themselves, so lively and amusing as he was. The only person who was not overjoyed was Mr Knightley, though Mrs Knightley was the only one to perceive it.

As soon as they could after leaving the table, Bella and her cousins escaped to a deep window embrasure to talk over the ball privately.

'I am not in the least surprised that Anna was angry with Selina, and left her behind,' said Bella. 'I thought she behaved very badly at the ball. Now her mother is at home I thought she would exert more control over Selina.'

'Not while she thinks Lord Urswick might be brought to the point,' said Emma. 'And while we are speaking of Lord Urswick, I must say he is hardly a paragon of virtue. Why must it always be the lady that is censured, while the gentleman is regarded with indulgence?'

'If a woman is to marry,' said Bella thoughtfully, 'she will guard her virtue, or at least she will behave with decorum in public. No man will marry her if she has a bad reputation.'

'Well Anna does not always behave with decorum,' said Georgiana, 'and no-one would dare to censure her to her face.'

'Anna is rich,' said Emma, 'and in the eyes of the world it is wealth and not charity that 'covers a multitude of sins'. Her behaviour is wilful and selfish, but I cannot believe she would ever do anything really wrong.'

'I hope you are right,' said Bella, 'but I will cap your quotation from the Bible with one of my own: 'Pride goeth before destruction, and an haughty spirit before a fall'.'

'I am tired of talking of Anna,' said Georgiana. 'You seemed to enjoy the ball, Bella. You danced every dance, and twice with Mr Churchill.'

'You are very observant, Georgiana,' said Bella with a smile. 'I must own I like Mr Churchill - I always have. He dances so well, and he has such an air - it makes a very pleasant change to dance with a gentleman of the world, instead of with these callow youths who are usually our partners.'

'Mr Walters is no callow youth,' said Emma, a little indignantly. 'He has wonderful manners, and his dancing is excellent.'

'I wish I could say the same of his brother,' said Georgiana.

'I can understand that you are out of charity with Master Tom,' said Bella. 'How dare he go off to Ireland and come back an engaged man? There are few enough gentlemen of marriageable age in Highbury, and not one as handsome as he is.'

They all laughed, and Georgiana thought, not for the first time, how pleasant it would be to live at home, surrounded by friends and loved ones, for the whole of one's life. Why should it be necessary to marry?

Later that day, when the John Knightleys had returned to Hartfield, Henry sought Bella out.

'What do you think of this business with Urswick and Selina Elton?' he asked her.

'I am afraid she is making a fool of herself,' said Bella. 'I have heard some ill-natured talk already, and I agree with the gossips in that I too think it would be impossible for him to have serious intentions towards her.'

'Not impossible perhaps,' said Henry, 'but very unlikely. I have spoken of the matter to him once already, and he almost admitted he was trifling with her. He is a sad fellow, but what else can I do? I was very disturbed by the degree of intimacy between them, which I had the opportunity of observing when I was in London.'

'Then it is fortunate that Anna has put a stop to all that,' said Bella. 'Selina is young - I expect she will get over her disappointment quite quickly; but beware, Henry, she might be in need of another object.'

Henry dismissed the idea with a smile, then went on: 'Rob Martin would make a good match for Selina. He has always liked her, but Selina has been guided by her mother to think he is not good enough. However, a few years without an offer may make her think very differently.'

'And by then Robert Martin will, I hope, be safely married to Miss Cox or Miss Hughes,' said Bella, bringing the discussion to a close.

While Henry was talking about Selina Elton, the young lady herself was passing an uncomfortable evening with her mother.

'What chance have you got now, you foolish girl?' Mrs Elton was saying, as she stabbed her needle vigorously into the tablecloth she was mending. 'You should never have defied Miss Weston. Wearing your hair plain instead of curled would have been a small sacrifice to make.'

'It wasn't that,' said Selina in a self-justifying tone.

'Then what was it, pray? What have you done to Miss Weston to make her cast you off? As if things were not bad enough! But I tell you, Miss, I will not be able to keep you when your father dies.'

Mr Elton looked up in some surprise from reading Fordyce's sermons.

'I assure you, Augusta,' he said mildly, 'I was never in better health in my life.'

'Oh, you know what I mean,' said Mrs Elton irritably. 'If anything were to happen to you, we should be turned out of the Vicarage with hardly time to gather our clothes together.'

'I thought you were raising Selina's hopes too high, even before the ball,' said Mr Elton, anxious that no blame for the debâcle should be laid at his door.

'Well, if she is not to marry Lord Urswick, who else will have her? I cannot have her moping about the house, pining for London.' She paused to bite off her thread. 'My mind is made up,' she said to Selina. 'You must go and stay with Augusta; perhaps she will be able to find you a husband.'

Mrs Elton was as good as her word, and wrote immediately to Augusta. The proposed visit was most welcome to her, for she had been feeling homesick and strange in her new surroundings. Her husband made no objection and her reply was sent with alacrity. Within ten days of her mother's letter, Selina Elton found herself on the first stage of her journey to Bath, where she was to be met by Mr Craig's servant. The weather was perfect for travelling, being mild and dry, but only two days after her departure there was a severe frost, followed by a week of rain by day and frost by night, rendering the roads treacherous.

Because of the severe weather, Emma and Georgiana had seen little of their friends since the ball. Anne Walters had relapsed into ill-health; Dr Perry looked grave, and said she was over-tired. Emma and Georgiana went to visit her as soon as the weather permitted them to walk out. It was a fine day in early November; the high winds had brought down most of the leaves, which now lay in sodden heaps in the ditches, but there was a pale sun and no wind, which made their walk to

Donwell Court very pleasant after the confinement of the previous fortnight.

Anne was in the parlour, lying upon the sofa, and had not strength enough to rise up to greet them. They were shocked at the change in her. At the ball she had been animated and glowing; now her face was the colour of parchment, and she had a dry cough. They had promised Mrs Walters that they would not stay long, but Anne was so pleased to see them, and enjoyed their chat so much, that they were astonished to find, when a visitor was announced, that they had been there more than an hour.

The visitor, whom they encountered at the parlour door, was John Knightley, come to visit Anne in his official capacity. With an air of portentous gravity he enquired for her. Mrs Walters ushered him into the parlour, then hurried out to speak to her departing guests.

'We had written to invite the Dixons,' she said, 'but, of course, all thought of that must now be given up. Tom will be very disappointed not to be able to present his betrothed to the neighbourhood.'

Georgiana was relieved. She had a certain curiosity to see Miss Dixon, but not until her own wounds had healed.

'Mr John Knightley has been very kind,' went on Mrs Walters. 'This is his third visit in a week, and I know Anne always feels the better for seeing him. Her cough is troublesome, but there is no fever. Thank God, Dr Perry has no fears for her lungs. I am most grateful to you both for coming,' she added, 'and I hope you will come again soon.'

Emma had had one letter from Augusta shortly after her marriage to Mr Craig. It was a sad little note, from someone who was trying to be resolutely cheerful in difficult circumstances. There was a hint that the children of Mr Craig's first marriage were being troublesome and could not accept Augusta as their new Mama. This came as no surprise to Emma, who knew that only five years separated Augusta and his daughter, Mary. The difficulties were implied rather than stated, but Emma's heart ached for poor Augusta. Georgiana did not take such a tolerant view. 'After all, Emma,' she said, with all the wisdom of just eighteen, 'she entered into this marriage of her own free will; nobody forced her.'

'Nobody except her own mother,' said Emma. 'To have her daughters married is Mrs Elton's only object, and in her eyes Augusta has made a good match. Not that anyone who could marry Mr Elton could be suspected of having too much delicacy.'

After Selina had been in Upton Prior for two or three weeks, there came another letter from Augusta, with kind regards from Selina. The tenor of this missive was very different. Mr Craig had exerted himself to amuse the young visitor, and there had been one or two excursions to Bath. Mary had taken a fancy to Selina, and spent long hours in her company, with the result that her behaviour toward Augusta had much improved.

Meanwhile, the Walters family were growing increasingly anxious about Anne. The weather was bitterly cold, and the November fogs did nothing for her cough. Emma and Georgiana were frequent visitors, and left each time hoping that their next visit would show a marked improvement. On one occasion Georgiana thought to amuse her by telling how the old refectory was being prepared for a ball.

'Oh, how I should love to go to a ball at Donwell,' said Anne, wistfully, 'but if it is to be before Christmas I fear I shall not be well enough.'

'Have no fear, dear Anne,' said Emma. 'We should not dream of dancing while you are unwell. Papa was only saying the other day that he had been meaning to have that part of the house set to rights for a long time. No date has yet been fixed for the ball. We will have it as soon as you are better.'

Georgiana was now becoming accustomed to meeting Tom Walters without resentment or embarrassment. He had such an endearing manner, and was so eager to please, that she rarely found it necessary to give him the sharp set-downs of the previous month. Emma and James Walters were still close friends, but she had seen little of him since the beginning of Anne's illness. She still felt almost sure of his regard, but sometimes wished he had a little of his brother's eager impetuousness. Mr James Walters would never become engaged on a whim.

Mrs Elton had called twice at Donwell Abbey, much to Mrs Knightley's irritation, to boast of Augusta's happiness in her marriage, and her pleasure in Selina's company. 'I do not believe she remembers that there is such a person in the world as Miss Weston,' she said, in a satisfied tone. 'Her visit to Upton Prior is to be extended until February. Augusta cannot do without her.'

One morning towards the end of November, John Knightley called at Donwell Abbey to announce in a heavy manner that Anne Walters was dangerously ill. She had suddenly developed a high fever, and Dr Perry was calling twice a day. After consulting with her mother, Emma filled a basket with all the choicest preserves and delicacies that Donwell could offer, and hastened over to Donwell Court, accompanied by Georgiana. Mrs Walters greeted them in the hall with an anxious expression.

'My dears,' she said, 'Anne is not well enough to receive you today, in fact she is very ill. I was up with her all night; not that I am complaining - who else should nurse her? We are anxiously awaiting Dr Perry's visit,' and with many thanks she accepted their basket of good things.

'She has hardly eaten a thing this week and more,' she said, clasping her hands together tightly. 'Perhaps when she is a little better she might be tempted by these preserved apricots. You are too kind . . .' here she broke off, and struggled to regain her composure.

'Is it her old trouble, ma'am?' asked Emma anxiously.

'No, thank God, Dr Perry thinks not. She has been so weak for so long that any infection could strike her down, he says. This began with a trifling cold, but now this fever makes me fear . . . I am sorry to be discourteous, but I must get back to her,' and pressing their hands warmly she motioned them into the drawing room, where her two sons were staring gloomily out of the window at the grey and dripping garden.

Mr Walters' face lit up when he saw Emma, and taking her hand he said: 'I am so glad that you have come, and am only sorry Anne is too ill to receive you. Your visits usually do her so much good.'

Feeling that they were in the way, the two sisters stayed only for a quarter of an hour, though pressed to stay longer by Mr Walters. As Emma was leaving, she said: 'You will send word if . . . if there is any news?' and was assured by him that they would be the first to be informed of any change. As they went into the hall the servant was just admitting Dr Perry, who looked grave, and with scarcely a 'good-day' hastened up the stairs.

The whole family at Donwell Abbey spent a very anxious evening, for Mr and Mrs Knightley were almost as fond of Anne as their daughters were.

'I wish there were something further we could do,' said Mrs Knightley. 'I sent one of the footmen over at seven o'clock to enquire, but they only sent word that she was much the same.'

'Perhaps you could play for us, Mama?' said Emma. 'Music would be soothing at a time like this.'

'I am sadly out of practice,' said Mrs Knightley, 'but if it would cheer you a little, my love, then of course I will play for you,' and going to the pianoforte, she looked over the music sheets, and chose a plaintive Irish air. Mrs Knightley played it very well, but when it was over Georgiana said: 'This is too melancholy for me, Mama; will you play something a little more lively?' and going to the pianoforte she picked up another sheet saying: 'This one is my favourite.' In other circumstances Emma might have been amused, for she had chosen an avowed favourite of Tom Walters'. Mrs Knightley began to play with spirit, then stopped abruptly. 'This is too lively, Georgiana. How would it seem to the Walters family if they could hear us? Poor Anne at this moment . . .' here she hesitated. 'Perhaps Papa would read aloud to us.'

'With pleasure, my dear,' said the obliging Mr Knightley, and he went into the library to choose a book.

'You do not think that Anne will die, Mama,' said Georgiana almost in tears.

'No, no, we must always hope,' said her mother, with forced cheerfulness. 'But who can that be at such a late hour?' They could hear footsteps and subdued conversation. The door opened, and Mr Knightley came in with Colonel Walters.

'I am sorry to call so late,' he said abruptly, 'but I wanted to bring you the good news myself. Anne is over the worst.'

There were exclamations of joy from the ladies.

'Yes, the fever got worse at about eight o'clock, and for half an hour we almost despaired. She was delirious, calling for her mother, who was sitting beside her the whole time. Perry has been very good. He came at five and has only just gone home. He had given her a draught which seemed to do her good, then the fever broke, and at nine o'clock she came to her senses and asked for a drink. She managed to swallow some water, and now she is sleeping quietly; please God, she is on the mend.'

He had been standing the whole time, holding his hat and gloves, which he would not relinquish to a servant.

'Won't you sit down, sir?' said Mrs Knightley gently, her eyes full of tears. 'May I offer you some refreshment? This is wonderful news - wonderful!'

'A glass of wine, if I may, ma'am, and then I must go home. Such kind friends as you are - I could not have you spoiling your night's rest with worry on our account.'

'Oh, thank you for coming, Colonel,' said Emma, pressing his hand and then bursting into tears. 'Forgive me, sir, I am just so relieved.'

'We all are, my dear sir,' said Mr Knightley, 'and if there is anything that we can do, we are at your service.'

Colonel Walters could only look his thanks and, as soon as he had drunk his wine, he took his leave.

Chapter 12

Now that their anxiety was over, for Anne grew stronger every day, Emma and Georgiana were free to make their preparations for Christmas. During the month of November everything else had taken second place to Anne's illness, and they had neglected to make their usual calls. They were particularly concerned for Miss Bates, though assured by Mrs Elton that *she* would take care of Miss Bates, who was always welcome at the Vicarage. One bright December morning, therefore, they made their way to Miss Bates's cottage, at the other end of Highbury. As ever, Miss Bates was delighted to see them, and enquired for the latest news of Anne. They were glad to assure her that Anne was so much recovered as to be up most days upon the sofa.

'Sadly, I am too infirm to walk so far,' said the good old lady, 'or I would have called to enquire myself. Such a charming family! Colonel Walters puts me in mind of Colonel Campbell, though he is much taller, and does not sport such a fine moustache. So, Miss Georgiana, Mr Tom Walters is to marry Miss Dixon. I never saw the Dixons but once, at dear Jane's wedding, you know. I wonder if Miss Dixon resembles her father or her mother most? He was quite a well-looking man, I remember, but she was plain, quite plain. Mr Tom called here, you know, oh yes, quite soon after his return from Ireland. I said to him: 'Mr Tom,' I said, 'are there no pretty girls to be met with in Highbury?' I did say to Mrs Elton once that I thought a certain young lady would ... but however she thought not, and so it has turned out. Are you warm enough Miss Knightley?'

Emma thanked her and said that she was.

'My shawl, you know, keeps me so snug. Dear Anna!' went on Miss Bates. 'Did I say she was coming to Highbury for Christmas?'

'No, ma'am,' said Georgiana. 'We are eager to hear all the news. Where will she be staying?'

'Mr Churchill is to bring her, and they are to stay at Hartfield. Mrs John Knightley is so hospitable; she must feel the loss of her little boys every day. They are both doing very well, she says; Frank cannot come home of course, but Mr John Knightley is going up to London to fetch Charles home for Christmas.'

'But Anna, ma'am, when is she to come?' asked Emma.

'I thought Selina would be coming home, but Augusta wrote so kindly to say they must spend Christmas at Upton Prior. Being a clergyman, Mr Craig must be very busy at this time - I remember my poor father - but what was I going to say?'

'Anna,' prompted Georgiana.

'Ah yes, Anna and Mr Churchill are to come the week before Christmas, and will stay until the New Year. Ah, here is Puss - see how he has grown! I am so grateful to dear Anna - he is such a good companion. And the little bell - it warns all the pretty birds to beware.'

On the way home the two sisters stopped at Ford's to look at the new Christmas display. Inside they found Bella, who had brought an unwilling Henry to carry her parcels. They were very pleased to see their cousins, and at first the talk was all of Anne's recovery.

'I have not had the opportunity to tell you,' Bella said, 'that Mr Churchill and Anna are coming for Christmas.' Bella was looking very pretty in a cherry red bonnet; it was a fresh, sunny day, but Emma did not think it was the weather which had put a sparkle in Bella's eye. 'Mama is delighted at the prospect of the house being full, and she is looking forward to seeing Charles, who is coming home for a few days.'

'Yes, we have just heard it all at Miss Bates's. I'm sorry, Bella; it is always particularly galling to have one's news disclosed by a third party.' Turning to Henry she said: 'Are we to have the pleasure of Lord Urswick's company?'

'I doubt if many people would call it a pleasure, Emma, but no, he is out of town at present, and has no immediate plans to return. But what of the ball? Dare we hope it will be before Christmas?'

'I'm not sure,' Emma said doubtfully. 'No, if we wait until January, Anne may be well enough to dance. We promised her it would not take place without her.'

'John would be disappointed if Anne were not there,' said Bella. 'He has been visiting her often as her pastor, and in the process he has become quite fond of the little thing.'

'Speaking of John,' said Henry, '. . . but we must not keep you from your purchases.' Georgiana assured him that they were in no hurry, so he continued: 'John is going down to Donwell Parsonage this afternoon to see how the work is progressing. We are going in the carriage so that we can help him move his books. Would you like to come with us?'

'We would like it of all things,' said Georgiana, full of enthusiasm, and it was agreed that the carriage would call for them at two o'clock.

On the way to Donwell Parsonage, Henry rode on the box with the coachman, well wrapped in greatcoat and muffler, to leave room inside for John's books. Even so, Bella and her cousins were forced to sit inelegantly crammed together, with their feet on sundry works of theology, while John occupied the opposite seat, alongside more of his books and a stuffed owl in a glass dome, which stared at them balefully. The horses went slowly, and it seemed an age before they had passed out of the avenue and travelled the long, rutted lane which led to the Parsonage. As they turned in at the sweep, Emma said: 'It is a handsome building, but it seems rather large for a bachelor establishment.' There was a porticoed entrance, with two long windows on either side of the front door, which had been left open to allow the house to be thoroughly aired. The building work and decorating had all been finished, but there was a strong smell of paint and fresh plaster.

They went up the steps and entered a wide hall with four large rooms opening from it, two on either side. The front room on the left proved to be a very handsome parlour, newly papered, and already furnished with pieces from Hartfield, and some elegant tables and chairs from Donwell Abbey. The rest of the rooms on that floor were empty, apart from one where the estate carpenter and his son were busy fixing a troublesome sash. John showed them the offices with great pride. Here there was every modern convenience, and John informed them that the housekeeper was to move in very soon, to make everything ready for her master. They returned to the parlour after being shown over the whole house, and Georgiana was in raptures.

'Now all you need is a wife, John,' she said playfully.

Emma blushed and looked down, but John seemed unconscious of her embarrassment.

'Indeed, and I think I may know where to find one,' he said archly, 'but we will not talk of that at present.'

Henry exchanged looks of significance with Georgiana.

'It is a very pleasant house, John,' he said. 'I quite envy you.'

'I should not have thought that sermonising would be much to your taste, Henry,' said Georgiana, laughing.

'Oh, saucy is it? You never know what I might achieve with the love of a good woman.'

They were interrupted by a 'Halloa' from the hall, and Mr Knightley strode in, having ridden over to see that all was well. John thanked him heartily for all that he had done, and was assured that Mr Knightley only awaited his instructions to have more furniture moved in.

'I think another week should do it,' said Mr Knightley, 'but which room do you propose to use for your study?' and they walked off to consult together. Meanwhile the coachman had carried in the books and stacked them in untidy heaps in the hall.

'I think it is time we went home,' said Henry. 'It looks as though John will be occupied with my uncle for some time yet.' They therefore took their leave, promising help in arranging his personal possessions as soon as it was needed. John said he would walk home, and they set off.

'Henry,' said Georgiana, 'you must tell us who this mysterious lady is. Can it be his friend's sister? I mean the friend he stayed with at Oxford.'

'Upon my life, I have no idea,' said he. 'John has never said to me that he wished to be married.'

'But you must have observed something unusual in his conduct,' she persisted.

'Oh, you know men never notice these things,' said Emma, anxious to put an end to the conversation.

To save the horses, Emma asked the coachman to set them down at the entrance to Donwell Abbey, and they walked down the long avenue together, huddling a little against the bitter wind.

'Do you think Henry will ever marry?' Georgiana asked Emma.

'I have never known him to be in love, though I think many girls would be glad to have him,' said Emma thoughtfully. 'Some young men, and I think Tom Walters is one of them, are forever falling in love. I think they are carried away by the romance of the moment, rather than by the reality. Then there are the others like John, who never seem to fall in love, but one day decide it would be pleasant to be married, and begin to look about them. I think any agreeable girl would do for John.'

'But what of Henry?' persisted Georgiana, 'He has never seemed to me to be seeking a wife, but I imagine he could fall in love if the right lady came along.'

'Once I used to think he was like John, only livelier; they both used to seem perfectly happy at home, then Henry fell in with Lord Urswick and Anna, and for a while he changed. Even Bella was out of patience with him. But now I am not sure; he is much more his old self, and I think perhaps he is capable of loving deeply after all. Only time will tell.'

Emma did not look at Georgiana as she was speaking, or she would have seen a smile of pure pleasure steal across her face.

Some nine or ten days later John was happily settled in his Parsonage, and his cousins were among his first visitors. After being shown all the improvements in comfort since they were last there, for all the rooms were now fully furnished and a fire blazed in every hearth, they were invited to take some refreshment in the parlour, now called the drawing room. As they ate their Madeira cake, and agreed with everything John said in praise of his house, they heard a carriage draw up, and soon Mrs Walters and Anne were announced. Emma and Georgiana were delighted to see she was well enough to be out, and said so.

'Oh, I could not rest until I had seen the Parsonage, after all that Mr John Knightley has told me about it.'

Both sisters were surprised to see how solicitous John was for Anne's welfare. Emma was asked to give up her seat by the fire to the invalid, and a screen was placed to ward off any draught. There was such affection in Anne's face as she looked at John that Emma wondered why she had never noticed it before. So this, then, was the young lady John had in mind! What was it he had said to Emma about the requisite qualities of a clergyman's wife? - 'sober and upright - with much to do about the parish.' Emma could scarcely suppress a smile. Here was Anne; small and thin, too frail to be like Mrs Elton, who was always busy in the minutest concerns of the parish, and so young. It must be love, thought Emma.

As the sisters took their leave, John was beginning to show Mrs Walters and Anne the various rooms, saying as he did so: 'The house is quite large, but easy to manage. The cook is delighted - says she has never seen a kitchen so well fitted up - and with a housekeeper, a man and two maids there would be very little for the lady of the house to do,' and he looked at Anne with a significant smile. Emma looked at Mrs Walters to see how she took his remarks, but she seemed happily oblivious of any particular meaning.

Mr Churchill and Anna were expected that very day at Hartfield, and Mrs Knightley was hoping they would call on the morrow, but late the same afternoon they called at Donwell to pay their respects, bringing Bella with them. Anna was looking as striking as ever, in a blue cloak trimmed with fur, but there was a change in her manner. With no sign of her former arrogance, she greeted Mr and Mrs Knightley with real affection, and was punctilious in her enquiries about their health and that of all her old friends. Mr Churchill seemed very glad to be back in Highbury, and brought apologies from Mrs John Knightley, who did not feel equal to accompanying them.

'But see, I have brought Bella instead,' he said jovially, as he joined the family seated around the fire. Georgiana, with no mischievous intention, asked Anna if she had seen Lord Urswick.

'I believe he is out of town at present,' she said as though the subject did not interest her. By her tone Emma thought that a coolness must exist between them. 'He said something about a slight indisposition,' Anna went on, 'and has gone to try the waters at Cheltenham, or Bath; I forget which.'

Their visit was, of necessity, short as they were tired after their journey, but they went away with an invitation from Mrs Knightley to dine at Donwell on Christmas Eve.

'I thought Anna was looking very well,' said Mrs Knightley to her husband when they had the drawing room to themselves, 'though she seemed a little subdued.'

'Anna subdued is a very pleasant prospect,' said her husband with a smile. 'I thought Bella was in particularly good looks - the cold weather has put roses in her cheeks.'

Chapter 13

Christmas Eve arrived, and Mr and Mrs John Knightley made their preparations for dining at Donwell. Mr John Knightley was in a bad humour, for he took no pleasure in evening engagements. He envied his son John who had pleaded a sore throat in excuse for his absence. His mother was fretting about him as she finished dressing.

'Poor John is not accustomed to preaching,' she said, in the plaintive tone she used when speaking of her children. 'I noticed he was a little hoarse yesterday; it would be too bad if he lost his voice altogether. I am not sure that Mrs Cooper is particular enough about airing the beds.'

'Oh, do stop worrying, Isabella,' said her husband. 'John is saving his voice for tomorrow by sitting snug by his own fireside. I only wish I could do the same.'

Bella made her toilet with extra care, and chose an ornament for her hair which Mr Churchill had particularly admired. Anna also dressed with care, aiming for elegance without ostentation. In the absence of Lord Urswick, it no longer seemed amusing to scandalise the company. Besides, Mr Walters was not impressed by anything flamboyant, and she was determined to win his attention away from Emma.

As Henry tied his cravat he was thinking of his cousin Georgiana. He had always been fond of her, and felt indignant on her behalf for the way Tom Walters had treated her. Last year she had been a girl, but now she was a beautiful young lady, and any man would be proud to claim her as his wife.

Colonel and Mrs Walters, with their family, had been invited to dine, but Mrs Walters wrote to say, with many thanks, that her sons were happy to accept the invitation, but she and her husband begged to be excused on Anne's account. Although

Anne was much recovered, her mother did not think she could stand the strain of an evening engagement.

The first people to arrive at Donwell were the Eltons, with Mr Walters and Tom, who had brought them in their carriage. They joined the Knightleys round the hearth, and Mrs Elton looked about her, determined to be gracious, and admired the great quantity of candles, and the noble fire.

'How brightly your jewels sparkle in the candle-light, Mrs Knightley,' she said. 'It says in the Bible that our children are our jewels, and that is enough for me. It is at a time like this that I miss my dear girls. Augusta writes very often, but it is not the same as having her at home. I had a letter from her only this morning.' She reached into her reticule as if to take out the letter, when the Hartfield family was announced, and Emma and Georgiana exchanged covert signs of relief.

'My dear Emma, and dear Mr Knightley,' said Mrs John Knightley, 'here we are at last! And here are Bella and Henry, and Mr Churchill and Anna will be here soon. Mrs Elton, how do you do? Have you heard from dear Augusta lately?'

Mrs Elton had no chance to reply for Mrs Knightley was already saying: 'We are so sorry not to have the pleasure of John's company his evening, but Christmas is a taxing time for clergymen.'

Everyone looked involuntarily at Mr Elton who was leaning back on the sofa, the picture of ease and indolence.

'Indeed it is,' said Mrs Elton. 'You have no idea how many people come knocking at our door, looking for charity in this cold weather. I am tempted to tell some of them they would not feel the cold if they worked a little harder.'

'Augusta,' protested Mr Elton, 'that is a little harsh, my dear. We must always try to help those less fortunate than ourselves.'

'Aye, that is just like you,' said his wife, 'but I say charity begins at home.'

Mrs Elton became aware that her words were not being received very kindly by her hearers, and changed tack. 'And as for his sermons,' she said, 'it takes him hours to write them.'

'He might save his breath to cool his porridge,' said Henry in an undertone to Georgiana. 'I cannot imagine that anyone ever listens to them.'

Mr Churchill and Anna were then announced, and room near the fire was made for them.

'I was just saying, Miss Weston,' said Mrs Elton, 'that I had a letter from Augusta this morning.' Anna looked as if she was not aware that such a person existed. 'Selina is staying there, you know, and Mr Craig is so kind. Nothing is too much trouble. Between ourselves I think Selina is quite a favourite.'

Anna made no reply beyond a slight inclination of her head.

'You will never guess who they met in Bath,' went on Mrs Elton. Everyone looked at her expectantly. 'It was Lord Urswick! Yes, I confess I was astonished. He behaved very civilly to Augusta and Mr Craig, being unknown to them before. Mr Craig asked him to dine, but he had another engagement.'

Emma looked enquiringly at Henry, who replied with a slight shrug. Anna said nothing, but looked somewhat put out by the news, and seemed glad that the announcement of dinner put an end to Mrs Elton's communication.

At dinner Anna was thwarted in her intention of fascinating Mr Walters, for she was seated beside her host, while Mr Walters was at the furthest end of the table, next to Mrs Knightley. Emma was delighted to be seated on his right hand, and observed that he was more animated than usual. They talked of Anne, and he told her that she had expressed a desire to learn Latin, and that John Knightley had volunteered to teach her. John's mother, overhearing her son's name, said: 'That is just like John - he is so kind. I remember how he nursed a sick puppy for weeks on end when he was only seven years old.'

'Yes,' called Henry from across the table, 'but if you remember, Mama, the puppy died.'

'I trust my sister will recover from his ministrations,' said Tom Walters, but was quelled by a look from his brother.

'John called this evening,' said Mr Walters, 'and stayed half an hour with us, just to see how Anne was faring. She scolded him for venturing out, and thought it wise in him to nurse his sore throat against the rigours of the morrow.' A faint smile showed that he meant to be satirical.

Emma noticed that Bella and Mr Churchill were deep in conversation, but on catching her eye he recollected himself and said: 'I have just been telling Bella about Enscombe.'

'It sounds wonderfully wild and rugged country,' she said.

'It is wild on the moors,' said Mr Churchill, 'but we have some snug valleys and rich farmland. I am obliged to go there in the spring, and was wondering if we might arrange for a party of friends to accompany me.'

Anna heard some part of this, and her expression darkened. Enscombe was hers, or would be one day, and she did not care for the notion of a party of friends, chosen by Mr Churchill, which included Bella. She was seated next to Mr Elton, and on a whim she turned to him and said: 'Poor dear Mr Elton; should you not be at home nursing your voice, as John Knightley has chosen to do?'

'Oh, these young fellows make much out of nothing,' he said, flattered by her notice. 'I have never had any difficulty in making myself heard in my own church.'

'And your voice has such a fine, manly tone; not deep, but sonorous. I would guess you sing tenor, Mr Elton,' Anna went on, her good humour restored by Mr Elton's susceptibility to flattery.

'Indeed, how clever of you to guess it, my dear,' said Mr Elton, his broad face, flushed with wine, beaming at her.

'Perhaps you would favour us with a song later,' said Anna. 'I should love of all things to hear you sing.' Mrs Knightley looked astonished, for she had never in her life had that pleasure.

'I remember Mr Churchill used to have a fine singing voice,' she began, trying to draw attention away from Mr Elton, who was beginning to look foolish, and thinking: 'He will pay for this when Mrs Elton gets him home.'

'My husband used to sing very well when he was a young man,' said Mrs Elton loudly, 'but he does not give performances. That would ill-befit his dignity as a clergyman;' which words and a venomous look at Anna, put a stop to that particular piece of amusement.

Anna then turned to Tom Walters and began asking him about his intended bride. 'I had a fancy that quite another young lady hereabouts had set her cap at you,' she said shamelessly. Tom hardly knew where to look.

'I am glad,' said Mrs Elton, 'that my daughters have never needed to set their cap at anyone. Here is Augusta very well married at nineteen, and Selina like to follow her example.'

'And who is Selina going to marry, do you think, ma'am?' asked Anna, with a dangerous edge to her voice. Mrs Elton wisely pretended not to hear, and busied herself with her knife and fork.

By the end of the meal Anna had succeeded in irritating or upsetting most of the company, and it was with some relief that Mrs Knightley signalled to the ladies to leave the gentlemen to their port. Mrs John Knightley was the only one who had not noticed anything amiss, her sweet nature not allowing her to see bad in anyone. Emma and Georgiana busied themselves about the tea and coffee, and Bella joined them.

'I seem to have offended Anna in some way,' said she, 'but I cannot imagine how.'

Emma and Georgiana, who had witnessed Mr Churchill's growing attentions to Bella, said nothing.

'Do you think Mr Churchill was serious about inviting some of us to Enscombe?' she went on. 'I hope so, for I should like it of all things.'

It was unfortunate that Anna, bringing her cup to be refilled, had overheard these remarks.

'My dear Bella,' she said with a smile, 'you must not believe everything that Frank says. He always feels mellow after a glass or two of wine. Poor Bella, you are not a woman of the world, are you? Your life is so confined. I expect Frank felt sorry for you, but you will find he has forgotten all about it in the morning.'

'You, of course, know your guardian better than I do,' said Bella, with quiet contempt, 'but I am surprised to hear you accuse him of not being a man of his word. I thought you would have more respect for someone who has been like a father to you,' and she turned on her heel, and went to sit by the fire with the other ladies.

Too late, Anna realised she had blundered, and to restore her self-esteem she went and sat by Mrs Elton, and set herself in earnest to charm her. This was no easy task, for Mrs Elton was deeply offended by Anna's conduct, which she thought had made her husband look a fool. In consequence her answers were short, and she looked straight ahead as she spoke. Mrs Knightley, understanding the situation, intervened.

'Mrs Elton,' she said pleasantly, 'you have had very little opportunity to tell us your news of Upton Prior. How is Augusta enjoying her new life?'

'Oh, she is very happy, Mrs Knightley,' said Mrs Elton, in a softened voice. 'Any little unpleasantness with the children has all been done away with by Selina. She is such a favourite, ma'am. Oh, yes, and there was one further piece of news.

Selina has had a letter from Harriet Cole with an invitation to visit her in London after Christmas. Of course, I shall give my consent. It will be a fine thing for Selina.' Looking at Anna, she said pointedly: 'We did think of Selina's being in London before this, but however it came to nothing. Some people can never be relied on to keep their word.'

Anna looked disconcerted, but said nothing.

'Ah, how is dear Harriet, and Mrs Cole, how is she, ma'am?' said Mrs John Knightley.

'Oh, dear Mrs Cole is no letter-writer, ma'am,' said Mrs Elton, with a pitying smile. 'I have to rely on the correspondence between the girls for any news of that family. They have settled in very well, apparently. William Cole now oversees his father's business, which seems to have improved its profits considerably, so I understand. Mrs Cole is the only one who longs to be back in Highbury.'

Their conversation was interrupted by the return of the gentlemen, and the two sisters were soon busily occupied in serving them with tea and coffee. Henry lingered to talk to them.

'I shall be out with the hunt on Monday,' he said, taking his coffee. 'Georgiana, I hope you and Emma will walk down to the Crown to see us off.'

'Certainly, if it is a fine day,' said Georgiana, and with a sidelong glance at Emma she asked: 'Is Anna proposing to go out with you?'

'I think not,' said Henry, with a smile. 'Our Master of Foxhounds would welcome the black gentleman himself, as long as he was suitably attired, but that tolerance does not extend itself to the female sex. Besides, she has left Bellerophon in London, where no doubt he is eating his head off, and growing unfit for anything. Mr Churchill was saying just now that he hopes she will sell him, and buy a more suitable lady's horse.'

'Anna rides very well,' said Georgiana. 'I quite envy her. I wish I could ride. We used to ride the old pony when we were children, but somehow we left off as we grew up; I don't know why.'

'If you really wish it, little cousin,' said Henry, 'I shall teach you as soon as the weather is warmer.'

'Oh, thank you, dear Henry,' cried Georgiana. 'Emma, would you like to learn to ride too?'

'No, thank you,' said Emma, decidedly. 'I fell off the old pony, if you remember, Georgiana, when I was thirteen, and after that I never wanted to go near another horse in my life!'

After singing some Christmas music, with everyone joining in, Mrs Knightley offered to play some country dances, while Mr Knightley, his brother, his brother's wife, and Mrs Elton settled down to cards. Henry immediately applied to Georgiana, Mr Walters stood up with Emma, and Tom rather reluctantly asked Anna.

'Bella has no partner,' exclaimed her mother, ever careful of her children's wellbeing. 'Mr Churchill, if you do not wish to take a hand at cards, perhaps you would dance with Bella.'

'I was about to suggest it myself, ma'am,' he said, getting up with alacrity, 'if Bella does not object to such an elderly partner.'

'No-one could ever call you elderly,' said Mrs John Knightley, fondly. 'You are a man in the prime of life.'

Bella rose from the sofa, leaving Mr Elton snoring gently at the other end, and gave her hand to Mr Churchill, who led her to the set.

Christmas Day and Sunday were spent quietly, but on the following day Georgiana rose early, hoping for a fine day for the hunt. It was still dark outside and very cold. The frost had made patterns on the inside of the window in spite of the good fire which had been blazing for an hour. She woke Emma, and they hurried into their clothes, then went down to breakfast. By nine o'clock the sun was showing as a red globe over the ploughed fields, and soon after, the two sisters set off for Highbury. The stream at the roadside was quite frozen over, and their breath hung in clouds as they spoke.

In Highbury all was noise and bustle as people hurried to the Crown to see the gentlemen on their fine horses and the farmers on their hacks. Little children ran about, in imminent danger of being trampled; horses tittupped and snorted, while the landlord of the Crown wove in and out of the throng with trays of steaming negus held high in the air. Mr Walters and his brother, dressed in dark green coats, rode over to greet them. As they tried to talk, amidst the hubbub of yelping hounds, and shouting children, Emma saw Mr Elton mounted on a stout cob, and a short distance behind him, Henry and Mr Churchill, looking very dashing in hunting pink.

The horn sounded, the hounds were whipped in, and the stately cavalcade moved off in the direction of Donwell. Bringing up the rear were George, and Rob Martin, who touched their hats in salute. Emma and Georgiana turned to walk home, and fell in with Bella near the entrance to Hartfield.

'I was surprised to see Mr Elton out with the hunt,' she said. 'Perhaps all that flattery from Anna has made him feel young again.'

'I expect he is one of those who go through gates rather than over them,' said Georgiana, with a smile. 'They have a fine morning for the meet, anyway.'

They left Bella and set off back along Donwell lane. Hearing the 'view-halloo' they looked over a gate, and saw a knot of riders on a distant hilltop start into life and disappear down the other side of the hill. Another ten minutes brought them to the entrance of Donwell Abbey, and at Georgiana's suggestion, instead of turning in, they walked on in the direction of Abbey Mill Farm, in the hope of catching another glimpse of the hunt. At the top of the hill they paused at a stile, from which could be seen the fields of Abbey Mill Farm, with the smoke of the farmhouse rising behind the orchard.

'Oh look, there's Papa,' said Emma, waving. 'He must have been over to Home Farm.' They watched Mr Knightley ride towards them at an easy jog-trot, then suddenly, out of nowhere, a riderless horse came galloping across his path. Mr Knightley reined in sharply, then set off in hot pursuit, and managed to seize the horse's bridle. The two horses galloped neck and neck for another half furlong, then slowed to a canter, then to a trot. Mr Knightley turned both horses, and brought them at a walking pace over to the gate by the stile.

'That looks like Mr Elton's horse, Papa,' said Emma in alarm.

There was a cottage a few yards down the lane, and the man and his wife, with three or four sturdy children had come out to see what was causing the commotion. Mr Knightley called to the eldest boy, a lad of about thirteen, to take Mr Elton's horse down to the Donwell stables, and calling to the man to fetch help, Mr Knightley wheeled his horse round, and retraced the steps of the bolting cob. The cottager immediately ran off to rouse his neighbours.

A few minutes later, both girls stood transfixed with horror, unsure what to do for the best, as a group of farm labourers ran across the furrows towards a copse, which had already hidden Mr Knightley from their gaze. One of the men was dragging a hurdle. The minutes passed slowly, and they were beginning to wonder whether they should return home, or fetch Mrs Elton, when their father, still on horseback, reappeared.

'We've found him,' he called across to them. 'Has anyone sent for Perry?' The cottager, who was only a short distance behind him, confirmed that his younger son had gone for Dr

Perry. As he spoke, the rest of the men emerged from the copse, dragging a heavy weight on the hurdle. Georgiana began to cry.

'Don't upset yourself, my love,' said Emma fondly. 'Go home; I'll stay here and help Papa,' and Georgiana, who was feeling faint, agreed with some reluctance to go and tell her mother what had happened.

The field gate was opened and somehow, for he was no lightweight, they got Mr Elton into the cottage. Emma caught a glimpse of him as the men carried him across the weedy path to the threshold. His eyes were closed, and there was a great gash on his temple. Mr Knightley dismounted stiffly, led his horse through the gate and closed it again.

'What happened, Papa?' asked Emma. 'Does anyone know?'

'I can only guess; something must have startled his horse, which reared up and threw him. My dear, you have had a shock; go home now,' he said gently.

'I thought I might be of some use if I stayed,' she said doubtfully.

'Leave it to Betsy Dawkins; she will know what to do until Perry comes. Now I must leave you, my dear. Someone must tell Mrs Elton,' and hauling himself back up into the saddle, he was off at a brisk trot. Emma had never thought of age in relation to her father; he was always the same dear Papa; but at that moment it struck her forcibly that Mr Knightley was growing old.

As she reached the gates of Donwell she paused as Dr Perry rode up at a great pace, and passed her with scarcely a nod. Matters must be grave indeed, she thought, to make Dr Perry discourteous. She found her mother and Georgiana sitting by the morning-room fire, and gave them what news she could.

The rest of the morning passed very slowly as they waited for Mr Knightley to come home. He came at last, his face grey with fatigue and worry.

'Sit down, Papa; let me get you something to drink,' said Emma.

'I own I am thirsty,' he said, sinking heavily into a chair. 'Some spruce beer, Emma, but nothing to eat. Poor Elton; it looks bad. I sent the carriage, my dear,' he said, turning to his wife, 'I knew you would not mind.'

'No, indeed. I would be happy to do anything. Mrs Elton - how did she take it?'

'Oh, she began to scold like any virago,' he said, with a wry smile. 'Blamed him for going out, - too old - foolish - on and on. I didn't listen to the half of it. I knew that after a while she would calm herself, and so it was. Thank you, my dear,' as Emma handed him his drink.

'Shall I go and sit with her?' said Mrs Knightley.

'That is kind, my dear, but no. I sent the carriage to fetch Miss Bates before it went on to bring Elton home. She is very fond of the Eltons, and although she has always talked too much, I think she can be strong in a crisis.'

'But Miss Bates! Are you quite sure?' protested his wife.

'Think what a hard life she has had, Emma. Her father died when she was a young woman, plunging them into poverty; then her sister dies too, leaving Miss Bates with an infant to rear. Then there were all those years spent in cramped rooms over a shop, looking after her old mother, who was as deaf as a post. Yet when did you ever hear her complain? No, Miss Bates is a strong character underneath that timid, fussy exterior. She will be more acceptable to Mrs Elton than anyone else, at least for the time being.'

After resting for a little while, Mr Knightley went round to the stables to find out from the coachman if there were any more news. The coachman had just returned, and was unharnessing the horses. He explained that having left Miss Bates at the Vicarage, he had driven on to Donwell, only to find he had been forestalled, Dr Perry thinking a farm cart a more suitable vehicle for carrying an injured man.

' 'Thank your Master,' says he,' said the coachman, ' 'and tell him it is better for Mr Elton to lie flat. However, I will borrow the sheepskins if I may. He must be kept warm.' That's what he said, sir, and I hope those sheepskins come back clean.' The coachman seemed more concerned with the state of his sheepskins than with the state of his Vicar, but in answer to a question from Mr Knightley he was able to report that Mr Elton was still insensible.

That evening, Mrs Knightley made up her mind that she would call at the Vicarage herself the following morning.

'We will both go,' said Mr Knightley. 'Mrs Elton will be finding it difficult to nurse Elton on her own, with the help of only two servants, who both already have too much to do. I have a plan which I will put to her,' but he would say nothing more until he had spoken with Mrs Elton.

Chapter 14

It was beginning to snow on Tuesday morning as Mr and Mrs Knightley drove down Vicarage Lane. Miss Bates opened the door to admit them, both servants being occupied in helping Mrs Elton lift the invalid into a more comfortable position, as she told them. Poor Miss Bates looked very tired, but said how glad she was to be of use. 'An old woman does not often get the opportunity,' she said, smiling.

Mrs Elton, when she finally came down, was far from her usual elegant self. She was wearing an old gown covered by a coarse apron, and her face was haggard. She seemed grateful for the visit, and for the basket of good things Mrs Knightley had brought.

'He is of course unable to eat anything yet,' she said, 'but this arrowroot and the calves foot jelly will be just the thing for him as he begins to recover. Dr Perry says there are no broken bones, but he cannot tell if there are any internal injuries. The blow to the head was severe.' She sat for some moments in silence, no doubt thinking of the extent of his injuries, then rousing herself, she said: 'All our neighbours have been so kind.'

'Mrs Elton, is there anything I can do for you?' asked Mrs Knightley. 'I will sit with Mr Elton while you take some rest, if you like.'

'Oh no, I could not think of sleeping. He may wake at any moment. I should be writing to Augusta to tell her the sad news. She will be very shocked; she always was her father's favourite. And Selina must come home. Oh, I cannot find time for everything!'

'Well, that at least I can do for you, if you will furnish me with pen and paper,' said Mrs Knightley decidedly, and Mrs Elton reluctantly agreed.

'Dear Mrs Knightley, you always did write beautifully,' said Miss Bates. 'Perhaps I could show you where everything is kept in Mr Elton's study? Oh wait, there is no fire . . .'

'No fire is necessary, I assure you, Miss Bates,' said Mrs Knightley. 'The letter will not take me long,' and the two ladies crossed the hall to Mr Elton's study.

'Poor Philip,' said Mrs Elton, her eyes filling with tears, 'who knows when you will be sitting in your own dear study writing your sermons?'

'Mrs Elton,' said Mr Knightley hastily, for he did not like tears, 'is there someone, your former housekeeper, or your old Nanny perhaps, whom I could fetch to help you?' Mrs Elton's eyes brightened.

'Nanny Hopkins lives with her son,' she said consideringly, 'at Keeper's Cottage in Torrington . . . but she is too old now, I think.' She paused. 'Mrs Hodge still lives at Old Mill Cottage, and I know she has not yet found employment since I was obliged to turn her off. Oh, but I would not be able to afford . . . that is, I can manage . . .'

'Forgive me, Mrs Elton, I would not offend you for the world, but by your leave I will fetch Mrs Hodge at once. She is a good soul, and an experienced nurse, and we will say no more about her wages. That will all be taken care of.'

'Oh Knightley, you are too kind. You always were a good friend to my *caro sposo*,' she said.

Mr Knightley rose quickly, and went to tell his wife where he was going. She was finding it difficult to compose her letter with Miss Bates standing over her, admiring every stroke of the pen.

'Miss Bates, I think Mrs Elton needs you,' he said to her, and to his wife: 'I shall be back as quickly as I can, but it may take some time for Mrs Hodge to pack her traps.'

Several long days and restless nights passed slowly for Mrs Elton, with little change in Mr Elton's condition. Mrs Hodge had duly arrived, prepared for a long stay, and Miss Bates went home. Dr Perry called twice a day, but could only give guarded replies to Mrs Elton's questions. She was immensely comforted, however, by the familiar presence of Mrs Hodge, and was aware of a marked change in the conduct of the other two servants. The house shone, and fires blazed in clean hearths. Mr Knightley had sent quantities of extra fuel, for the whole house needed to be kept warm. Mrs Knightley's letter to Augusta had been dispatched, but no reply had been received. Mrs Elton was ready to go mad with worry, when one snowy morning in early January the longed-for letter arrived. Mrs Knightley happened to be calling at the time, as the housekeeper came in with the letter on a silver salver.

'Here, ma'am,' she said cheerfully, 'this is what you have been waiting for! Perhaps Miss Selina is already on her way home.'

Mrs Elton opened the letter quickly, and scanned the contents. Mrs Knightley could see that it was but a short letter.

'I hope it is not bad news, Mrs Elton,' she said, seeing her expression change.

'Yes it is - very bad news. Oh, it is too provoking!' and getting up, Mrs Elton began to pace about the room. 'Augusta says she cannot come at present, though she is very concerned for her father. Mr Craig cannot be spared, and he will not hear of Augusta's travelling alone. Well, well; it is only what I expected, but Selina - it is really too bad.' She returned to her seat, picked up the letter she had hastily thrown down, and read aloud: '. . . *unable to travel at present* . . . (ah, here we are) . . . *Selina had already departed for London some days before I received your letter. I wrote to her at the Coles' straight away, but so far I have received no reply. Perhaps, as you are so much nearer to London, it might be better if you wrote to her yourself.* There! you see. What is that silly girl about? I expect she is gadding about, enjoying herself, and not caring a fig for her poor father.' She sat down again, her face contorted in an effort not to weep before Mrs Knightley.

'I am sure there must be a rational explanation for all this,' said Mrs Knightley, gently, 'but you are wanting to write straight away, ma'am, so I will bid you adieu.'

'Yes, I will write to Mr Cole himself, and tell him to *make* Selina come home. Thank you, Mrs Knightley; I am sure you will excuse me.'

The snow began to clear away, and could no longer be used as an excuse for the slowness of the mails. Anna happened to be calling on Mrs Elton when the letter from London finally arrived. The letter had been written by Mr Cole, and it contained Augusta's letter, unopened. Putting Augusta's letter to one side, Mrs Elton seized the hastily folded sheet; reading it through with exclamations of horror and disbelief, she cried out in agony: 'She is not there! Oh, where can she be, Miss Weston?'

'Mrs Elton, calm yourself,' said Anna. 'What does the letter say?'

'Here, read it for yourself; I cannot take it in,' said she, twisting her handkerchief, and tapping her foot nervously. 'Oh Selina, you wicked girl! As if I did not have enough to vex me!'

Anna took the letter, and read the following:

Dear Madam

Mrs Cole and I were very sorry to hear of Mr Elton's riding accident. Be assured of our best wishes for his speedy recovery. As to your daughter, Selina, she is not here, nor ever has been. The letter which you say is from Augusta, and which I enclose, has lain here unopened for some time. We were perplexed about it, and did not know what to do for the best. Harriet wrote to Selina before Christmas certainly, but there was no invitation to stay here at the present time; not but what we would always be glad to see any member of the Elton family, but Mrs Cole is unwell at present, being indisposed with a bad cold.

We were not alarmed, ma'am, until we received your letter, for Harriet, thinking Selina must be staying with Miss Weston, and that Augusta had mislaid her direction, expected her to call here any day.

Try to stay calm, ma'am. Selina may turn up here still, and when she does I shall send her home straight away. I have not heard any reports of an accident to the Bath Mail.

With compliments from your obedient servant,

J. Cole

'I am sure you have no need to worry, ma'am,' said Anna. 'There is a misunderstanding here which I am sure will soon come right.'

'None of this would have happened if you had not cast Selina off,' said Mrs Elton bitterly.

'You are distressed, ma'am,' said Anna, 'so I will not remain to add to your troubles.'

As soon as she could after returning to Hartfield, Anna sought Henry out and, briefly telling him the details of Selina's disappearance, awaited his opinion.

'You think Urswick has had a hand in this?' said Henry.

'It seems the most obvious explanation,' said Anna. 'I am surprised her mother did not think of it. Henry, my conscience is troubling me. Mrs Elton was right when she said if I had not cast Selina off this would never have come about.'

'Anna, you must not judge yourself so harshly,' said Henry. 'I have known Selina Elton all her life, and she has always been a vain, empty-headed little flirt.'

'So she may be, but she is also very young, and innocent of the ways of the world. If she has gone off with Urswick, it is because she thinks he means to marry her.'

'He has no intention of *that*, I assure you,' said Henry.

'Where can they have gone, do you think?' asked Anna. 'Perhaps we could go after them.' Henry thought for a few moments.

'We could try his London house at least. Look, Anna, can you think of something that needs your attention in London? Then I could offer to convey you there in my father's carriage. I think Mr Churchill would be reluctant to leave Hartfield at present.'

'Oh, Frank must never know!' said Anna, in alarm. 'He would condemn me, and rightly, for my part in this.' She stood pondering, then said: 'I usually consult with my mantua-maker at this time of year, to order new clothes for the spring. That would be a good enough excuse, I think.'

Henry promised to explain to his mother that he was going away for two or three days, and would escort Anna and her maid to St James's Square at the same time.

They were ready to leave shortly after one o'clock, to travel the sixteen miles to London. Snow still lay in neglected hollows, but the turnpike was clear. They made good progress, but it was already dark when Henry set Anna down in St James's Square. Though she pressed him to come inside and take some refreshment, Henry insisted on going straight to Lord Urswick's house, half a mile away.

'If he is there without Selina, I can be sure of a bed for the night,' he said. 'Otherwise I will put up at an inn, but I will come back as soon as I have any intelligence of Selina's whereabouts.'

The butler was a little put out by Anna's unexpected arrival, and there was much bustling about, and lighting of fires. Anna ordered some tea, and sent Marie to the mantua-maker to arrange an appointment for the morrow. Anna wanted to tell as few lies as possible, and she may also have thought that although her errand was serious, she need not therefore be deprived of a new spring gown.

Anna was just about to sit down to a late dinner, for which she had ordered the butler to set two places, when Henry arrived. 'No luck, alas,' he said, joining Anna at the table, then waiting for the servants to withdraw before continuing. 'I went to Urswick's house where the housekeeper told me she had been expecting her master for several days, but that he had not yet arrived.'

Both of them ate and drank mechanically, without noticing the tenderness of the veal cutlets, or the excellence of the wine, while they pondered what to do.

'Could he be staying with his aunt at Richmond?' said Anna.

'It is possible,' said Henry slowly, 'but we could hardly go there unannounced - it would look so odd.'

'You could write a note to Lady Maria, enquiring for Lord Urswick,' said Anna eagerly, 'and I will send a servant with it at first light tomorrow morning.'

He agreed that this was the best plan, and took his leave soon after, promising to call again on the morrow.

Anna found it difficult to sleep, and when sleep came she was disturbed by bad dreams, full of Selina and Lord Urswick. She rose late, having fallen into a heavy slumber about five o'clock, and after breaking her fast, she spent an hour with her mantua-maker, ordering new gowns and a cloak. Henry arrived shortly after eleven o'clock, and Anna was relieved to see him. Having someone to confide in was an inexpressible comfort. A footman had ridden over to Richmond early, and was expected back at any time.

'You don't think they might have gone to his estates in North Lonsdale, do you, Henry?' said Anna.

'No; this is no weather for travelling, and besides, if he is conducting some sort of *amour* it would be here in town. You must know that one's every action is observed by someone in the country.'

They went into the drawing room and Anna ordered some refreshment. The butler duly brought in the Madeira, and a note from Lady Maria at the same time. Anna took it eagerly, scanned the contents, then handed it to Henry in disappointment. It was a scrawl, with her ladyship's compliments, to say that the last time she had heard from her nephew he had been in Bath.

'Oh, it is too provoking!' said Anna, almost in despair, when the door opened and the butler announced Lord Urswick.

'Henry, my dear fellow,' he said amiably, 'I had not expected to find you here. Anna, my dear, how lovely you look,' and he took her hand and kissed it.

'Urswick, we have been looking for you everywhere,' said Henry impatiently.

'Well, now you have found me, my boy. Anna, a glass of Madeira if I may.'

Anna sat, immobile, staring at him as if she expected him to vanish at any moment.

'Oh, of course . . .' and getting to her feet, she went to pour him some wine.

'Your very good health, my dear,' said Lord Urswick, raising his glass, then downing the contents in one gulp. 'Ah, that's better. So, children, why have you been seeking me up-hill and down-dale? I received Henry's message late last night when I returned home, and here I am, at your service.'

'Where is Selina?' asked Anna bluntly.

Lord Urswick looked momentarily disconcerted by this frontal attack, then recovered his composure, and made himself comfortable on the sofa.

'Where is Selina?' he said thoughtfully. 'That puts me in mind of the old song: *Who is Silvia? What is she?*'

'Come on, Urswick,' said Henry, 'tell us where she is.'

'I am just asking myself what possible business that could be of yours,' said he, looking at Henry coldly.

'Lord Urswick,' said Anna, in a more persuasive tone, 'Mr Elton is lying dangerously ill. He has had a bad fall from a horse, and has not yet recovered the use of his senses. Mrs Elton is ill with worry, fearing for his life, and wants Selina very much to go home.'

'Does she indeed?' said he with a sneering smile. 'And would she be prepared to receive her into the bosom of her family?'

'I do not understand you,' said Anna.

'Oh, I think you do,' said Lord Urswick. 'Selina was kind enough to bestow her . . . company upon me, and is now living in a sweet little house in Chelsea under my protection.'

Anna gasped with horror as Henry stepped forward as if to strike him, crying: 'You devil!' But holding up a restraining hand his lordship said sharply: 'Have a care, sir. If you wish to speak to Selina you had better keep a civil tongue in your head. She is not a prisoner, you know. Come; my carriage is at the door. I will take you there myself.'

The house in Chelsea was small and charming like a doll's house, with a prospect of the river, but Anna was in no mood to admire the architecture or the situation. The door was opened by a neat maid, and they were ushered into a parlour overlooking a garden at the back of the house. There was a light footstep on the stair and Selina rushed in, crying 'Roly, I heard the carriage, and I knew . . .' She stopped short on seeing her other visitors. She was wearing a velvet tiring-gown, richly adorned with lace, and her fair curls were tumbling down her back.

'Miss Weston,' she said, faltering, 'I had not thought to see you here . . . and Mr Henry Knightley. Pray take a seat . . . If you will excuse me, I will go and dress.'

'There is no time for that, miss,' said Anna sharply. 'Sit down, Selina; we are here on a disagreeable errand.'

Lord Urswick had helped himself to some wine from a decanter, and was now sprawled in a chair by the fire. The other three were standing.

'I am not coming back,' cried Selina, rushing to stand behind Lord Urswick's chair, as if for protection. 'Who sent you? How did you find out where I was?'

'Oh sit down, all of you,' said Lord Urswick irritably. 'Selina, they are not going to steal you away. Listen to what they have to say, there's a good girl.'

'Selina,' said Anna, 'your father is gravely ill. He fell from a horse, and received a severe blow to the head. You must come home.'

Selina sank into a chair, looking shocked.

'When did this happen?' she asked.

'It was on the Monday after Christmas - the twenty-seventh.'

'But that was the day I . . .' she began to cry, '. . . the day I left Bath to come here. Oh, poor Papa!'

'Tell your maid to pack your clothes, Selina, and we can be off straight away,' said Henry.

'How can I?' said Selina, and began to cry afresh.

Henry began to feel thoroughly uncomfortable, and at a glance from Anna said: 'Look here, Urswick, we had better leave the ladies alone.'

'Very well,' said he, rising. 'Perhaps you would care to take a turn round the garden.'

'Don't leave me, Roly,' cried Selina piteously.

'Have no fear, my love; I shall not go far,' and with that the two gentlemen left the room.

'Selina,' said Anna more gently, 'this has been a great shock to you. Are you not sorry for your poor Papa? Your Mama is deeply distressed, and needs you. We can make up some story about where you have spent the last weeks; no-one need ever know.'

'I cannot leave Roly,' said Selina. 'I could never be happy without him.'

'Does he mean to marry you, Selina?'

'Yes . . . no; I expect he will if I stay by him; but if I go home I will never see him again. They would never let me come back.'

'Selina, what you are doing is wrong; you must know that; you - a clergyman's daughter. But it is not just wrong - it is foolish. What will you do if he casts you off? You can never be received in polite society again.'

'And who are you, Miss Weston, to tell me how to behave?' cried Selina angrily. 'You who rode astride in a horse-race against Mr Henry Knightley for a wager of thirty guineas. Who dressed as a boy to take fencing lessons, and the other things too shocking to mention. Oh yes, Roly has told me everything, so do not presume to lecture me!'

There was a long silence. Anna got up and walked to the window, where she stared out at the bare garden, and Henry and Lord Urswick walking up and down.

'What am I to tell your mother?' she said at last.

'I suppose you must tell her the truth,' said Selina defiantly. 'When I am Lady Urswick, I don't suppose she will care how I came by the title. And now, Miss Weston, I will bid you 'Good day'. I trust you will not find it necessary to call here again,' and Selina left the room. Anna rang the bell for the maid, and sent her into the garden to ask the gentlemen to return.

'Well, Anna, has she agreed to go back with you?' said Lord Urswick, with a smile which already anticipated the answer.

'No, you have trained her well. She is like that little spaniel you used to own; cringing and fawning,' said Anna with contempt. 'Come, Henry, we can do no good here.'

'My carriage is at your disposal,' said Lord Urswick, still smiling.

'Thank you, but I prefer to walk,' said Anna, sweeping out of the room with as much dignity as she could muster, Lord Urswick's derisive laughter ringing in her ears, and closely followed by Henry, who was beginning to wish he had called Lord Urswick out.

It was a long walk back to St James's Square, but Anna hardly noticed the distance, being too occupied with unpleasant thoughts. She was deeply shocked by her encounter with Lord Urswick, feeling she had never known him before, and wondering how she herself had escaped unscathed. They arrived back at St James's Square, but Henry refused to come in, saying he thought Anna must be tired, and nothing could be gained by further discussion. He left, promising to call for Anna the following morning, to take her back to Highbury.

It was a chill, damp day, with a thick mist coming off the river, as they left London. For the first half hour neither of them spoke, then Anna, rousing herself, said in a hopeless tone: 'What am I to say to Mrs Elton?'

Henry cast a warning glance at Marie, who sat huddled in a corner, staring out at the grey streets.

'Oh, do not worry about her,' said Anna carelessly. 'She prides herself on not speaking a word of English, *n'est-ce pas*, Marie?'

'Mademoiselle?' said Marie with raised eyebrows.

'You see,' said Anna, 'you may speak freely. Now, what am I to tell her mother?'

'There is no occasion for you to tell her mother anything,' said Henry. 'She will find out soon enough.'

'Oh, I cannot leave her in suspense; anything is better than that. She will be fancying all manner of things, each one more terrifying than the last. Perhaps she will go to Selina and persuade her to come home. At least no-one else knows at present.'

'You are forgetting the Coles,' said Henry. 'They must know by now that Selina is missing. They also know she lied about going to stay with them. The truth is bound to come out before much longer.'

With this cheerful thought to speed them on their way, they continued their journey to Highbury.

Chapter 15

Henry and Anna were welcomed back with great cordiality by Mrs John Knightley. She was full of concern for their wellbeing, and anxious to be assured that they had not taken cold from their journey. Fortunately, she asked no questions about their visit to London, and beyond a few desultory enquiries about the spring fashions from Bella, neither did anyone else. Although she was tired from her journey, Anna lay awake most of the night wondering what she could tell Mrs Elton, if indeed she should tell her anything at all. Finally, she resolved to call on Mrs Elton the following day, disagreeable as an interview with that lady might be, and fell asleep just as the clock was striking three.

Anna told Henry of her decision, but did not mention it to anyone else. She found, however, when she sat down to breakfast, that the talk was all of the Eltons. Mr John Knightley had been out early, and had met with Dr Perry coming from the Vicarage. The news was grave; Mr Elton's condition was giving rise to some alarm, and Dr Perry, with much head-shaking, indicated between themselves that he had only days to live.

Anna found that she no longer had any appetite for breakfast, and it was with a heavy heart that she prepared to go out. The sun was shining as she walked down Vicarage Lane, and in a sheltered corner of the Vicarage garden a solitary snowdrop bloomed. The house was very quiet as she was admitted, and it was some time before Mrs Elton joined her in the parlour. She looked thin and haggard, but was quite composed.

'So kind of you to call, Miss Weston,' she said, gesturing for her to be seated, 'but there is no good news, I'm afraid. Dr Perry says my dear husband cannot last much longer.'

There was a certain pathetic dignity about her, which made Anna want to weep. She said what she could, but it was obvious Mrs Elton was lost in her own thoughts.

'I have had another letter from Augusta, Miss Weston. As you know, I have been frantic with worry about Selina, but now . . . I really don't know what to think.'

'Was Mrs Craig able to throw any light on the situation, ma'am?' asked Anna, trying to assess the situation before committing herself.

'Miss Weston, without a husband or a brother to consult I am at a loss to know what to do for the best,' she said, her composure beginning to crack. 'If I tell you something, will you *swear* not to reveal it to anyone?' Anna was eager in her assurance. 'Augusta says that Selina was conveyed to Bath in Mr Craig's carriage, to take the Bath to London Mail, at least that was what she understood. But, after receiving my letter and knowing how anxious I was, she questioned their coachman. He was reluctant to say anything, but eventually owned that Miss Selina had been met by a gentleman in a carriage, and we have all too much reason to suspect it was Lord Urswick.' She broke down, and began to weep. 'Miss Weston, I have no-one to send to find her; I am at my wits' end. Perhaps they are married, though I cannot believe Selina would behave in this underhand fashion if that were the case. There would be no need for concealment. Oh God! If only I knew one way or the other.'

'Are you sure, ma'am?' said Anna. 'The news might be . . . not very good; you might prefer to remain in ignorance.'

'What do you mean?' said Mrs Elton wildly. 'You know something, Miss Weston! For the love of God tell me; tell me!'

'Mrs Elton, it is indeed bad news. Mr Henry Knightley and I went to London on purpose to find Selina . . .'

'And you found her?' said Mrs Elton, her tone rising sharply.

'Yes, we found her, ma'am. I almost wish that we had not. You were right in thinking she had left Bath with Lord Urswick. She went with him to London, and now . . . oh, how can I tell you? - she is established under his protection in a house in Chelsea.'

Mrs Elton sat in stunned silence.

'We begged her to come home, Mrs Elton, but she refused. Lord Urswick has not offered her marriage, and she thinks the only way to secure such an offer is to stay with him. I am sorry to be the bearer of such bad tidings, ma'am, but if you were to go to see her . . .'

'Oh no,' said Mrs Elton with reviving spirit. 'Oh no, - the very idea! By behaving in this fashion she has forfeited all right to be called my daughter. No, she has made her bed, and she must lie on it.' Anna thought this rather an unfortunate metaphor in the circumstances, and was hard put to it not to smile.

'If you should change your mind, Mrs Elton, my guardian would be happy to put his carriage at your disposal.'

'Change my mind? Certainly not! I would not have that wicked, ungrateful girl in my house if she begged me on her knees. I thank God my poor husband has been spared this terrible disgrace.'

Anna tried to soothe Mrs Elton, who was growing angrier by the minute.

'If you had not introduced Selina to that monster, this would never have happened,' she said bitterly.

Anna could not find fault with the logic of this statement, and soon after, took her leave.

That evening, after dinner, they received word that Mr Elton had died.

John Knightley had been a frequent visitor at the Vicarage during Mr Elton's illness, and he it was who conducted the funeral service. He was particularly eloquent on the subject of Mr Elton's virtues as a clergyman, and many in the congregation left with the feeling that they had never known their Vicar. Mrs Elton had confided something of Selina's situation to John, and asked for his advice, though really only wanting to be told she had done the right thing.

'You must forgive her in your heart, ma'am,' he said soberly, 'but you cannot insult your neighbours by asking them to receive her. Shakespeare was right when he wrote the lines: 'How sharper than a serpent's tooth it is to have a thankless child.' A heavy burden has been laid upon you, Mrs Elton.'

Only two weeks after the funeral Mrs Elton left Highbury for ever. She went to her daughter, Augusta, at first, but hoped to find a cottage to rent in Upton Prior eventually. After Mrs Elton had called to take her leave, Mrs Knightley remarked to her husband: 'I can see how it will be: she will make herself so comfortable at the Parsonage that she will have no inclination to remove to a cramped cottage, and she will spend her time scolding the servants and Mr Craig's children, until there is no peace left in the house. Poor Augusta! How I pity her.'

The old Vicarage, the happy scene of Miss Bates's childhood, and the house to which Mr Elton had brought his bride, now stood empty and neglected. A curate rode over once a week from Torrington to conduct a hasty service, and that was all. Mr Knightley, in whose gift the living lay, tentatively offered it to John, but he was unexpectedly firm in his opposition to pluralities, and could not in conscience accept it.

Miss Bates was the only one who truly mourned the passing of the Eltons, though Robert Martin, hearing the gossip about Selina, could not help feeling heartily sorry for her at least. Mr Churchill returned to London the day after the funeral, leaving

Anna still a welcome guest in Highbury. She had a marked reluctance to return to London, after her unsuccessful interview with Selina. She now loathed and despised Lord Urswick, and was ashamed that she had never understood before the corruption of his nature. Mr Churchill was making plans to return to Enscombe at the beginning of March, and Anna longed with all her heart to be there; to ride out in the clear, cold air, and put all her foolishness behind her.

Bella and her parents had received an invitation to visit Enscombe, but Mr John Knightley had made it abundantly clear that he never stirred from his own fireside except on business. Mrs John Knightley, who would never be separated from her husband, claimed that her health would not permit her to undertake a long journey. Bella was bitterly disappointed, and for a while all was in suspense until a letter from Mr Churchill made everything easy. He wrote to suggest that Bella should choose another companion with her parents' permission. So it was with renewed optimism that Bella called at Donwell Abbey, one morning in late February, to solicit the company of one of her cousins. Emma, reluctant to leave Highbury because of her growing affection for James Walters, hoped Georgiana would seize upon the idea of a pleasure trip with her usual enthusiasm. However Georgiana had no intention of leaving Donwell. She disliked Anna, and did not relish the thought of a month or more in her company.

'I am sure Emma would be the best companion for you, Bella,' she said firmly. 'You are more of an age and, in any case, Henry has promised to teach me to ride, and we are to begin next week.'

Emma had no alternative but to accept, with the *appearance* at least of pleasure; and on the first day of March, in brilliant sunshine, she was conveyed in her uncle's carriage to London, together with Bella and Anna, on the first stage of their journey to Yorkshire.

It seemed very strange at first to Georgiana to be without Emma, for they had never been apart for more than a day in their whole life. One morning, about a week after Emma's departure, Georgiana was feeling in particularly low spirits. Her father was out, her mother was closeted with the housekeeper, and she was almost regretting her decision to remain at home when Henry arrived. He was on his way to Home Farm, and had called to offer Georgiana a riding lesson on the following day. She accepted eagerly, and agreed to meet him in the paddock which lay beyond the Abbey ruins.

'I shall have Bella's horse brought up for you,' he said. 'She is a quiet old thing, just suited to an inexperienced rider, and I am sure Bella would be glad for her to be exercised by you while she is away. It will be dull for you without Emma,' he added with a smile. 'I shall have to see what I can do to make your life more interesting.'

After Henry had departed, Georgiana could not settle to any tame employment; she wanted to run and skip like the lambs in the Abbey meadows. She decided she would go to visit Anne, and ran out into the grounds to gather an armful of daffodils to take with her. When she arrived at Donwell Court, she was shown straight into the parlour and found that Anne already had a visitor. John Knightley, true to his promise, had been giving Anne a Latin lesson. Georgiana was amused to see Anne with her list of verbs and a Latin grammar that John had had as a schoolboy. They exchanged a few pleasantries and John took his leave.

'What lovely flowers!' said Anne. 'I must arrange them myself,' and she rang the bell for a maid to bring vases and water. As she snipped the stems and dripped water on the carpet, Georgiana thought she had never seen her look so animated, all smiles and blushes.

'Can you keep a secret?' she asked shyly, turning to Georgiana, who was seated by the fire.

'Of course!' said Georgiana, full of curiosity. 'What secret is this?' She wondered fleetingly if Anne had heard the gossip about Selina Elton, and wondered what she would say if Anne mentioned it, the subject having been forbidden as a topic of conversation by Mr Knightley.

'John has spoken to me about . . . marriage,' said Anne, turning away and busying herself with the flowers.

'Marriage?' said Georgiana in surprise. 'Do you mean 'the honourable estate of matrimony' where N takes M? I should not have thought you would need lessons in the Book of Common Prayer.'

'No, silly,' said Anne, laughing. 'John has asked me to be his wife, and I have accepted.' Georgiana was shocked into silence.

'I see that this has come as a surprise to you,' Anne went on; 'but you know I have always had a great affection for John, right from the first. He was so good to me when I was ill, and that was when I came to love him.'

'I knew you were fond of John, certainly,' said Georgiana, 'but I thought he was just like another brother to you. Have your parents given their consent?'

'Mama was against it at first; she said I was far too young, but John was very persuasive. Both my parents think very highly of him, and at last they agreed to an engagement. They want to be sure that my health continues to improve, so the wedding must wait a while, but I am feeling better every day. Oh Georgiana, I am so happy!'

'I can see you are,' said Georgiana affectionately. 'If this is what you really want, then I am delighted for you,' and she kissed her. 'Your parents could not have thought when they came here that they would have a son and a daughter engaged before they had been here a year.'

'No, indeed,' said Anne, 'and speaking of Tom, did you know that the Dixons and Sophia are coming to stay in Donwell?' Georgiana could only look her surprise. 'They should be here by Friday.'

'I shall look forward to meeting them,' said Georgiana, making a heroic effort to appear normal; but finding two shocks in one morning rather too much to absorb, after a little while, she made her excuses and left.

At the gate she met Tom Walters coming in, and he turned back to walk with her.

'I hear we shall soon have the pleasure of meeting your future bride,' said Georgiana, trying to disconcert him.

'Yes, we expect them on Friday,' said Tom awkwardly. 'But what of your sister? I hear that she has gone to stay at Enscombe, but I do not know where that is exactly.'

'It is *exactly* four miles north of the Derbyshire border, which places it in Yorkshire.' Tom made a wry face, but did not reply.

'How long do the Dixons propose to stay with you?' asked Georgiana, unable to leave the subject alone.

'They have been invited to spend a month with us at least, and they will be very sorry to have missed Mr Churchill. He is their very old friend.'

'Perhaps he will visit Highbury again before they leave,' said Georgiana.

'Perhaps,' said Tom, and there was another long silence.

'Henry is going to teach me to ride,' said Georgiana brightly. 'My first lesson is tomorrow.'

'I think you would make a very good horsewoman,' said he, considering. 'You are very graceful, so light and quick. It should not take you long to become accomplished.' Georgiana was overcome with confusion and blushed.

'Mr Henry Knightley is a bold, fearless rider himself,' he went on. 'I hope he understands how to be patient with a novice and one, moreover, who might be apprehensive.'

'My cousin Henry is kindness itself,' said Georgiana, with spirit. 'I have never heard him utter a sharp word in his life, so I don't expect he will begin now, however clumsy or stupid I may be!'

'I did not mean to imply . . .' said Tom, in some confusion.

'Mr Walters, it is getting late, and I am wanted at home,' said Georgiana, for they had been dawdling along. 'If you will excuse me, I will just run on - we are almost there,' and without waiting for a reply she ran lightly down the lane, and turned in at the gates of Donwell, leaving Tom Walters standing, open-mouthed.

With the help of her maid, Georgiana spent an evening altering a riding-habit of her mother's. It was old-fashioned, but the material was good, and a very pretty shade of deep blue. When it was finished to her liking she put it on, and went down to show her mother.

'That colour is very becoming, my love,' said her fond Mama. 'I am glad Henry is going to teach you - you need something to occupy your time while Emma is away.'

'Mama,' said Georgiana slowly, 'Anne told me the Dixons are coming to stay at Donwell Court. Did you know?'

'Yes, your aunt called this morning while you were out and told me; she met Mrs Walters in Ford's. It will make a pleasant change for us all, after the gloom of the past months. I hope, Georgiana, that you will make a point of being very kind to their daughter. Apart from the Walters family, she has no acquaintance in the area. We must try to make her feel welcome.'

Georgiana said nothing, thinking privately that Miss Sophia Dixon was not a welcome visitor to *her*.

'Georgiana,' said her mother, a little severely, 'I hope you have put all thoughts of Tom Walters out of your head. He is an engaged man, remember.'

'I am hardly likely to forget it, am I, with Sophia Dixon coming here,' said Georgiana, a little petulantly, and went to change out of her habit.

All her good humour was restored, however, after a wonderful morning spent with Henry. Bella's horse was gentle and obedient, and after only a few circuits on the lead-rein, Georgiana felt confident enough to walk round the paddock on her own.

'I suppose the turns I had on the old pony when we were children must help,' she called out to Henry. 'It's all coming back to me.'

'You must not overtire yourself, Georgiana,' said Henry, 'Perhaps we had better stop now,' but she was enjoying the experience so much she hardly knew how to leave off. In the end, the old groom, who had been looking on, muttered something about Miss Bella's horse being spared; Georgiana dismounted reluctantly, and Bessie was led away.

'You will come again tomorrow, Henry, and give me another lesson?' said Georgiana eagerly.

'You must ask your father if he can spare me,' said Henry, laughing. 'I have not been attending to estate business so much lately, and I think he wishes me to interest myself in the old cottages that are to be pulled down.'

'If you can leave it until the end of next week I shall be able to ride well enough to go with you,' said Georgiana, persuasively.

'Oh, very well,' said the good-natured Henry. 'Why do I feel it is I who am on a lead-rein, and not old Bessie? Do you always get your own way, Georgie?'

'Usually,' she said pertly, 'because I never entertain any doubts in the matter; and do not call me 'Georgie'. I am a grown woman, and not six years old!'

Chapter 16

The Dixons and their daughter arrived late on Friday, and were introduced to the neighbourhood. Miss Bates was delighted to see them, and spent an hour and more talking about her dear Jane to the kindly Mrs Dixon. Georgiana could not help being curious to see Sophia Dixon, and it was not long before her curiosity was satisfied. Mr Knightley had waited on them on Saturday, and the following day they all met together after morning service. Georgiana hung back a little, studying the gravestones, which were so overgrown with lichen as to be illegible, while her parents smiled and chatted with the Walters family and their guests. Miss Dixon was holding Tom's arm in a very proprietorial way, while he looked stiff and awkward, as if wishing himself elsewhere. On first observation Georgiana was inclined to be critical; Sophia was not pretty, though elegantly dressed in colours to suit her reddish hair; no, she was decidedly plain. Georgiana was ashamed to find herself feeling pleased about Sophia's lack of beauty. 'I must not judge her hastily,' she said to herself, 'though she is decidedly short and plump. She may be animated and charming on closer acquaintance, but at the moment she is about as lively as a currant bun,' then chided herself for the vulgar thought.

On her way home from church Georgiana told her father how much she was enjoying her riding lessons.

'I am to have another one tomorrow, Papa; or at least, Henry says I must ask your permission first. He is afraid you will think he is neglecting estate business.'

Mr Knightley smiled wryly at the thought; Donwell Abbey had been prospering as a private estate for nigh on three hundred years, without the assistance of Mr Henry Knightley.

'Oh, I think he can be spared, Georgiana,' he said, smiling indulgently, 'but when he realises how *exigeante* you are, I think he may come back to his duties with renewed enthusiasm.'

Georgiana also learnt from her mother that they were to dine at Donwell Court the following evening.

'Mrs Walters says the Dixons wish to get to know us better,' said Mrs Knightley. 'They used to be such friends of Mr Churchill's, they know us all by repute already. Your aunt has written to tell Mr Churchill of their visit, so he may return to Highbury sooner than expected.'

Monday morning was fine and dry, enabling Georgiana to go on with her riding practice. She cantered with great confidence, and even persuaded Bessie to jump over a fallen log.

'On Friday, if the weather is still fine, I am going over to those cottages I told you about. Would you like to go with me?' asked Henry.

'I should love to, Henry,' she said, her eyes sparkling. It no longer seemed such a tragedy that Tom Walters was affianced.

As he was about to leave, Henry said: 'We heard from Bella today. Her whole letter is full of praise for Enscombe, but no doubt my mother will tell you all about it this evening.'

'Oh, of course, we are all dining at Donwell Court,' said Georgiana, a little downcast.

'Take comfort, my sweet, in the fact that you are a hundred times more beautiful than Miss Dixon. Tom Walters must be a great blockhead to have preferred her to you.'

Georgiana could only smile. Henry had called her 'my sweet' and told her she was beautiful. She wanted to call after him that she had never cared for Tom Walters, but he had already ridden off through the copse.

The drawing room at Donwell Court was already full of people as Georgiana and her parents arrived. Anne hurried over, and took Georgiana on one side.

'I have told Sophia all about you, and she is longing to meet you,' she said. 'Let us go and talk to her now.'

Georgiana felt that she had nothing at all to say to Miss Dixon, but her natural good manners made her try very hard to be civil. Miss Dixon, though young, had the air of one to whom nothing was a novelty. When Georgiana mentioned that she had been riding, for her head was full of it still, Miss Dixon said, with an affected smile: 'Forgive me, Miss Knightley, but you seem a trifle old to be learning to ride. Why were you not taught when you were young?'

'I hardly know,' said Georgiana. 'I suppose I had no inclination to do so.'

'I have had my own horse since I was five years old, and I cannot remember when I was not able to ride.' She smiled complacently. 'Papa says I have good hands.' She seemed to be waiting for a compliment, but when none was forthcoming she changed the subject. 'Miss Knightley, I hear from your aunt that her daughter is staying at Enscombe.'

Georgiana agreed that that was so, and asked her if she was familiar with it.

'Oh yes, it is a sweet place. You probably know that Mrs Churchill was brought up by my grandparents. Poor thing! She would have been nobody if they had not had the charge of her; living in poverty over a shop, with only that dreadful aunt for company.'

Georgiana could not believe that Miss Dixon could be so insulting, and was very angry.

'I have a high regard for Miss Bates,' she said sharply. 'She loved her niece dearly, and did everything she could for her comfort.'

'Oh, I don't deny it, but the old thing is such a talker. *I* could not be in her company for more than five minutes. How happy Miss Fairfax must have been to have been taken in by my grandfather. He owed her no obligation, you know, and yet he treated her almost like a daughter.'

An even sharper retort rose to Georgiana's lips, but she saw a look of alarm on Anne's face, and held her tongue.

'If you will excuse me, Miss Dixon,' she said coolly, 'I must speak with my aunt,' and she joined Mrs John Knightley on the sofa, to be regaled with the contents of Bella's letter.

At dinner Georgiana was seated near enough to Miss Dixon to observe her closely, and watched while she spoke to Tom Walters in a childish voice, or whispered in his ear. His thoughts seemed to be elsewhere until he noticed that Georgiana was looking at him, whereupon he began to be very animated, offering Sophia a dish that she had just refused. Georgiana suddenly found herself being addressed by Mr James Walters, who wished to enquire for her sister.

'We had a letter only this morning,' said Georgiana. 'She is finding everything so strange; Yorkshire is not like Surrey, Mr Walters.'

'But she is happy there?' he asked, a trifle uncertainly.

'She is enjoying the novelty, but she misses home very much, and asks to be remembered to all her friends.'

Mr Walters was finding that he missed Emma's presence more than he would have believed possible. It was a pleasure to him to talk to Georgiana about her, and they chatted together until the next course was served. Mr Walters then turned his attention to Mrs Dixon, who was seated at his right hand, and Georgiana was at liberty to look about her. She found that Sophia Dixon had transferred her attention from Tom, and was bestowing it on Henry, who was being his usual charming self. This made Georgiana uneasy, but she did not know why.

After dinner, as she helped Anne with the tea and coffee, she was approached by Miss Dixon.

'Your cousin, Mr Henry Knightley, is a very fine gentleman,' she said. Georgiana agreed that he was. 'My dear Tom tells me that he is to inherit the Donwell estate. Your elder sister must find that very galling.'

'It is not a matter that has ever been discussed between us,' said Georgiana, with a look that told her she was being impertinent.

'Oh, you must forgive my easy Irish ways,' said Miss Dixon, not at all put out. 'I always speak my mind and cannot change now.'

Georgiana turned away to pour out some coffee, and was surprised when she turned back to find that Miss Dixon was still there.

'I am amazed that Mr Henry Knightley is not married yet,' she said. 'He would be a great catch for any girl.'

Henry was just approaching the table with his cup and saucer in his hand.

'Henry,' said Georgiana mischievously, 'Miss Dixon wishes to know why you are still unmarried.' Miss Dixon had the grace to blush. 'She thinks you would be . . . 'a great catch' I think you said, Miss Dixon?'

'Oh, that was just between us girls,' she said, trying to look roguish. 'The gentlemen are not to be admitted to our confidences.'

Henry paused for a moment, then said seriously: 'I am obliged to you for your concern, Miss Dixon, but I could never like a woman who tried to 'catch' me, as you put it. There is something so cold and artificial in the notion. We all want to be loved for ourselves alone, regardless of our wealth or position. When I find such a one I will marry her.'

He looked at Georgiana as he said it, and the look pierced her to the heart. In a moment she knew it was Henry she had always loved, even as a child; she had only made the mistake of thinking she loved him like a sister. How she would hate him to marry a scheming, vulgar girl like Miss Dixon. Tom Walters was welcome to her!

There was music later on, and Miss Dixon was eager to perform. She played very well, but her voice was thin, and her style affected. She was followed by Anne and Georgiana, who both played well enough, and their simple airs gave great pleasure. In the absence of Bella and Emma there was no dancing, and Georgiana found that she was disappointed not to be standing up with Henry.

As Georgiana was about to follow her mother out to the carriage, Henry stepped forward to remind her of the riding lesson the following day.

'I shall meet you in the paddock at ten o'clock if the weather is fine,' he said.

'May I join you?' asked Miss Dixon eagerly. 'I have been longing to see Donwell Abbey, especially the old ruins.'

Good manners forced Georgiana to agree readily, but she was very put out, suspecting that Miss Dixon came only to demonstrate her superior equestrian skill.

'Tom will bring me over, won't you, dear?' she said, turning to him.

Tom looked embarrassed but agreed.

'There now, Mr Henry Knightley,' she said exultantly, 'we shall all be friends together. Perhaps we might go for rides about the countryside, and see some of the famous beauties of Surrey ... when Miss Georgiana is able to ride well enough.'

'Georgiana is already a competent rider,' said Henry, with a smile. 'She only needs a little reassurance,' and in an undertone to Georgiana he said: 'I hope you will not find their company too disagreeable.'

Georgiana looked out of the window early on Tuesday morning, hoping for rain, but she was greeted by a bright blue sky, and a soft breeze shaking the blossom off the blackthorn. After breakfast she went down to the paddock a little early, hoping for a private word with Henry, but found to her dismay that Tom Walters and Miss Dixon were already there, both mounted. Miss Dixon's habit was bright scarlet, which Georgiana thought drained all the colour from her face.

'Where is your horse, Miss Georgiana?' called Miss Dixon. 'We have been waiting an age.' Georgiana was annoyed by her familiarity and said: 'It wants ten minutes to ten o'clock, which is the time Henry and I agreed, Miss Dixon.'

'Oh, please call me Sophia - everyone does. We are to be such friends, I hate to stand on ceremony. Perhaps you could show us the Abbey ruins while we wait for Mr Henry Knightley.'

'Oh, here is the groom with my horse now,' said Georgiana, 'and Henry is sure to be close behind. We had better wait until after our ride. The grass will be dry then; you must not draggle your fine habit.'

'Do you like it? I was not sure that scarlet would suit me, but Tom says it is his favourite colour.'

Georgiana was saved from the necessity of replying by the arrival of Henry, who suggested they ride over to Lower Farm, where the cottages were due to be pulled down. Georgiana mounted with some trepidation, and they set off, with Henry leading the way.

'Stay close to me, Georgie,' he said, 'and you will be quite safe.'

Their style of riding did not suit Miss Dixon, and when they came to the open grassland which led down to Lower

Farm Lane, she set off at a brisk canter, closely followed by Tom. Henry reined in his horse, and Georgiana was glad to catch her breath.

'Miss Dixon rides so well,' said Georgiana.

'She does, and so will you one day,' Henry told her, as she watched the couple reach the bottom of the hill. 'You have made great progress in less than a week; and there is another thing. You ride because you enjoy it; Miss Dixon, at least at the moment, rides only to be admired, and to put you in the shade.'

'I wish Anna were here,' said Georgiana, surprising herself. 'She could show Miss Sophia what riding is.'

'I hope that is not your ambition; to ride like Anna, I mean,' said Henry. 'You would be more likely to break your neck!'

'You have no confidence that *I* might win thirty guineas one day?' said Georgiana, looking at him demurely.

'Certainly not, and I beg that you will not shame me by mentioning that episode again,' said Henry trying to look stern, but failing dismally, and they descended the hill at a brisk pace, both of them laughing.

None of them, except Henry, had seen the cottages before, and finding much to amuse them, idled away an hour, looking into the cramped rooms, and climbing up to the loft to stare out of the tiny windows. One of the cottages had stood empty for some time, but the tenant of the other, a frail old man, had only recently died before he could move into the almshouse.

'Why must they be pulled down, Henry?' asked Georgiana. 'I can see that *that* one is rotting away, but this one is quite neat and clean; and see, some spring planting has already been done in the patch behind the house. It seems such a pity.'

'The thatch even on this one is rotten,' said Henry, 'and they are both damp and insanitary. If one of the workers needed housing it might be worth the expense to the estate to put this one, at least, in good repair, but they are so far from any other habitation, and so low-lying, that no-one wants to live here.'

At that moment Sophia, who had been peeping in at all the windows, now wanted Henry to come down to the other end of the cottage garden, where she thought a hen had been laying. Georgiana and Tom were left alone. There was a long, awkward silence, then Georgiana made some commonplace remark, but was interrupted by Tom, who said violently: 'It's no good, Georgiana; I cannot bear it any longer.'

'What?' she cried in alarm. 'What is it you cannot bear?'

'I have made a terrible mistake,' he said, trying to take her hand. Georgiana snatched it away, saying: 'Mr Walters, control yourself!' and turned to walk after Henry and Sophia.

'I should never have asked her to marry me,' he said, in a desperate tone. 'In fact, I believe I never did ask her. It just seemed to happen.'

The expression on his face was so comical that Georgiana was tempted to laugh. 'I cannot listen to this,' she said firmly. 'No,' as he tried to speak, 'not another word, if you please. None of this is any business of mine.'

'But it is,' he protested. 'I love you. I have loved you all along, only I didn't know it until now. Seeing you so happy with your cousin breaks my heart.'

Georgiana was so shocked she could say nothing; as she stood there, feeling rooted to the spot, a rat ran across her path, and up the side of the derelict building. Georgiana screamed involuntarily, and Henry came running back, to find Georgiana weeping. She was almost grateful to the rat for frightening her, as it gave some excuse for her tears. Henry was all solicitude.

'Perhaps we had better go home now; you must be tired,' he said, and helped Georgiana into the saddle.

On the ride back Sophia was the only one who showed any animation, though she directed one or two curious looks at Tom, as if surprised at his silence. They came out at a field gate just opposite the entrance to Donwell, and Georgiana was obliged to invite them all into the house for some refreshment. Sophia eagerly accepted, but was hurried away by Tom.

'But we have only seen the ruins from a distance,' she protested, smiling over her shoulder at Henry.

'That will do for another day,' said Tom. 'Your mother will be wondering where you are.'

Henry sent both horses back with the groom, saying he needed to speak with his uncle, and would walk home later.

'You seem out of spirits, Georgiana,' he said, directing a keen glance at her as they walked up the avenue to the main entrance. 'Is there something you would like to tell me?' She nodded, and Henry went on: 'Come, let us take a turn about the grounds before going in,' and offering her his arm, he took a path to the east, and they were soon in the lime walk, where the trees were just beginning to bud. At the end of the lime walk they stood in silence, looking over the low wall at the view of Abbey Mill Farm. It was a pleasant prospect, the sun was warm, and Henry suggested they sat for a moment, keeping Georgiana's arm clasped in his own.

'Now tell me what is troubling you,' he said affectionately.

'Oh Henry, I hardly know what to say, I think you will be angry.'

'You could never make me angry, Georgie,' he began, but she interrupted him.

'No, not me . . . I meant that you would be angry with Tom Walters. He has been saying foolish things to me.'

'What things? What foolish things has he been saying?' asked Henry sharply.

Georgiana began to weep.

'He said he had made a mistake. That he did not love Sophia, and . . . and that he loved me,' she said, ending in a whisper. Henry cursed under his breath, then there was a long silence, broken only by the cooing of the wood pigeons. 'I was very angry,' she went on, recovering her composure, 'and told him not to speak to me of it. He would have said more, but then the rat startled me, and you came back. I have never been so glad to see anyone in my life as I was to see you.'

'If he were to break his engagement, would you wish to marry him?' said Henry, not looking at her.

'How can you ask me such a question, Henry?' cried Georgiana. 'No, of course not. How could I ever trust a man who was so fickle? Besides, he is in honour bound to Sophia unless she chooses to end it.'

'I thought you liked him once,' said Henry.

'Well, perhaps I did, like every other young lady in Highbury and Donwell. Two such handsome men coming amongst us - it was bound to cause a stir; but I soon realised that Mr Tom Walters is . . . shallow and selfish. He is just a foolish boy, who wants to collect hearts like trophies, but let us hope he has met his match in Miss Sophia!'

'So I have a chance then?' said Henry, looking at her for the first time. 'Could you ever stop regarding me as a brother, and learn to love me as a husband? I want you to marry me, Georgie.' Taking her hand, he pressed it to his lips.

'Oh, I do love you already, and I will marry you, Henry . . . on one condition; that you stop calling me Georgie!'

Half an hour later they walked into the house, hand-in-hand. Enquiring of the butler where his master might be found, Henry was told he was in the library, and went there straightaway. Georgiana ran into the morning-room, and flung her arms round her mother's neck.

'Be careful, child,' said Mrs Knightley, startled. 'You might injure yourself on my needle.'

'Mama, never mind your embroidery,' said Georgiana. 'I have something to tell you,' and she proudly gave her the joyful news.

Mrs Knightley, always quick to assess any situation, passed from surprise to joy in moment. One of her girls to be mistress of Donwell, and to be married to her favourite nephew! How could she ever express her delight?

'Where is Henry now?' she asked eagerly.

'He is with Papa in the library. He *will* give his consent, won't he, Mama?' Georgiana asked anxiously.

'I am sure of it,' said Mrs Knightley, ' but here they are now. Henry, my dear, come and give me a kiss.'

Mr Knightley's joy was even greater than his wife's; he was not a man who displayed his feelings easily, but his heart was full of deep, quiet satisfaction.

'My dear Georgiana, I have just told Henry he is the most fortunate of men. I could not be more delighted. You will have a good husband, and one day you will be mistress of Donwell like your dear mother before you,' and he kissed her heartily.

Henry soon hurried away to bring the good news to his mother and father. He hoped that his mother would be pleased, but knew from experience that all change was repugnant to her. When John had announced his intention to marry Anne his mother had been deeply shocked, and it had taken all John's persuasion to win her over. Now she accepted the notion and loved Anne as another daughter, but Henry feared she would not accept the news of *his* engagement with equanimity.

In this, however, he found that he was wrong. Mrs John Knightley's conscience had long made her uneasy that the enrichment of her son would mean, if not the impoverishment of her nieces, then at least the loss of a much loved home. Now everything was perfect; Henry would inherit Donwell, but not until many years had passed, she hoped, and Georgiana would succeed to her dear mother's place. They had been invited to dine at Donwell, and even Mr John Knightley showed less than his usual reluctance to spend an evening away from home. For her part, Mrs John Knightley was eager to talk over with her sister the wonder of Henry's engagement, and in the meantime she sat down to write a letter to Bella, to pass on the good news.

Just as her aunt was sitting down at her writing desk, Georgiana was halfway through a letter to Emma. Her mother had wanted the privilege of conveying such exciting information; but Georgiana was certain that *her* communication, full of underlinings and exclamation marks, would prove more informative and entertaining to Emma. Meanwhile, after a hurried repast, Henry was on his way to Donwell Parsonage, to spread the good news still further.

He found John in his study, making an early start on Sunday's sermon, and in a few words told him what had taken place.

'Well done, my dear fellow,' cried John, clapping him on the shoulder, then shaking his hand. 'You have made a wise choice. I thought at one time that you and Anna might make a match of it, but that would have been a terrible mistake. When is it to be? - the ceremony, I mean. Bless me! It will be my first wedding. I shall be as nervous as the bride!' and John continued to bless himself, and wonder, in great good spirits for some time.

The two families met that evening, and there was a good deal of laughter at very little, which always signifies a happy family occasion. George, who was making a rare appearance in evening clothes, was teased and told that he would be next. He smiled complacently, and thought fondly of Henrietta

Martin, who had taken to smiling at him in a special way every time they met. Georgiana was in great good looks, and could not bear to leave Henry's side for a moment.

'I wish Bella were here, and dear Emma,' was the gentle complaint of Mrs John Knightley.

'They will be home before you know it,' said Mr Knightley jovially, anxious that no-one should cast a gloom on such a happy occasion. 'And when they are home we shall have a ball here at Donwell, before Georgiana and Henry are married.'

The date for the ball was set for a Friday towards the end of April, and invitations were sent to Enscombe. Meanwhile, news of the engagement had spread throughout the parishes of Highbury and Donwell. Henry and Georgiana together had called on Miss Bates, who said she was delighted, and assured them that she would order a new bonnet in honour of the occasion. Word had also got round of the ball, and Ford's was overwhelmed with orders for muslin, fine lawn, and even silk. The nuptials were to take place in May or June, though a date had not been fixed, and Georgiana was amused to hear a rumour that her gown was to come from Paris.

The visit to Enscombe was cut short, both Bella and Emma being desirous to be home at such a time, and the whole party arrived back in St James's Square on the 8th of April. Anna was the only one who was sorry to be back in London; Enscombe was her spiritual home, she decided, and as soon as she could after the wedding of Henry and Georgiana, she would persuade Frank to go back with her. It would also be a means of cooling the friendship that was developing between him and Bella. Frank would never marry again if Anna had anything to do with it!

Chapter 17

The morning after their return to St James's Square, amidst the hubbub of deliveries from the hatter and mantua-maker, and visits from morning callers, Anna found that there were two letters awaiting her, both in the same hand, which had not been re-directed to Enscombe. On opening the earlier one, she discovered it to be from Selina Elton wishing to speak with Anna urgently and asking her to call. The letter was dated the 3rd of April, and Anna hastily opened the second, dated the 6th of April. It contained apologies for her former rudeness, reproaches and a frantic plea for Anna to call upon her in Chelsea at once. Anna was seriously alarmed, for the tone of the letter was almost wild, and making an excuse to Mr Churchill, she ordered the carriage and was conveyed to Chelsea immediately.

This visit seemed like a re-enactment of the previous one; again she was admitted by a neat maid, and was shown into the parlour. Immediately she heard a light step on the stair, and Selina rushed into the room wearing the same tiring-gown as before. When she saw Anna her look of hope vanished, and she began to weep violently.

'I thought you were Roly,' she said between sobs.

'Is Lord Urswick not here?' asked Anna.

'No; that is why I wrote to you, Miss Weston. Oh, why did you not come? I have been almost out of my mind with worry.'

'I came as soon as I could, Selina,' Anna said in a soothing tone, ignoring her petulance. 'I only arrived in London yesterday; we have been visiting Enscombe. Now come and sit down, and tell me why you need to see me so urgently.'

Selina did as she was bidden, and sat next to Anna on the sofa.

'Roly left me more than a week ago,' she said, striving to be calm. 'We had a violent argument. He said he never wanted to see me again, and rushed out of the house.' She hid her face in her hands and began to weep afresh.

'Selina, if I am to help you I must know everything,' said Anna, then listened as it all came pouring out.

They had been very happy at first, according to Selina, and he had been lavish in his gifts and attentions. Anna was in no mood to listen to this, and hurried Selina along. Then she told how his visits became less frequent; she suspected that he was tiring of her, and accused him of being unfaithful. There had been many quarrels, each one more violent than the last. Finally, she begged him, on her knees, to marry her. At this point in her narrative she became hysterical, and Anna rang for a glass of wine to calm her. This last desperate plea had proved too much for Lord Urswick, and he had left the house in a terrible rage, vowing never to return. Since then she had been waiting for him to come back, the rent had not been paid, and her debts were increasing.

'Have you any notion where he has gone?' asked Anna.

'I am not sure, but I think . . . to his aunt in Richmond.'

'Then to Richmond we must go at once,' said Anna firmly. 'Go and dress, Selina; my carriage is at the door.'

In half an hour, for Selina had made a very hurried toilet, they were on their way to Lady Maria Dalton's. Selina, who had absolute faith in Anna, was feeling more hopeful, but Anna dreaded the thought of a confrontation with Lord Urswick. Fortunately, Selina sat in silence for most of the journey, which gave Anna an opportunity to marshal her thoughts.

As the carriage drew to a halt before the grand entrance, Selina began to weep again; to be once again at the scene of former happiness in such altered circumstances was too much for her. They were admitted to the hall, the butler took Anna's card, and they were at leisure to wait and feel nervous. Selina, feeling all the weight of Lord Urswick's ancestry staring down at her from the many portraits, was almost too afraid to speak. When she did venture a remark, her voice echoed, and she grew silent again.

After some time the butler returned, looking a little foolish, and told them his mistress was not at home. As they turned to go, Lady Maria appeared, and called: 'One moment, if you please, Miss Weston.' Dismissing the butler with a wave of the hand, she joined them where they stood at the front door.

'Miss Weston, I am willing to hear what you have to say, but I cannot receive that . . . person in my house,' she said in a haughty tone, not looking at Selina. Anna thought quickly; her first instinct was to sweep out with her dignity intact, but that would be of little use to Selina, so, asking Selina to wait in the carriage, she followed Lady Maria into a small room which opened off the hall.

Once inside, with the door closed, Anna felt even more affronted. This was obviously a room for the transaction of business, being very small and furnished only with a large desk, neatly stacked with ledgers, and two chairs. Lady Maria did not offer Anna a seat, and remained standing herself.

'Miss Weston, I have guessed your errand and beg that you will be brief.'

'Lady Maria,' said Anna, adopting a similar tone, 'I do not deserve to be treated in this uncivil manner. I am here to inquire for Lord Urswick. I understand he is staying here.'

'He is,' said Lady Maria unwillingly, 'but he has left instructions that he is not at home to anyone. You dare to call me 'uncivil', but it was not very civil of you to bring that woman here.'

'*That woman*, Lady Maria, is not yet eighteen years old. She was . . . persuaded by your nephew to leave her family and friends, to live under his protection, as no doubt you know, and now he has cast her off.'

'And what interest have you in the matter?' she said, scornfully.

'I am ashamed to say that, knowing what he was like, I nevertheless brought them together, and I have come here today to beg him to do right by her.'

'You mean that you expect him to marry her,' said Lady Maria, with a sardonic smile.

Anna was silent, knowing that Lord Urswick could never be prevailed upon to marry a girl without fortune, or birth and connections.

'My dear Miss Weston, you must allow that it would be impossible for such a match to take place.'

'It would be unusual, certainly . . .' began Anna, but Lady Maria raised a hand for silence.

'I see you do not know my nephew as well as you think you do. It would be impossible, Miss Weston, because *he is married already*.' She sat down suddenly, and indicated that Anna should take the other chair. 'Roly has always been wild, even as a child. Four years ago, when his debts were mounting, he contracted an imprudent marriage with the daughter of a tradesman in the North of England. She was much older than he was, and no beauty, but she was very rich. I make no excuses for him, Miss Weston. There was no love on either side; she wanted a situation, and he needed her fortune. She stayed with him only six months, then returned to her father's house, accusing him of the direst cruelty. None of it was true, of course, but it made life very unpleasant for Roly. He left his estates in North Lonsdale, where his neighbours knew something of the situation, and took pleasure in cutting him, and settled in London. The rest you know.' She suddenly looked very tired. 'You cannot imagine that I have viewed this latest liaison with complaisance, Miss Weston, but there is little I can do. No doubt the girl used her wiles to ensnare him. And now, if you will excuse me, I am feeling a trifle unwell.'

Anna took this as a dismissal, and left the house without waiting for the servant, almost too shocked to know what she was doing.

As she descended the long flight of steps to the gravel sweep she saw a man on horseback talking to Selina through the carriage window. When he saw Anna, he touched his hat and rode off. The coachman handed Anna in, the door was shut and Anna turned to Selina in amazement.

'Was that Lord Urswick I saw speaking to you just now, Selina?' she said.

'It was,' said Selina, looking down. 'I came back to the carriage, just as you told me to, and had been waiting but a minute or two, when Roly came riding up the avenue. I must confess I put down the window, and called to him, and he came over to see me. He was quite unpleasant to me at first, - said he knew you were behind this, after meddling in his affairs before. I think he had warned his aunt not to receive you, but I suppose she was curious to see what you would say. We talked, and he seemed to soften, - told me to dry my tears and so on. In short, Miss Weston, we are completely reconciled; he has told me to go home, and he will join me in Chelsea this evening.'

'Selina, wait,' said Anna urgently. 'I have spoken with Lady Maria, and she has told me something . . . something which alters your situation.'

'Miss Weston, you do not understand. All is well; Roly loves me, and I am to keep the house in Chelsea. He is sorry for being angry, and all will be as before.'

'Selina, you gave me to understand that you were staying with Lord Urswick in the hope that one day he would marry you; but I have just discovered that that is impossible. Lady Maria has told me that he has a wife already.'

'Yes, I know,' said Selina calmly. 'She was monstrous horrid to him, then went home to her father. Roly never loved her, Miss Weston.'

Anna was silenced. For the first time she was tempted to echo Mrs Elton's words: 'wicked, foolish girl!' She was relieved when they reached Chelsea at last, and she could be rid of Selina.

The following morning, just before they were about to start for Highbury, a note arrived for Anna from Selina Elton. It was short and exultant.

Dear Miss Weston, (it said)

My thanks for conveying me to Richmond yesterday. You will be pleased, I am sure, to know that my dear Roly called as promised, and told me he intends to leave London for Italy on Friday, the 15th of April, and I am to go with him! There, are not you surprised? It is to be a secret, but I could not go without taking my leave of you, dear Miss Weston.

Lord Urswick sends his compliments.

I remain, dear madam, your devoted friend,

Selina Elton

Anna reflected that Lord Urswick was no doubt flying to escape his creditors, and was not averse to having a travelling companion. With a wry smile she threw the letter into the fire.

Chapter 18

It was some time after Emma's return before she was at leisure to have a long conversation with Georgiana. The house was alive with morning callers, come to welcome Emma home, and to offer their warmest good wishes for Georgiana's happiness; and there was scarcely a room downstairs that was not busy with servants scrubbing, sweeping and polishing in preparation for the ball. Mrs Walters and Anne had been amongst the earliest callers, but Georgiana had taken care that there was no opportunity for private conversation. As for the Dixons, they had gone to London to visit friends, and were expected back the day before the ball, giving Georgiana a welcome respite from Sophia's company.

Emma had not enjoyed her visit to Enscombe, and was relieved to be home. She had felt strange without Georgiana, and while she could not help admiring the rugged grandeur of the scenery, it seemed to her cold and inhospitable. Anna had not seemed in good spirits, and had rebuffed any friendly overtures from Emma, while Bella was in raptures with everything to do with Enscombe. Emma had also observed a growing tenderness between Bella and Mr Churchill, which made her feel uncomfortable and excluded. The news of Georgiana's engagement to Henry had come as a great surprise, but she was delighted by her sister's obvious happiness. Georgiana had hinted something of Tom Walters' improper remarks to her, and Emma wished to hear more. One wet and windy morning, therefore, they escaped to their bed-chamber, where a comfortable fire was burning, Mrs Knightley being no believer in the popular assumption that Spartan conditions were morally improving for the young.

When Emma heard the whole of Georgiana's story, her indignation against Tom Walters was increased.

'How could he speak to you so, when his future bride was only yards away?' said Emma. 'His impudence knows no bounds!'

'It would have been inexcusable even if Sophia had still been in Ireland,' said Georgiana firmly. 'I spoke very sharply to him, but I could see he was in a very difficult situation. I imagined he would go home and break off his engagement straight away, since he had owned that he did not love Sophia. I have taken care to avoid them both since the unfortunate incident, but if he had broken with Sophia I am sure I would have heard of it.'

'The Dixons are in London, you say? Isn't it possible that there has been a quarrel, and they have gone to be out of the way?'

'Perhaps . . .' said Georgiana thoughtfully. 'No, Anne mentioned some time ago that the Dixons would be visiting friends during their stay. I think Tom Walters has been avoiding me since Sophia went away, but I shall have to meet him at the ball. I will not be able to look him in the face.'

'*You* have done nothing wrong, Georgiana,' cried Emma. 'If he had any decency he would stay away; in fact, I am beginning to wish the whole family had never settled here.'

'My dear Emma,' said Georgiana, 'just because Tom Walters is a . . . foolish young man, we cannot shun the others. Colonel and Mrs Walters have been kindness itself to us, and Anne would be so hurt by any coldness on our part.'

'I was thinking of Mr James Walters,' said Emma sadly. 'There was a time when I thought . . . but that can never be. I want nothing more to do with him.'

'You cannot mean that, Emma. He has missed you, I am sure. I cannot tell you the number of times he inquired for you when you were at Enscombe.'

'If I spend any time with him I am sure to say something disagreeable to him about his brother, and then he will never like me again.'

'He will want to dance with you at the ball,' said Georgiana doubtfully, 'and you will not be able to refuse him.'

'Then I shall take care to fill up my dance-card,' said Emma stoutly, and began to talk about what they should wear for the ball.

Anna was not looking forward to the ball with any pleasure. She had returned with her guardian to Hartfield because it was expected of her, but found that everything had changed. Her old, easy friendship with Henry, which she once idly thought might blossom into love, had come to an end with his engagement. Henry spent more than half his time at Donwell, and when he was at home he seemed to Anna to have lost all his old sparkle, and was dull, and no longer amused by her *bon mots* or outrageous behaviour. She had encountered Mr James Walters one morning out riding, and they had had a pleasant enough conversation. Perhaps she would dance with him at the ball; if she tried hard she felt sure she could dazzle him, but somehow, it did not seem worth the effort.

Anne Walters was one of the few young ladies whose pleasure was unalloyed. She would dance for most of the evening with her dear John, and when she grew tired he would sit out with her and keep her amused. She was concerned for her brother Tom, who was not his usual bright self. This she attributed to his pining for his dear Sophia. Anne was too gentle ever to dislike anyone, but when she was with Sophia she sometimes wished that Tom had made a match of it with Georgiana.

On the evening of the ball, the two Knightley families, with Mr Churchill and Anna, dined early together at Donwell, and when the other guests began to arrive they were all waiting around the fire in the large drawing room. Emma had been asked to dance by Henry, John, and Mr Churchill, but she was hoping for all the spaces on her card to be filled before the arrival of Mr James Walters. Emma looked with a feeling almost of envy at Georgiana, radiant with happiness, standing next to Henry; Mr Churchill was whispering something to Bella which she was finding amusing; the only person besides herself who did not look very happy, apart from her uncle, Mr John Knightley who hated all such occasions, was Anna. Emma was deeply disappointed; for years she had longed for a ball at home, and now that her wish had come true, instead of delight and anticipation, she felt flat and dreary as if nothing mattered.

The room was rapidly filling up, the guests were drinking their tea and coffee, and the Walters family and the Dixons had not yet arrived. Emma had added several other names to her dance-card, but there was a blank by the two first, and the two supper dances. Although she had made up her mind not to dance with Mr James Walters, she was now feeling mortified and disappointed at not being asked. More guests were announced, and the drawing room was becoming crowded. Emma did not notice Mr Churchill hurrying to the door to renew his acquaintance with the Dixons, or that they were closely followed by Colonel Walters and his lady, for she was too busy studying her dance-card, and wondering who might be prevailed upon to ask her to dance. Her reverie was disturbed by a familiar voice at her elbow.

'Miss Knightley, I am delighted to see you again. Am I too late to solicit the honour of the two first dances?'

Emma looked up and saw Mr James Walters smiling down at her, confident that she would be delighted, and said coolly:

'It is customary to secure the two first some time in advance. It would be shameful for me to own at this late hour that I lacked a partner.'

She was hoping he would press her, but he merely looked grave, and said: 'Perhaps you would save two other dances for me?'

Emma agreed and filled in the blank spaces by the supper dances. Mr Walters bowed and walked away without saying anything. Seeing her cousin George nearby she called him to her.

'George, do you know how to dance?' she asked him.

'I am nimble enough to avoid treading on your toes, but will not condition for more,' said he, laughing.

'Then will you partner me for the two first?'

'Oh Emma, I was just about to ask Henrietta Martin!' he protested, then seeing the look on her face, he added: 'Oh, very well; I suppose you and Mr Walters have quarrelled, for I am sure I heard him ask you a minute ago. I must just run across and put my name on Henrietta's card for later on,' and he left her and disappeared into the crowd.

'Emma, my dear,' said her father, coming up to her, 'Are you engaged for the two first dances? We are about to move into the ballroom, and you and Georgiana must lead.'

'Yes, I am just waiting for my cousin, George.'

'What? That young scamp? What has happened to Mr Walters?'

Emma made no reply, but the tears started to her eyes. Mr Knightley pressed her hand fondly.

'Well, well; George it must be, unless you wish for another partner. Mr Dixon would take it as an honour, I am sure . . .'

'Please Papa, I am happy to dance with George,' and she moved away to the door, where Georgiana and Henry were already waiting.

The ballroom looked like something out of a fairy tale; even Emma's spirits were lifted by the brilliant light from hundreds of wax candles, reflected in the large looking-glasses. The floor was highly polished, and there were delicate gilt chairs for sitting out, upholstered in red velvet, which Emma could not recall having seen before. Flowers from the hot house filled every corner, and made the air fragrant with their scent. Through the window she saw the rising moon, illuminating the Abbey ruins. This was no time for repining, Emma told herself; there would be much to enjoy in the dancing and the handsome supper her mother had provided for the interval.

The musicians were tuning their fiddles as Emma and George followed Henry and Georgiana, who were to lead the dancing in honour of their engagement. Emma found that the other affianced couple, John and Anne, had come to stand behind her. Anne seemed a little reserved, and looked at Emma with reproachful eyes. As she waited for the rest of the sets to be formed, Emma looked about her and saw Bella walk up with Mr Churchill, and after them, Tom Walters with Sophia Dixon, who smiled and waved. Mr James Walters, she noticed with a pang, had asked Anna, who seemed to be delighting in his company, and was at her most polished and elegant.

The musicians struck up a merry tune, and Emma was agreeably surprised to find that George could dance very well. They had nothing to say to each other, beyond the merest commonplaces, George being occupied in smiling and nodding to all his acquaintance. Once Emma looked across to the other set, and found that Mr James Walters was regarding her, his face unsmiling. He looked away quickly, and paid attention to his partner, who was gay and animated. It was a small comfort to Emma to think that he did not look as though he were enjoying Anna's company, however hard she tried to be fascinating. The dances were over all too quickly, and as Emma returned to her seat she was joined by Anne, who said timidly: 'It is a long time since we have had the pleasure of your company at Donwell Court, Emma. Have I offended you in any way?'

'My dear Anne, of course not. I am sorry if you think I have been neglecting you, but really, there has been so much to do since my return from Enscombe that I have not had a moment to spare. Will you forgive me?'

Anne took her hand affectionately. 'There is nothing to forgive; but, Emma, I should be distressed to think there might be any coolness between our two families. My brother James says he asked you to dance with him, and that you seemed reluctant to do so. Pray tell me what he has done to offend you? He would never willingly give you pain.'

Emma was saved from having to reply by the advent of her partner for the next dance. 'We will talk later, Anne,' she said, as she rose and walked on to the dance floor.

It was time for the two dances before supper, and Emma was growing increasingly apprehensive. She was aware that she had been curt with Mr Walters, and now she was sorry and wished to make amends. He had done nothing to offend her, she reasoned; it was all his brother's doing. She noticed that Tom Walters was wisely keeping away from anyone with the name of Knightley, dancing only with Sophia, or wandering in and out of the card-room.

Mr Walters came to claim her, and led her to the set without speaking. Emma felt constrained to say something, but felt it was not for her to praise the decorations of the ballroom or the elegant dress of Mr Walters' relations, which was all that sprang to mind. When the musicians began to play, a smile of unfeigned pleasure lit up her face.

'This is one of my favourite tunes,' she said, smiling at him for the first time.

'I am glad,' he said, returning her smile. 'Miss Knightley, it is a great relief to me to see you in good spirits once again. I was beginning to wonder how I could have offended you.'

'I assure you, *you* have not,' she replied, but for some time was not at liberty to say more, being forced to pay attention to the dance.

As the first dance came to an end, Mr Walters said: 'A ballroom is no place for rational discussion. Perhaps you would care to sit out for a little while before supper.'

Emma was about to say that dancing never tired her, then guessed his meaning and agreed. The ballroom was very warm, and a charming place had been prepared for those who wished for a respite from dancing. Long and narrow, it had formerly been an orangery, but was now filled with leafy plants, and chairs and tables set at intervals along its length. Emma led the way, and they were soon seated at the first table nearest to the entrance, where they were shielded from the gaze of the two or three other couples who were also sitting out by several large potted palms. Through the glass walls they could see the Abbey ruins bathed in moonlight.

'Mr Walters,' Emma began, 'I owe you an apology for my behaviour; you must think me very rude. There is an explanation, but . . . it would be very difficult to . . .' she paused, at a loss to know how to continue.

'Miss Knightley, do not distress yourself by trying to explain. I know it all. My wretched brother is at the bottom of it.' Emma could only look her surprise. 'He has confessed everything to me; that he spoke to your sister most improperly - telling her he loved her - that he had never loved Sophia. No wonder you were angry; I was minded to box his ears myself. This engagement to Sophia has been a mistake from the start; in his defence I can only say that she led him on; yes, I know that is no excuse, but remember, I was a witness. She was so importunate that he hardly knew what he was doing.'

'If he really felt he could not love Sophia, he should have told her so, like an honest man,' said Emma firmly. 'Georgiana would not have welcomed his addresses even if the engagement had been broken, but to speak to her within yards of Sophia, in imminent danger of being overheard . . . that was foolhardy indeed!' She paused. 'There, Mr Walters, I knew I should be led on to say more than I intended. I am sorry. Oh, how could you like anyone who insulted your brother?' and she turned away from him in distress.

'My dearest Emma,' he said tenderly, clasping her hands in his own, 'you have said nothing but what is true and just. Your love of your sister might reasonably compel you to say much more. Oh Emma, you must know how greatly I admire you and love you. Will you allow the fickleness of one brother to separate you forever from the other? I am not like Tom, Emma; I have no talent for pretty speeches, but I offer you my hand and heart with all my devotion, and they will be yours for the rest of my life,' and so saying, he took her in his arms.

Emma had never in the whole of her existence heard sweeter words; they brought immeasurable joy and consolation to her heart, now that she knew she had not lost him by her capriciousness.

'I believe I have loved you since the first day we met,' she said, after a little while. 'There was a time (it was foolish of me, I know), when I thought you were displaying symptoms of tenderness towards Anna.'

'Oh Emma,' he cried reproachfully, 'how could you think so for a moment? I ought not to speak disrespectfully of Anna, as a close connexion of your family's, but she is everything I dislike in a woman; vain, proud and overbearing. From what I hear, she has done irreparable harm to Selina Elton, and by all that nonsense over the pocket-handkerchiefs she almost created a rift between us two. But come,' he said, kissing her, 'we shall be missed. I would not wish anyone to guess at our betrothal before we tell them of it. Let us go into supper, and tomorrow, my love, I will call on your father.'

It was a delicious sensation that Emma felt; to take his arm, and go back into the ballroom, knowing that she, like Georgiana, would soon be a bride. She hugged her secret to her in silent satisfaction, not knowing that her mother, seeing her flushed face and shining eyes as she entered the supper-room with Mr Walters, had guessed immediately, and was full of joy.

After Emma and Mr Walters had gone in to supper, a silent figure remained seated in the shadow of the palms, where she had not been observed by the lovers. Anna had heard everything that had been said and, angry and mortified, was wondering how she could use the information she had just obtained. She had gone there innocently enough, meaning only to escape the attentions of Mr Cox, who had drunk too much wine. After overhearing the first few words, and recognising the speakers, she felt it would be awkward to reveal her presence, and in any case she was curious to hear more. Thus she stayed, to hear herself traduced by Mr Walters; she owned she was proud, but 'vain' and 'overbearing' - she could not bear it. Someone would have to suffer for this insult!

Emma sat at the supper table, ate her food and drank her wine, but could not have told whether the meat were chicken or cold ham, or the wine hock or claret. She replied gaily to those who spoke to her, without knowing what she said, and had to try very hard not to keep gazing at the perfection of Mr Walters' profile. Both her mother and Georgiana looked curiously at her from time to time, as if they could not believe this was their steady, sober Emma.

After supper the dancing began again. Henry had been sent to fetch his mother's shawl, and Georgiana was waiting impatiently for his return, seated by her mother and aunt.

'Anna does not seem to have danced many dances,' said Mrs John Knightley. 'I hope she is not ailing. I thought she looked pale yesterday, and I asked her if I should send for Dr Perry, but she dismissed the thought. She does not mean it, of course, but Anna can be quite sharp-spoken at times.'

'Now you mention it, I do believe Anna did not come into supper,' said Mrs Knightley. 'She can act strangely sometimes, but I am sure she is not ill. Do not alarm yourself on her account, my dear Isabella.'

'Look Aunt; Anna is sitting over there and she looks perfectly well to me,' said Georgiana. 'She has been talking to Sophia Dixon for some time. What *can* they have in common?' The two older ladies turned their heads just in time to witness the extraordinary sight of Sophia Dixon running from the ballroom in hysterics. Tom Walters had at that moment strolled out of the card-room, and seeing her go, ran after her crying: 'Sophia, stop! What is the matter?' Mrs Knightley, concerned, conferred briefly with her sister.

'You must send Colonel Walters after them, Emma,' said Mrs John Knightley; 'He will know what to do.'

'Whatever could Anna have said to upset her so much?' wondered Mrs Knightley, annoyed that the elegance of her party was being destroyed. All the chaperones were staring, and talking in undertones. Meanwhile Anna had thought it expedient to quit the ballroom, and finding an outer door open to let in some air, she went outside on to the terrace.

Henry returned with his mother's shawl, and asked Georgiana to dance. As they walked down to the bottom of the set, Georgiana told Henry what had happened.

'Ah, that explains it,' he said. 'Miss Dixon rushed past me in the corridor in floods of tears, then Tom Walters caught up with her, and they went into the library.'

'Do you think Anna has found out what happened that day we went to the cottages at Lower Farm?' asked Georgiana fearfully.

'How could she?' asked Henry. 'I have not mentioned it to a soul, upon my honour. Have you told anyone?'

'I told Emma,' said Georgiana doubtfully, 'but Emma would never betray a confidence, particularly to Anna. No, Henry, I am being foolish. Anna probably told her there was a great rent in the back of her gown, or that pink ribbons do not become her. She is quite capable of *that*, I am sure,' and laughing, they joined the set.

As Anna stood on the terrace, she was joined by Robert Martin.

'It is a warm evening, Miss Weston,' he said.

'Yes; I came out because I needed some air, Rob. It is too hot in the ballroom.'

Robert had witnessed the scene between Anna and Sophia Dixon, and had drawn his own conclusions as to why Anna had chosen to be elsewhere.

'You have not danced much this evening. I hope you are not unwell.'

'No, I thank you. I have not spirits enough for dancing,' she said, her cheeks still burning from the excitement of her encounter with Sophia Dixon. She began to fan herself vigorously.

'You must not stay to be cold,' said Robert gently.

'Rob, I have a fancy to walk,' Anna said abruptly. 'Will you walk with me?' Robert was silent. 'Oh, you think it would be improper, do you? Well, tonight I care nothing for impropriety. If you will not come, I shall go alone.'

'Let me at least fetch your shawl,' said he.

'No, I am not cold; come,' and she moved quickly to the steps that led down to the Abbey ruins. The moon was at its highest point in the heavens and almost full, casting deep shadows round the ruined walls and pillars. They walked about the worn flagstones for a while, then Anna found a seat on a large piece of fallen masonry, near the edge of the stream. All was tranquil; the only sound the ripple of the stream, and Anna grew calmer.

'Are you happy with your life, Rob?' she asked. There was a pause.

'That is not a question I ever ask myself, but yes; I can imagine no other,' he said, maintaining a respectful distance.

'I do not believe I have ever been really happy,' said Anna slowly. 'I remember my mother only as a gentle presence. After she died my father changed, giving in to my slightest whim, as if to make up for her loss. Sadly, it only made me capricious and hard to please.' She smiled momentarily. 'The happiest times I remember were those spent in the fields and orchards. I was better at climbing than any boy. What sport we had! Do you remember?'

'I remember very well. You were also the best at running and riding, but children must grow up, and wild young girls become ladies. Miss Weston, I think we should go back.'

'Will you ever marry, Rob?'

'Indeed, I hope so; but it cannot be for a long time.'

'Perhaps I will choose a wife for you,' she said, getting up eagerly and coming towards him. 'Some young lady with good sense, not too fine, who can brew and bake, and manage a dairy like your mother. Would that suit you?'

'My mother was not always the farmer's wife you see now,' he said, smiling. 'My grandmother used to laugh when she remembered what a pretty, dainty little thing she was. She knew nothing of household management, let alone managing the dairy or the poultry. And she was terrified of the geese!' He laughed. 'But a young woman can always learn if the desire is there.'

'Could I learn, do you think?' asked Anna, standing close to him.

'Not in a thousand years,' said Robert soberly. 'Miss Weston, you might find it amusing for a season to play at being a farmer's wife, but then the novelty would pall, and you would wish to be off - to travel to foreign lands as you have been used to do; and you would miss the gaieties of London.'

'I am sick of London,' said Anna.

'For now, perhaps,' said Robert, still sounding serious. 'Miss Weston, I think we have talked enough. You will regret speaking so frankly to me in the morning.'

'No, Rob; I could never regret that. We were such friends in those days; even sweethearts in our childish way. Can that never be again?'

'Miss Weston, we have grown too far apart. I will never be anything but a farmer, and you are a fine lady.'

'You are a *gentleman* farmer, and an educated, sensible man. So far I can see no distance between us.'

'I am a country-man; I like quiet pursuits and the rhythm of the changing seasons. When I think of my life it is here that I belong, in the woods and fields, and not in ballrooms or theatres, or the streets of London. Now I think we had better go back to the ballroom, Miss Weston,' and turning away he walked purposefully towards the house.

It was growing late as Anna slipped quietly into a corner of the ballroom, and a few families had already gone home, amongst them the Dixons. Emma, who had seen nothing of Sophia's hysterics, was dancing with Mr Walters when he was approached by his father. James stepped out of the set to speak to him, and returned in a few moments.

'My dear Emma, you must forgive me; I am wanted at home. My parents are about to leave, and my father is insistent I go with them. I cannot understand it, but I will tell you all when I call tomorrow.'

With a hasty 'goodnight' he was gone, and Emma left the set to go and sit with her mother.

'Emma, has Mr Walters gone home?' asked Mrs Knightley, in some surprise. 'Colonel Walters took his leave just now, saying Miss Dixon had been taken ill, but I see no occasion for Mr Walters to leave also. Can you throw any light on the situation?'

'No, Mama; Colonel Walters spoke privately to Ja . . . Mr Walters, but merely said what you heard yourself.' Emma blushed, but her mother wisely pretended not to notice.

'Do you intend to dance again, my love?' Mrs Knightley asked her. 'If you do not, will you take my place here? I must go and speak with the housekeeper; there is little point in keeping the servants from their beds any longer. If anyone wishes to speak to me, I shall be in the housekeeper's room, or you may fetch your Papa, who is still in the card-room, I think.' So saying, Mrs Knightley went off on her errand, and Emma was left with her Aunt Isabella.

'I hope poor Sophia Dixon will soon recover,' said that lady, in the plaintive tones she always used when discussing anyone's health. 'The fit came upon her very suddenly; one minute she was sitting with Anna, smiling and fanning herself, so Georgiana said, then Anna spoke - I cannot think what she could have said, but it did not take more than a minute, perhaps less - and suddenly Miss Dixon started up in hysterics, and ran off out of the ballroom. It is so strange. What can have happened, Emma?'

'I should not care to hazard a guess,' said Emma, as perplexed as her aunt. 'No doubt we will hear more tomorrow.'

At two o'clock even the most indefatigable dancers were tired, and by three o'clock the last guests had departed. Emma, happier than she had ever been, was too tired to give Georgiana the good news of her engagement, and fell asleep before she had time to relive in memory the happy events of the evening.

Chapter 19

On the morning after the ball everyone rose late except for Mr Knightley, who was up at six as had been his custom for the past forty years. As soon as they had broken their fast, Mr Knightley retired to the library, and Mrs Knightley to the morning room. Telling Georgiana that she needed to speak privately with her mother, Emma quickly followed her, saying: 'Mama, I have something to tell you. Mr Walters has asked me to marry him, and I have accepted.'

Mrs Knightley, who had observed with pleasure her daughter's growing attachment to that gentleman, wept tears of joy.

'My love, I am so glad for you, and wish you very happy in your choice. Mr Walters is a charming young man with an abundance of good sense. I could not have chosen better for you myself. Both my girls engaged; I can scarcely believe it! Is Mr Walters coming to speak to your Papa this morning?'

'He said he would; in truth, I am surprised he is not here already. Mama, I cannot sit still, I am so happy. I must go and tell Georgiana,' and Emma went out into the hall. Mr Walters was just being admitted and waited for the servant to be gone before saying: 'My dear Emma, I am sorry I could not be here sooner, but there have been such happenings at home that I could not get away. I will tell you all about it later, but now I must speak to your father. Where is he?'

'He is in the library,' she said blushing, as he kissed her hand, and leaving him to his serious business she hurried up the stairs to find Georgiana.

Sitting beside the fire in their bed-chamber, with Georgiana an attentive listener on the other side, Emma confessed how foolish she had been before the ball, and then related the details of her present happiness. Georgiana embraced her, saying: 'I always knew you would make a match of it, but I did not think it would be so soon.'

In less than half an hour they were sent for to come down to the drawing room, where they found their mother and father with Mr Walters, and there were hearty handshakes and good wishes. Mr Walters was invited to spend the day at Donwell Abbey, and readily accepted. Henry arrived soon after, and was told the good news. He had always liked James Walters, and congratulated him on finding a treasure in Emma.

'I suppose you will be carrying her off to Ireland as soon as you are married,' said Henry.

'Oh my dear,' said Mrs Knightley to Emma, before Mr Walters had time to answer, 'I had not thought of your going so far away. What will I do without my Emma?'

'You must be our first visitors at Innisdoon, ma'am,' said Mr Walters. 'Come as often as you like, and stay as long as you like. It is indeed a long journey, but we must not become strangers.'

'I hope that some part of every year will be given by you to Donwell,' said Mr Knightley. 'That would make both families happy, and I could part with my dear Emma on no other terms.'

Mr Walters, deeply in love, readily agreed to any arrangements the two families cared to make on their behalf, and soon the four young people left them happily discussing the wedding arrangements, to take a walk in the grounds.

While Georgiana and Henry made their way to the lime walk, Emma and James walked down to the Abbey ruins, and found a seat on the same stone which Anna had occupied the previous evening. After talking of themselves and their own happiness for a while, Emma was curious to know what had happened to delay James earlier that morning.

'The whole household was in turmoil when I left,' said he; 'I was glad to get away. I managed to get most of the story out of Tom last night. As you know, we were forced to leave the ball early because of Sophia's indisposition. That was all I thought it was at the time. We were home half an hour after the Dixons, and learnt that she was still in hysterics, and her mother was trying to calm her. You can imagine the scene: Mr Dixon pacing up and down; everyone trying hard to be polite, and privately wondering what on earth was going on. Eventually Mrs Dixon came down, having given Sophia some drops to calm her. Tom begged to be allowed to speak to her but was denied, very coldly, I thought. Everything was to be left until morning.'

'Did Tom know at this point what ailed Sophia?' asked Emma.

'Yes, in part; we all retired for the night, but I cannot imagine that anyone slept very well. Tom came into my room as I was preparing to go to bed, flung himself into a chair, and told me as much as he knew himself.'

'If he told you in confidence, then I should not even inquire further,' said Emma.

'I believe you have a right to know,' said he. 'Sophia has convinced herself that Tom is in love with your sister, and has therefore broken off the engagement.'

'I do not understand,' said Emma. 'I thought Anna had said something to hurt or upset her, but that is something Anna could have no way of knowing. Georgiana has told no-one but me; of that I am certain. You and I talked of it in private, but told no-one else, which only leaves Tom. Could he have said anything?'

'Tom is indiscreet sometimes, but he would not have told *Anna*. Believe me, Emma, it is not worth speculating about; the truth will come out eventually. Tom was to have a private conference with Sophia this morning and no doubt I will hear all the details this evening. Now, come; you have made me the happiest of men by consenting to become my wife; I have talked over my prospects with your father, who seemed to be perfectly satisfied with them; now all I need to know is how soon we can be married.'

They returned to the house to find more welcome callers; Bella, with Mr Churchill and Anna, had made Donwell the object of their walk. Mrs Knightley had been telling them the good news about Emma and James, when the lovers themselves came in, to be almost overwhelmed with good wishes. Georgiana and Henry then came in, and there was a great deal of banter and general merriment. Mr Churchill approached Emma and said, very kindly: 'My dear, you remind me so much of your mother when she was young, and I am sure you will be as happy with your James as she has been with your father.' He looked so much as if he meant it that Emma was touched. Anna, too, said what was proper, but there was no benignant light in her eye as she regarded Mr Walters.

Under cover of the general conversation Bella was able to take Emma aside. She was eager for all the details and asked when and where she had received Mr Walters' proposal. Emma blushed, and said it was when they were sitting out in the orangery.

'Ah yes, it was delightfully cool in there after the heat of the ballroom,' said Bella. 'I was there before supper with Henry and Georgiana, . . . and Mr Churchill,' she added, looking down. 'When we first went in we saw Anna sitting alone. It was so strange; we invited her to join us, but she said she was about to return to the ballroom, and only wanted to be left in peace. I sometimes think Anna has a rather rude way of speaking . . . but what is wrong, Emma? You look startled?'

'When we came into the orangery we saw a group of people seated at the further end, but did not recognise who it was because of the dimness of the lights. There was no sign of

Anna. I shudder to think that she might have been . . . eavesdropping on a private conversation. Where exactly was she sitting when you saw her?'

'It was somewhere near the door; let me see; just inside the door was a carved wooden seat next to a table and some chairs, then there was a great bank of ferns, and palms, and Anna was sitting close on the other side of them. She was still there half an hour later when we went into supper, because Henry asked her who she was avoiding.'

Emma was now convinced that Anna had heard at least some part of her conversation with James, and was filled with horror. She found it difficult to believe that even Anna could behave so dishonourably, and then to use information gleaned to do serious damage to both Sophia and Tom, who had never done her any harm - surely there must be another explanation. Her first instinct was to confront Anna, who was at that moment laughing with Henry as though she had never harboured an uncharitable thought in her life. On reflection she decided to wait until she had an opportunity of talking the matter over with James.

That night, as Georgiana undressed and Emma sat brushing her hair, they talked over the day's events. Once again Georgiana mentioned Sophia Dixon and Anna, wondering aloud what could have been said. Emma decided that this would be a good time to enlighten Georgiana as to the source of Anna's information, and to apologise for having spoken of it at all.

'You could not have known Anna was listening,' said Georgiana. 'I sometimes wonder if that girl has any scruples at all. Why didn't she stand up as soon as she heard your voices and announce her presence?'

'My love, you are so honest yourself you could not begin to understand a mind such as Anna's. I am sorry the information came from me, however unintentionally, but otherwise I think it may turn out well in the end. It was quite plain from the beginning that Tom did not love Sophia, but I did not observe much love on her part towards him. Possessiveness, yes; but not love. They might have married and been miserable.'

'I think, Emma,' said Georgiana, getting into bed, 'that you will go to any lengths to find an excuse for him, because he is to be your brother. Is that not so?'

'Perhaps you are right,' said Emma with a smile, 'but I make no apology for it. Family harmony, like sleep, is a state devoutly to be wished,' and kissing Georgiana goodnight, she blew out the candle.

The next day was Sunday, and the Knightleys, the Walters' and the Dixons all met at church. (Emma had gone with James to Donwell Court the previous afternoon, to be welcomed and kissed by his family, but the atmosphere was strained, Miss Sophia still keeping to her room. They stayed but a short time, Emma promising to come for the day on Monday.) In honour of the occasion, Mr Knightley invited both families back to Donwell to celebrate the young people's engagement. Sophia was not at church, and the Dixons therefore made their excuses, with many thanks, but urged Colonel and Mrs Walters to go, and they agreed reluctantly, saying they would not be long away.

Once comfortably ensconced in the drawing room, Mrs Knightley and Mrs Walters were soon deep in conversation exchanging views on marriage in general and comments on their children in particular, in terms highly agreeable to both.

Mr Knightley told Colonel Walters how delighted he was with the match. 'Emma has made a wise choice; your son is a most estimable young man,' he said.

'Yes, James has never given me a moment's anxiety,' said Colonel Walters soberly. 'I could only wish that his brother had half his sense. He is not a bad fellow, Mr Knightley, but he never foresees the consequences of his actions. Perhaps I should have kept him by me when he was young,' he said, musing, 'instead of sending him home to England. I believe he was not happy at school, and his uncle had good reason to be severe with him on more than one occasion. It has made him all too eager to seek amusement where he can find it, without a thought as to whom he might be injuring. I will not say more, Mr Knightley - he is, after all, my son. I hope you will overlook his light conduct.'

Mr Knightley, who had very little idea of what Colonel Walters meant by all this, readily agreed, and with a hearty handshake assured the Colonel that Tom would turn out well in the end.

Colonel and Mrs Walters did not stay long with the Knightleys, wishing not to seem discourteous to the Dixons. Anne was to return with John to spend the day at Hartfield but, making the excuse of borrowing some of Emma's music, she sought a hasty private word with her.

'Emma, the past few days have been hateful,' she said. 'I felt sorry for Sophia at first, thinking she was genuinely broken-hearted about Tom's ill-conduct, but she has behaved very badly herself.'

'I am sorry to hear it,' said Emma, a little surprised, for she had never heard Anne utter a critical word about anyone.

'Oh, she is so spoilt,' said Anne. 'I am sorry to be so uncharitable, but she has led her poor mother such a dance, not to mention the rest of us. There has been such screaming and crying and banging of doors; my mother's head positively ached. Then, after returning Tom's letters, and a lock of his hair, she took a china shepherdess that Tom had given her and threw it down the stairs. It narrowly missed a housemaid, and smashed to pieces on the tiles. By now the story will be all over the village!'

Emma was amused in spite of herself by the picture Anne had painted, but thought such childish behaviour was probably typical of Sophia.

'I think it is her pride that is hurt, for I never believed she loved Tom,' Anne continued. 'We are all too thankful that she is to go away tomorrow, though, of course, we will be sorry to lose her parents. I hope this will not create any difficulties for you, my dear Emma, once you are married. They will be your nearest neighbours in Ireland and, no doubt, Tom will visit you there.'

'The absence of Miss Sophia's company will be no loss to me, I assure you,' said Emma. 'In any case, I should not be surprised if she did not find herself another young man very quickly, to replace the one she has lost.'

Mr Dixon called upon the Knightleys that evening to bid them farewell, excusing the absence of his wife by saying Sophia could not be left in her present state. Emma could not help looking at Georgiana, who lifted her eyes in mock exasperation. He was as cordial as ever, though Georgiana fancied a little coolness of manner towards *her*. Had she heard his earlier conversation with her father she would have known it was only embarrassment which made him awkward. He could not stay long as he was expected at Hartfield to take leave of his friends there.

'I hope Anna will have the decency to keep to her room while he is in the house,' said Emma in an undertone to Georgiana. Though Emma guessed her mother suspected Anna's hand in the trouble between Tom and Sophia, the subject had not been raised between them.

The following day the Dixons departed, and the parishes of Highbury and Donwell returned to their accustomed calm.

The whole episode, and especially Sophia's tantrums, had been a source of entertainment to the servants and their like, but they accepted the change philosophically, reasoning that some new event, a wedding, a funeral, or a fire would soon occur to amuse them in the future.

Anna, sensing the chill in the atmosphere, was also anxious to be gone. She thought she might return to London, and had dropped a hint or two to Mr Churchill, but he either could not or would not understand her. Every day now it was his custom to sit next to Bella at table, and to spend much of his leisure, of which he had a limitless supply, in her company. Mrs John Knightley often exchanged meaningful glances with her husband, and Miss Bella's wedding was openly talked of in the servant's hall, but Anna wilfully refused to accept their growing attachment.

A week or more after the departure of the Dixons, it was decided that Emma and James, and Georgiana and Henry, should be married in June at the same ceremony. John graciously said he would perform that office, as if it were something extraordinary, and not part of a clergyman's regular duties. Tom had called once at Donwell Abbey; the visit was of necessity short and full of embarrassment for both him and Georgiana. She could not be angry with him for long, however, in deference to Emma's feelings, and now that Sophia had gone she could view him with something like her old affection.

Once the wedding date had been announced, Anna insisted that she and her guardian should return to London so that she could order some new clothes in honour of the occasion. Mr Churchill reluctantly agreed, and took fond leave of Bella. It was not yet warm enough to travel in an open carriage, but Anna could not help observing the fresh green of the hedgerows through the carriage window, and was reminded of her beloved Enscombe.

'Frank, I think we should return to Enscombe after the wedding is over,' she said in her usual imperious way.

'I may have to go sooner than that,' he said coolly. 'I have passed my time so pleasantly at Highbury that I have been in danger of forgetting my duties.'

'Oh, that is wonderful!' cried Anna. 'I shall only need a few days to complete any business I . . .'

'Anna, I should prefer it if you would remain in St James's Square.'

Anna was angry and astonished. 'May I ask why my society has suddenly become irksome to you?' she said haughtily.

There was a long silence, then Mr Churchill said: 'I have been loth to introduce this subject, Anna, before now, but I must say something, painful as it might be to us both. Bella has told me of your part in the quarrel between Tom Walters and Sophia. It was a shabby, spiteful trick, Anna, and I am ashamed of you. The Dixons are my very good friends, and I have known Sophia from a child. What harm has she ever done to you?'

'Oh,' said she, trying to adopt a light tone, 'I am not privy to what Bella has said of me, but I am sure she exaggerated. She probably saw me speak to Sophia in the ballroom; that is all. How can I help it if Sophia is so easily offended?'

'I know everything, Anna,' Mr Churchill went on, in a tone of calm displeasure. 'Bella heard some part of it from Emma, then Henry told her the rest; Bella herself saw you in the orangery, where it was obvious you deliberately listened to a private conversation, whilst remaining concealed. I am your brother, Anna, and I have tried my best to be a father to you since our father died, but I now conclude I never knew you.'

Anna felt some compunction at this uncharacteristically harsh assessment of her behaviour, then grew angry again, and, desperate to justify herself, cried recklessly: 'It is 'Bella' this, and 'Bella' that, until I am sick of the sound of her name. Are you blind and deaf, that you do not know how she is using her wiles to entrap you? Bella Knightley would do anything to become mistress of Enscombe.'

'Now you have said enough,' he said sharply. 'You are attributing your own base motives to an innocent girl. Yes, I love Bella, and I would have asked her to marry me long ago if it were not for the disparity in our ages. Twenty years is too great a gap, or at least I thought so, but now I am not so sure.'

'What do you mean?' asked Anna, in a faint voice.

'Because I made you my ward, Anna, you have always assumed that Enscombe would one day be yours. I suppose I thought so too. I had no intention of marrying again, and there are no other heirs; but your conduct over the past months has made me see that you are totally unfit to have charge of the estate.' He paused and looked out of the window. 'When I return to Highbury, I mean to ask Bella to marry me. I have reason to believe she returns my affection and, if she accepts, we will make our home at Enscombe.'

'But what about me?' Anna was on the verge of tears.

'You have your own fortune, Anna, though you will not have the complete management of it until you are five-and-twenty. If you regulate your conduct to my satisfaction, I am willing to assist you in setting up your own establishment. I am sure you will agree that, in the circumstances, it would be inappropriate for you to reside at Enscombe.'

Anna sat in shocked silence for some minutes, then as the realisation dawned she struggled to hold back her sobs. Never to live at Enscombe again; she could not bear it; she would faint! Bella Knightley would take her place. She would marry

Frank and bear him many children, who would ensure that Anna would never have any claim on the estate. It was too much even for Anna to bear, and for the first time since her father's death she began to weep.

Chapter 20

M r Churchill spent only two or three days in St James's Square before departing for Enscombe. His purpose in going there was twofold: the first was to order the redecoration of several bed-chambers, and to make some minor changes that would please Bella; the second was to seek out a small house for Anna, somewhere on the estate at a sufficient distance from the main house. He had not mentioned this to Anna, intending to punish her by allowing her to believe that she was banished from Enscombe forever; but when she had suffered enough, he reasoned, and had learnt to be civil to Bella, he would permit her to come home. Thinking about his private plans had restored his customary good humour, and his parting from Anna was cordial.

The weather was fair and his journey was uneventful. As he crossed the moors, on the final stage of his journey, he caught a glimpse of Enscombe, its grey mass standing out clearly against the afterglow of a particularly fine sunset. For a while he reflected on the sadness of his life after the death of his dear Jane, then felt renewed hope as he thought of Bella. There could hardly be a greater contrast between the two women; Jane so shy, delicate and reserved, a perfect model of good breeding; and Bella, used to the rough and tumble of family life with five brothers; merry, confident and full of life. Surely, a woman born to be the mother of fine sons!

Anna, for her part, had spent many painful hours. Her eyes had not closed at all the first night in London, but by the second day she grew calmer; and as soon as Mr Churchill had departed she began to plan for her own future. She resolved, first of all, that she would not return to Highbury for the wedding in June, nor, when Mr Churchill returned in a month's time would he find her meekly sitting in St James's Square with her embroidery in her hand. She needed something to distract her mind and, filled with a sudden resolve, she sat down and wrote to friends in Bath and Weymouth, where she had been received before. The letters were dispatched, and Anna went to bed hoping for some speedy replies. By the end of that week she had received two invitations to join her friends in their summer pleasures. After some thought, Anna wrote first to her friend Miss Kerr, in Bath, saying she would be delighted to spend a month with her before joining her other friends in Weymouth. In Weymouth she hoped to make up a party to go on to Brighton later. Once resolved on any course of action, Anna was no dawdle, and only three days after receiving the invitation, she and her maid were on their way to Bath.

After attending to estate business for several days, Mr Churchill was at leisure to look for a house for Anna. His agent had made a list of the available houses on the estate that might be suitable for a lady. Of these, one was dismissed as being too small, leaving two others, both suitable in their way. Mr Churchill rode across the park one morning to view the first. It was a handsome house, in a very good state of repair, and his agent thought this would be the obvious choice, but Mr Churchill was put off by its situation, less than half a mile from the great house. He did not relish the thought of having Anna wander in whenever the mood took her, which she would be bound to do, living in such close proximity.

The other house lay farther off, in a village three miles from Enscombe. It had once been a small manor house, which had been improved some fifty years earlier, and painted white, which gave it its name. The White House was charming, situated on the main street of a small village, and backing on to the moors. It was soundly built, but would need a number of improvements to suit Anna's taste. Mr Churchill rode home feeling very pleased with himself. Anna could not fail to be delighted.

Meanwhile Anna had been received very cordially by her friend, Miss Kerr, who resided in one of the elegant Nash terraces, and was soon caught up in a round of engagements. They visited the theatre, and Miss Kerr's friend, Lady McGregor, gave a dinner in Anna's honour. One morning in May as the two ladies were on their way to visit Miss Kerr's aunt, whose house lay some six miles from Bath, they happened to pass through Upton Prior, and Miss Kerr suggested that Anna might care to view the parish church, which was of great antiquity. Anna, amused at finding herself in the village to which Mrs Elton had removed, readily agreed. Not that she had any intention of calling at the Parsonage, but one could never tell what might happen by accident. Leaving the carriage by the lych gate, they walked up the path through the ancient yews to the west door and entered the church, finding the cool, dim interior refreshing after the heat of the sun.

As they wandered about at the back of the nave admiring the Norman font and the carvings on a tomb, they heard voices coming from the chancel, and Anna recognised the strident tones of Mrs Elton.

'Come, Augusta, must I do everything by myself? There are four more vases to be filled. Why do you droop about in that languid fashion? It cannot be the heat. Mary, fetch some more water.'

Anna drew closer and, concealed by a pillar, stood witnessing the scene played out before her. Mrs Elton was kneeling on the chancel steps arranging some flowers and foliage in a vase. A young woman, who had been seated in a choir stall, rose slowly to her feet and knelt down next to Mrs Elton.

'So this is Augusta,' thought Anna. 'How pale she looks. Her mother's presence is obviously irksome to her.'

Mary returned carrying a pail of water, closely followed by Mr Craig.

'What an excellent arrangement, ma'am,' he said, beaming. 'Your talents are wasted in a country church.'

'I do my best,' said Mrs Elton modestly. 'Augusta, I shall not always be here; you must learn to do the flowers yourself.'

'Yes, Mama,' said Augusta meekly.

'I can never look at that carved angel without thinking of Selina,' said Mary. 'Do you remember, Papa, you used to tell Selina she had a face like that angel?'

'Hush, child,' said Mr Craig, his expression darkening.

'Mary, come here and gather up these leaves,' said Mrs Elton hastily.

At that moment Anna was joined by her friend. 'Here's a fine family piece,' said Miss Kerr. 'Papa and Mama with their two daughters! If you are ready, Anna, I think we must not keep the horses waiting any longer,' and they left the church with only one backward glance from Anna.

In Highbury and Donwell preparations were under way for the wedding. Bella was feeling excluded, and was in low spirits as a consequence. She had had news of Mr Churchill but once, in a letter to her mother. Mrs John Knightley had invited him to stay at Hartfield during the wedding celebrations, and he had written to say he would arrive sometime in the first week of June, in good time for the ceremony. His message to Bella was short; he sent his good wishes and said that the avenue of chestnuts was in full bloom, and he wished she could see it. Bella had been envying her cousins, but the message, short as it was, gave her renewed hope, and she could view with equanimity the procession of packages, parcels and boxes which were delivered to Donwell Abbey every day. Henry was in excellent spirits, and went about the house whistling, which caused his mother to remonstrate feebly with him.

Mrs Knightley had had a short letter from Anna, making her excuses for not attending the wedding: 'a previous engagement - impossible to get out of it' and so on. The letter arrived while the family were at breakfast, and Mrs Knightley read it aloud.

'Well,' said Georgiana, 'that is all I need to make my happiness complete. We were obliged to ask her, but I am so relieved she is not coming.'

No-one attempted to argue with her, though Mrs Knightley, thinking of Anna's mother, felt a pang of regret that she could not like Anna better.

After the wedding the two couples were to spend some time at the seaside, and hearing that Anna was to be in Weymouth at that time, they settled upon Sidmouth as their venue. The new Mr and Mrs Walters planned to return to Donwell with Georgiana and Henry before leaving for Ireland in September. A house on the Donwell estate was in process of being renovated for Henry and Georgiana. 'Until the smell of the paint had gone', as Henry put it, he and his wife were to reside at Donwell Abbey.

Bella was not the only young lady who had been feeling out of spirits as the preparations went on. Anne could not help repining, reflecting that it would be many months before she could be married. She now felt completely well, and looked blooming; her figure had filled out, and she was certain she had grown an inch. Her poor John was always in her thoughts, in what she thought of as his cheerless bachelor household, though in fact he had an excellent cook, and was generally well looked after. Not that his cook was overburdened with work, since he dined several times a week at Donwell Court.

Mrs Walters observed the change in Anne's health with satisfaction and, after a private word with the Colonel, they gave their approval for a September wedding. Quiet little Anne was overjoyed, though none but her mother could have discerned it.

At the beginning of June, Mr Churchill, in a new carriage, returned to Highbury and was made particularly welcome at Hartfield. Bella had been longing for his return, but now he was actually here at Hartfield, joking with her father and being charming to her mother, she felt shy and imagined she had lost all power of pleasing. The first evening passed in an agony of suspense for Bella, as she waited and hoped for Mr Churchill to speak to her privately, but she was disappointed. The following morning, after a restless night, Bella resolved to spend the day at Donwell, knowing she could be useful to her cousins. She announced her intention at breakfast, and Mr Churchill offered to drive her there in his new carriage. The offer was accepted with eagerness; Bella ran lightly up the stairs, singing to herself, and chose her most becoming bonnet. Whether it was the beauty of the bonnet that brought Mr Churchill to the point seems doubtful, yet it is certain that as the carriage rolled down the avenue at Donwell Abbey Mr Churchill and Bella were engaged.

In all the excitement of the wedding preparations, Emma and Georgiana were uncomfortably aware that they had been neglecting Miss Bates. One fine morning, therefore, having been urged to go by their mother, they set off to walk to Highbury. It was a beautiful sunny day, and they were glad to be out in the air after having been confined to the house for several days by persistent rain. They were also glad to escape from all the bustle and upheaval the marriage festivities were causing. Their progress down the High Street was slow, as they were stopped by kind friends and neighbours, full of good wishes.

'I am beginning to regret we did not come in the carriage,' Georgiana said, as they finally reached their destination. 'I never realised that a wedding was such a *public* occasion. It almost makes me feel we are putting on a play for the benefit of the residents of Highbury and Donwell!'

Emma laughed. 'You must endure it as well as you can, my love,' she said. 'It will soon be Bella's turn, not to mention Anne, and we shall be quite in the shade.'

Miss Bates was delighted to see them, and bustled about as usual.

'So kind of you to visit an old woman when you have so much to do,' she said happily. 'Miss Georgiana, I fear you are in a draught.' Georgiana had taken a seat as far away from the fire as she could, the day being very warm. 'Miss Knightley, I hope you will take a glass of my elderberry wine,' and ensuring that her visitors were happily settled, she took a seat herself.

'Mr Churchill was so kind as to call a few days ago to tell me the good news. I was never more astonished in my life, for I never thought he would marry again after my poor Jane . . .' Here she paused to wipe away a tear, before going on in forced cheerfulness. 'You must not think I am one of those who believe happiness cannot be found in a second attachment. Dear Bella! I think she will make him an excellent wife, though how poor Anna will take it, I do not know. She has always loved Enscombe, you know.'

'I understand that Anna will not be living at Enscombe,' said Emma.

'Oh no; Mr Churchill said not, and he did not have to tell me why. I hear things, Miss Knightley; I know about Anna's part in poor Selina Elton's downfall. I had it from Mrs Elton herself before she departed for Upton Prior, but I never mentioned it to a soul that I am aware of. And she was no friend to Miss Dixon; the poor girl came to see me, and it all poured out. Not that I blame you, Miss Georgiana; it was none of your doing.' Georgiana blushed, and Emma, trying to change the subject, made some mention of Miss Bates's garden. 'Oh yes, the roses. Anna will miss the rose-garden at Enscombe . . . but what am I thinking of? I meant to tell you that Anna wrote to me a week ago, and sent me a parcel,' and ringing the bell, she sent her servant to fetch it. The little maid soon returned, bearing something encased in layers of tissue, which Miss Bates removed to reveal a beautiful *moiré* silk gown in dove grey.

'Anna said she thought I would need a new gown for your wedding, and sent me this. How clever of her to guess my size, though I recall the last time she was staying in Highbury she sent her maid, Marie, to make a small alteration to my best black. I am not as well set-up as I was, though still perfectly healthy. This gown is so beautiful I shall not know myself, and only needed a tuck or two on the waist to make it fit perfectly. Dear Anna has always been so kind to me; I hate to hear the unpleasant stories that are being circulated about her. She made no mention in her letter of Mr Churchill, or Miss Bella, though he told me this morning he had written to tell her of his engagement. They are to be married here in Highbury, you know, and Mr Churchill says Anna will return for the wedding. It is to be a summer of complete pleasure for me. My new silk gown will be quite worn out with all the merry-making!'

The wedding day was one of great rejoicing for the two Knightley families in particular, though one might suppose they were not alone in that. Mrs Knightley was overjoyed to see both her girls so well married; her only sorrow being Emma's imminent departure for Ireland. Even that cast but a small cloud on her happiness; she must make her dear Mr Knightley bestir himself, she reflected; he must be prepared to leave his beloved Donwell and make the long journey to visit their daughter, for if he would not, they would never see their grand-children. Her great comfort must be that she would have Georgiana always with her.

Mrs John Knightley, perhaps for the first time in her life, was completely happy; not even a slight threat of rain early on could discompose her. Her younger sons were doing well in their chosen professions; Bella was engaged; her dear John would soon be married and, best of all, her favourite son, Henry, would be established near her, to be a comfort in her old age.

Bella and Anne, as they followed the bridal train up the aisle, were reflecting with satisfaction that their own nuptials would shortly take place. Bella now thought of Enscombe with equanimity; during her visit she had been somewhat over-awed by its splendour and, snubbed by Anna, had sometimes longed for home; but to return there as mistress was quite another matter! She was glad that Mr Churchill had forgiven his sister, and even gladder that Anna would not be making her home with them.

After receiving a brief acknowledgement of his first letter, Mr Churchill wrote again to Anna, telling her of the alterations he was making to the White House to make it a fit residence for a lady. He had enjoyed planning this surprise for her, but if he had hoped for gratitude or meek acquiescence to his wishes he was sadly disappointed on receiving Anna's reply.

My dear Frank, (she wrote)

It is very kind of you to make available to me a house on the estate. I have often passed the White House whilst out riding; it used then to be occupied by the bailiff, I believe. No doubt the smell of the pig-pen still lingers. Three miles is a convenient distance from the great house - to you, I mean, knowing you would not wish me to be the cause of any embarrassment to your wife or your guests.

You will mark how eager I am to see this dwelling when I tell you that, as soon as my sojourn in Brighton comes to an end, I mean to go abroad. My friend, Lord Urswick, has a villa on Lake Maggiore, and has been pressing in his invitations to spend the winter there. I regret it will not be possible for me to attend your wedding in September, since I shall be leaving for Italy in August. I am sure you know how warm my wishes are for your happiness.

> *Your loving sister,*
> *Anna Weston*